I0580248

BOOKS BY BRENDA S. ANDERSON

THE MOSAIC COLLECTION
A Beautiful Mess
A Beautiful Christ-mess
(a short story In *Hope is Born: A Mosaic Christmas Anthology*)

THE POTTER'S HOUSE BOOKS
Long Way Home
Place Called Home
Home Another Way

WHERE THE HEART IS SERIES
Risking Love
Capturing Beauty
Planting Hope

COMING HOME SERIES
Pieces of Granite
Chain of Mercy
Memory Box Secrets
Hungry for Home
Coming Home – A Short Story

A BEAUTIFUL mess

A NOVEL

Vivant Press
A Beautiful Mess
Copyright © 2019
Brenda S. Anderson

ISBN-13: 978-1-951664-00-8

Scripture quotations are from The ESV® Bible (The Holy Bible, English Standard Version®), copyright © 2001 by Crossway, a publishing ministry of Good News Publishers. Used by permission. All rights reserved.

This novel is a work of fiction. Names, characters, places, and incidents either are the product of the author's imagination or are used fictitiously. Any resemblance to actual events, locales, organizations, or persons living or dead is entirely coincidental and beyond the intent of either the author or the publisher.

Cover Design by Think Cap Studios
Palette image by Image by Clker-Free-Vector-Images from Pixabay

Printed in the United States of America

19 20 21 22 23 24 25   7 6 5 4 3 2 1

Welcome to

THE MOSAIC COLLECTION

We are sisters, a beautiful mosaic united by the love of God through the blood of Christ

Beginning August 2019, this international group of authors will release one book each month for the next twelve months, as we explore our theme, Family by His Design, and share stories that feature diverse, God-designed families. All are contemporary stories ranging from mystery to women's fiction, humorous fiction, and literary fiction. We hope you'll join our Mosaic family as we learn together what truly defines a family.

To keep informed about The Mosaic Collection books, subscribe to Grace & Glory, the official newsletter of The Mosaic Collection. You will receive monthly encouragement from Mosaic authors as well as timely updates about events, new releases, and giveaways.

Subscribe:
www.mosaiccollectionbooks.com/grace-glory/

Learn more about The Mosaic Collection at:
www.mosaiccollectionbooks.com/

Join our Reader Community, too!
www.facebook.com/groups/theMosaiccollection

Books in

THE MOSAIC COLLECTION

When Mountains Sing by Stacy Monson
Unbound by Eleanor Bertin
The Red Journal by Deb Elkink
A Beautiful Mess by Brenda S. Anderson
Hope is Born: A Mosaic Christmas Anthology

COMING SOON!

Novels by

Lorna Seilstad, Janice L. Dick, Angela D. Meyer,
Sara Davison, Johnnie Alexander,
Regina Rudd Merrick, and Hannah R. Conway

Learn more at www.MosaicCollectionBooks.com/Books

To Stacy Monson
for walking alongside me on this very messy road
of writing and publishing!
I couldn't have traveled it without you!

"As we pour out our bitterness, God pours in his peace."

— F.B. Meyer —

Chapter One

Today was a good day to live again.

Erin Belden rubbed the wrist she'd had tattooed a few weeks back. It was still healing, but at least she was now free of wearing a wide bracelet or long sleeves. Another sign of life.

She strode across her bedroom and folded open the closet doors. What to pack . . . She drummed a finger on her chin then chose a pair of jeans and a couple of hoodies. No need for dressing up, this weekend was all about comfort. And she wouldn't have to worry about hiding her scars or faking emotions she wasn't capable of feeling.

Her best friend knew the truth.

Going on the weekend retreat with Debbie was exactly the jumpstart she needed before diving into her new home business on Monday. No longer would she allow her ex-husband to rule over her thoughts and actions. Maybe she'd even start dating again. There was that cute newcomer at church . . .

Thinking about him made her feel . . .

She pinched her eyes shut and tried dredging up those feelings that made themselves known only around rare people, like anger with her ex, frustration with her daughter, peace with her best friend.

Excited. Yeah. That was what she felt when she thought of that guy at church. New beginnings, new relationships without strings—or pasts—were exciting.

Now she was getting ahead of herself. *Slow down, Erin!* She had more important things to worry about than daydreaming about a new relationship. That last and only one had failed miserably.

She glanced out the bedroom window. Snowflakes were already starting to swirl through the air, and many more would join them as the minutes wore on. The forecasters warned of an approaching snowstorm, maybe a blizzard, an April Fool's joke played four days late. If they didn't get on the road soon, the roads could become treacherous. Thank goodness Debbie was punctual.

Problem was, her ex wasn't.

She jotted a mental to-do list while packing a bag of toiletries and important meds. Send Michaela off with her father. Hooray for that! Finish packing. Don't forget her Bible, chocolate, a couple of mindless adventure flicks and only one chick flick. Neither she nor Debbie cared for them. They had been her ex's favorite.

"Do I have to go?" Michaela's all-too-familiar pubescent whine sounded from Erin's bedroom doorway. What Erin would give to have the girl back who couldn't wait to go to her daddy's new home where she'd be lavished with expensive gifts and treated like a princess. Oh, how she'd adored her daddy. That glow had worn off too quickly once her stepsister was born.

Shoot, just like that, Corey had wormed his way into Erin's thoughts. She shoved him aside and did her best not to reply to her daughter with snark, by forcing a smile. "Mik, I'm going to be gone this weekend. I can't leave you home alone."

"Then I'll go to Hannah's house. Her mom said I could stay."

"No can do. It's your father's weekend for you."

Mik snorted and formed horns with her fingers on her head. "Tell that to the wicked stepmom."

Erin might be poor at identifying body language, but that she understood clearly. Erin clenched her teeth together and spoke through them. "Your stepmother is not that bad." Well, not exactly true, but Erin always tried to paint both her ex and his new wife in a positive light, letting Mik draw her own conclusions.

"But they give all their attention to the brat."

One . . . two . . . three . . . Erin continued to count under her breath. This was just adolescence rearing its dragon-like head. She sat down on her bed and patted the space beside her.

Mik trudged across the carpet as if her feet were dragging fifty-pound weights. To think, this was just the beginning of teenage drama. How would Erin make it through the next five years without throttling her daughter?

It seemed to take forever, but at last Mik slumped down on the bed, her shoulders hunched as if they bore the same weight that dragged her feet.

Lord, give me strength. Erin stretched an arm around her daughter's back and drew her close. Erin might not like hugs, but her daughter thrived on them. "That's just the way three-year-olds are. They require a lot of attention."

Mik sighed, heaving her shoulders along with it. "I know, but why should I be punished because Dad couldn't keep his pants zipped?"

Erin jerked back as if slapped. "Michaela!" She knew about her father's affair? Oh, boy. That meant it was time for another talk, but not tonight. Nothing was going to spoil this weekend, so she tucked her daughter's head against her shoulder. "That's a question I've asked myself numerous times, and there's no good answer. But I've decided I can't wallow in it. I can't be bitter. Not anymore. And I need to move on with my life." Nearly four years of wallowing had been too long. His selfish actions would no longer steal her joy.

"Dad's moved on. You're moving on." Mik sniffled and dragged an arm across her nose. "Can't I move on, too?"

"Your father loves you."

"Right. That's why he abandoned me." She propelled off the bed.

"Mik, please."

Without turning back, Mik stomped across the room and out the bedroom door.

Lord, help me. Erin massaged her forehead while throwing mental darts at her ex-husband. If only he could see the damage he'd left in his selfish wake, leaving her to pick up all the shattered pieces of their family.

There she went again. Grrr. Reminders of Corey's indiscretions would steal no more seconds of her weekend. Mik would go to his place, she'd end up having fun, and then come home and complain that Erin never did anything fun with her.

So, she did waste another second.

She sighed while adding a few items to her suitcase, including a family-sized bag of Sixlets that likely wouldn't last the weekend, and rolled her luggage out to the living room. Debbie should be here soon. Facing Corey was always easier when another adult was around to keep her from throwing things—okay, she'd only thrown things one time, but that time had been immensely gratifying.

As soon as Corey picked up Mik—who was probably sulking in her bedroom—Erin would be off on a fabulous retreat, surrounded by nature and not a thirteen-year-old drama queen.

God's voice would certainly break through.

Oh, she needed to hear His voice!

The doorbell rang as she set her suitcase by the front door. No surprise, Debbie was right on time.

She pulled open the door, and a brisk, biting wind pushed through the opening. "Are you as ready—"

Her gazed connected with Corey's and tension zapped through her body. He was early? The man was never on time, much less early.

"Hey, sorry I'm early." He combed gloved fingers through blond hair that curled over his ears, landing on his shoulders, hiding the earring she knew he now sported. It all made him look like the artist he'd become. A lazy smile edged up his lips to the left. What did that mean? That he didn't have a care maybe? Or that he was peaceful?

What she did know was that he looked good. Better than when they'd been married, even, and he'd always been a head-turner.

She shook her head to escape from her over-analytical thoughts and crossed her arms. "You're right on time for once. And I need to warn you that puberty is hitting full force."

He shrugged. "Guess we had to expect it. She'll be fine."

Stupid small talk. She always hated this part of the child exchange. Someday she'd never have to see him again. Well, except for graduations and weddings and . . .

Oh, who was she kidding, she'd never be rid of him. But she'd do her best to show he didn't bother her.

She looked beyond Corey's shoulder, glancing between the snowflakes. Where was Debbie, anyway?

Corey followed her gaze. "Looking for something?"

"Just a friend. We're retreating this weekend, so please don't bother me unless it's an absolute emergency."

"I promise."

"I'll get Mik." She closed the door, leaving Corey outside in the cold, with hardly a tinge of guilt. She strode from the entry and through the living room, and down the short hallway to Mik's room. She knocked. "Your dad's here." No reply, which wasn't a surprise. Mik would eventually make her way out, probably hauling a storm cloud darker than the one outside.

On the way back to the front door, Erin glimpsed herself in the hallway mirror. Oh, she was a frumpy mess. She should have freshened up her makeup, her hair. Too late now. Besides, what she looked like to Corey shouldn't matter.

Corey had stepped inside and shut the door behind him. "Is she ready?" He looked past Erin, down the hallway.

Erin shrugged. "Her bag is packed."

"But she doesn't want to come with me." Something unidentifiable flickered on his face as he sighed and looked down at his snow-caked boots. "I'm sorry, Erin."

He was sorry? Three important words spoken far too late, for which she had no response.

Debbie, where are you?

A door slammed behind her, announcing that Miss Attitude was on her way. She slunk into the living room, suitcase in hand, her gaze riveted downward. Oh, Corey and bride were going to have a fun weekend. A wicked smile forced its way out, but Erin quickly tucked it back in. She didn't feel sorry for him, not one little bit.

"Hey, Sixlet, good to see you." He took the suitcase from her and tried to give her a hug, but she pulled away.

"Don't call me Sixlet." She shoved past him, flung open the front door, and trudged in flip-flops across the snow-dotted sidewalk toward his Prius.

That girl was going to be the death of her.

"Mik, your coat." He snatched her winter jacket off the closet hook, but he got the silent treatment. He puffed out a breath and shook his head. "You warned me. This is going to be fun."

"Welcome to my world. At least you don't have to deal with her every day of the week." Erin grabbed Mik's snow boots from the closet and handed them to her ex. "Shouldn't you be going?"

"Uh, yeah." He kicked his heel on her entry rug and looked toward her, but his gaze avoided hers. What did that language say? Was he about to lie? Or was he avoiding something? "Actually, there's a reason I got here early. We're taking Six to see the Grizzlies tonight and need to get on the road."

Corey was going to a hockey game?

The surprise must have shown on her face, because he laughed. "Yeah, it's time I started realizing our daughter isn't going to be an artist, and I need to support her passions."

Erin had nothing to say. Was he finally looking beyond his own wants—not likely!—or did he have an angle?

"Also." Corey looked back at his car then at Erin. "I wanted to ask you, could we, uh." His Adam's apple danced down and back up. "Could you and I get together some time to talk?"

She set her jaw and crossed her arms. "I have nothing more to say to you."

"Yeah, I get that." He drew his fingers through his hair again.

If only she had an interpreter beside her to tell her what Corey's signals were. She always felt as if she was missing half the conversation.

"But there are things I need to tell you." His gaze finally connected with hers. "Things I should have said long ago."

And give him peace about what he'd done to her and Mik? Uh-uh. Sure, listening and forgiving would be the Christian thing to do, but her attitude toward him was anything but Christian. "It's not a good idea."

"Think about it?"

"Maybe." Maybe not. Give him the satisfaction of a *mea culpa*? Hoping she'd absolve him of his guilt? Wasn't going to happen.

She opened the door wider, hoping he'd catch the hint that she wanted him to leave, just as Debbie pulled to the curb behind Corey's car. "My ride's here." Debbie to the rescue once again.

He nodded and stepped outside then turned back. His easy smile had been replaced with a grim line. "We'll have her home Sunday night."

"After eight. I'll be gone until then."

"Will do." He strode down the sidewalk, meeting Debbie halfway. They exchanged terse nods but no words. There was no love lost between those two either.

Debbie grimaced as she climbed the steps to Erin's home. "I'm sorry. Jerry was called into a last-minute parent meeting and got home late, making me late."

"I survived." Erin put on her winter jacket and boots. "Now it's time to get away and pamper ourselves."

"You've earned it." Debbie picked up Erin's toiletry bag.

And Erin grasped her suitcase handle. "*We've* earned it." Besides being a part-time marriage and family therapist, Debbie was mom to three children, including one not too much younger than Mik. The woman deserved a break.

Minutes later, the house was locked tight and they were heading toward the highway, singing like teenagers on a joy ride. Even with the wipers struggling to keep pace with the falling snow, the tension Corey always gifted her with melted away. Nothing was going to spoil this weekend.

Brake lights flashed on the car in front of them, and Debbie's SUV brakes pulsed as her vehicle fishtailed on the black ice.

Erin screeched as the SUV stopped inches behind the car in front of them, and her heart raced faster than the falling snow.

Debbie's hands clenched the steering wheel, her gaze riveted toward the rearview mirror. "Stop. Please stop."

"Oh no!" Erin gripped the sides of her seat, bracing for impact, while watching the vehicle in her side mirror spin a donut. Its trunk barely missed the SUV as it slid into the ditch. A pickup truck followed that car.

Silence.

Followed by ragged breaths, and then nervous giggles. Other drivers stopped to help the ditched cars as Debbie inched her vehicle forward. "How's that for an exciting beginning to our weekend?"

"I'd prefer to keep it a little less dramatic." Erin craned her neck to see beyond the vehicles in front of them. "See anything?"

"Just a lot of traffic. This storm hit earlier than the forecasters said it would."

"There's a surprise." Not really. A preschooler could predict the weather as accurately as the TV news anchors, it seemed. "Good thing we're not going too far. As it is, we'll be on the road for an extra hour."

"Then I suggest we make the best of it." Erin cranked up the volume on the sound system and the women jammed to an eclectic playlist from Skillet to musicals to Michael W. Smith. A little snowstorm would not ruin this weekend.

Two hours of grueling driving later, Debbie pulled into the recently plowed driveway of a lakeside A-frame log home with two bedrooms and two baths, one she'd found on a vacation home rental site. With the snow falling, it could be on a postcard.

"It's perfect." Erin clapped her hands together. "Let the retreating begin!"

A half an hour later, the two women were cozied up in the living room, covered in blankets, a fire warming the open space, and hot cocoa heating their insides. *While You Were Sleeping*, the one chick flick she enjoyed, played on the big screen TV. Even better, cellphone reception was almost non-existent, so interruptions would be minimal. If someone really needed to get in touch with them, they'd have to call the homeowners who lived about a mile away. Now this was the life.

"Why have we not done this before?" Erin grabbed a handful of very buttery popcorn.

"Good question." Debbie stretched her blanket-covered legs on the ottoman the two women shared. "The kids have been getting on my nerves, and even Jerry recognizes that as a sign that it's time for me to get away."

"It's paradise, isn't it? No phones ringing. No Mik whining that a pimple just broke out. Or worse, that I won't let her date until she's sixteen. I'm the worst mom ever! At least I have her father's backing on that one. We don't want a repeat of our fiasco." Dating at thirteen. Pregnant and married at twenty. Just because they practically grew up together, everyone thought they were a shoe-in for life-long love. Puhlease. At least his parents took her side in the divorce. Erin stuffed another handful of popcorn into her mouth.

Debbie laid a hand on Erin's arm. "I'm sorry it worked out that way. And it reminds me to give thanks for Jerry. We haven't had the perfect marriage, but it's been good. He's a good man, and I hope there's an equally good man out there for you."

"Ha!" Erin snorted and popcorn flew from her mouth. "Oh, sorry." She wiped her mouth with a napkin. "Corey cured me forever of wanting a romance." Well, unless it was that eligible guy from church.

"That's a good thing. Too many people focus on romance and forget that it's really about relationship." Debbie pointed at the TV screen. "Sandra Bullock is dreaming of romance with that guy with caterpillar eyebrows. Don't know what she sees in him, but I digress. What she gets is a friendship and a relationship with Bill Pullman, and a love that goes beyond feelings."

Erin laughed—oh it felt good to laugh, to feel and even identify what that feeling was. Debbie brought that out in her. "That's the corniest thing I've ever heard." She lowered her voice, speaking in a radio-announcer tone. "Dr. Debbie expounds on relationship advice found in *While You Were Sleeping*."

Debbie laughed back. "Hey, we're retreating. You can't expect deep, intellectual thoughts this weekend. I left those back in the office."

"Touché." Erin raised her cocoa mug and clinked it with Debbie's. "No deep thoughts. This is a give-your-brain-a-vacation retreat."

"I'll drink to that." Debbie sipped at her cocoa. "But I still think some romance would be good for you."

"Sure. Fine. When Mik graduates from high school, I'll start dating again."

"Is that a promise?"

"Sure. Why not. Maybe that cute guy from church will still be available."

"Ha! I knew you had your eyes on him."

"As does every other single woman in our church." Erin pointed at the TV screen. "This is my favorite part." Not really, but anything to get away from talk of romance. Corey had spoiled its allure for good.

Too quickly, an hour and a half passed, and Bullock and Pullman were riding off into the sunset together. Corny, but cute.

And now it was time for bed and a date with a novel. When was the last time she'd read something for fun? She said goodnight to Debbie, cleaned up, and donned flannel pajamas with footies. Yeah, she was all about romance, baby. Then she snuggled beneath the covers on the queen-sized bed and engrossed herself in the latest Charles Martin novel. Now, he knew how to write romance!

Fifty pages into the book, a pounding came from the main room, propelling Erin from the bed. She hurried from the room, into a dark hallway and bumped into something. Or someone? "Debbie?" *I hope.*

"You heard that too."

"Uh-huh." Erin felt the wall for the switch, and light flooded the living room.

Pound. Pound. Pound.

On the front door?

Shivers tingled down Erin's spine as the two women approached the door.

"One second." Erin grabbed the poker from the fireplace and stood to the side of the door as Debbie opened it.

A burly man stood thigh-deep in snow on the stoop. "Erin Belden?" He looked from Debbie to Erin and to the poker.

"Who wants to know?" Erin backed away and held the poker like a baseball bat.

"Wendell Horton, ma'am."

Oh, the homeowner. Erin lowered the poker but kept it ready just in case. "What do you need?"

"Got a phone call. There's been an accident."

Debbie gasped.

"An accident?" Erin kept her voice steady. No sense jumping to conclusions when she didn't have all the facts to analyze.

"Yes, ma'am. Involving one of your daughters."

The two women shared a wide-eyed glance, and Debbie managed to eke out, "Do you have a name?"

"Uh, yeah." He removed his gloves and tugged a wrinkled piece of paper from his pocket. "A Michaela Belden."

Chapter Two

"Mik!" A thousand questions whirled through her brain that processed information far too slowly. But the main question finally passed her lips. "Is she all right?"

Not waiting for an answer, Erin looked around for her coat, but all she saw was an image of her daughter laying crumpled in a pool of blood. She barely felt Debbie's arm wrap around her shoulders.

"Please come in, Mr. Horton." Her friend's voice was unbelievably calm. How could Debbie remember her manners at a time like this? Erin could hardly recall her own name.

"'Preciate it." He stepped inside with snow caked up to the top of his boots. "It's nasty out there."

"What happened to my daughter?" Erin couldn't restrain herself any longer. Normally, she wasn't given to displaying emotion, but when it came to her daughter's wellbeing, she became a mama bear.

Mr. Horton's lips drew into a straight line. "She's okay, Mrs. Belden. Banged up good, has a mild concussion, but otherwise came through fine."

He couldn't have said that at the beginning?

Still, Erin practically wilted with relief as she reined in her feelings and tucked them away where they belonged. "Thank you for letting us know. May I use your phone to call her?" Mik needed to know she'd be there as soon as she could.

"That's not all." Mr. Horton removed his bomber cap and held it close to his chest. "I'd prefer you talk with Mr. Monson. He's the one who called."

"Jon." Erin thought out loud. One of the 3 Sixlets—an artist, a nerd, and an introvert— who'd formed what they'd thought was an unbreakable childhood bond with her and Corey. Corey not only broke their marriage vows, he'd broken up the 3 Sixlets and stole Jon's friendship along with it.

Erin shook her head, trying to wrap her mind around Mr. Horton's words. Accident. Michaela. Jon. Corey?

"Corey. Is he all right?" Erin finally spotted her winter coat hanging on a coat tree right by the door.

"I couldn't tell you anything else ma'am. Just that Mr. Monson wants to hear from you as soon as possible."

"What are we waiting for?" Erin grabbed her coat and squeezed her footie-pajama-covered feet into her boots. Ignoring Debbie's and Mr. Horton's pleas for her to take it easy, she ran outside into snow falling so thick, she couldn't see Mr. Horton's vehicle.

Seconds later, she felt Debbie at her side, tugging her in a different direction. And then they were in some vehicle, driving through a thick forest, veiled by even thicker snow.

Corey had to be all right. Sure, he'd wronged her and Mik, but that didn't mean he deserved to be hurt. Mik needed a father. Erin couldn't raise their daughter on her own. But it would be just like Corey to shirk out of his parenting duties as he'd skipped out of his husband role.

Why was she assuming the worst?

Because Mr. Horton wouldn't be so evasive if Corey were okay.

Somehow, she found herself inside Mr. Horton's house, seated by the fireplace with a cup of hot cocoa in her hands, and wrapped in a blanket.

"She's in shock." Erin heard Debbie say through a dense fog. "I'll see if I can get her to talk."

Her shoulder shook. "Erin. Jon's on the phone. He needs to speak with you." The phone was placed in her hand. She stared at it then raised it to her ear. She could do this. She cleared her throat. "Jon?"

"Erin."

"How's Mik?"

"She's fine. Not even a broken bone. She has a mild concussion that'll give her headaches, some blurred vision, dizziness, but she'll be okay."

"Is she there with you?"

"Yeah, she is."

"I need to talk to her."

"She's resting."

"I don't care. Put her on. I need to hear her voice."

"I guess you do. One second."

Erin tapped her foot, waiting too long for that one second.

"Mom?" Mik said through a sniffle.

Erin breathed out a sigh. "How are you doing, sweetheart? I want to be there. I'm coming as soon as I can." She needed to see her daughter, even hug her, let her know her mom would never abandon her like her father had.

"I . . ." More sniffles. "I just can't . . ."

"Can't what?"

More infernal silence. What was going on at that hospital?

"Hey Erin, Mik is having difficulty talking. She's pretty upset." He sniffled.

He sniffled? Wait. Jon does not sniffle. He does not cry.

What weren't they telling her?

"How's Corey?"

More sniffles.

Even she could read that language. Erin looked upward and blinked. "He's gone. Isn't he?"

"No. He's not, but . . ."

She waited, listening to more silence. No surprise, the attorney knew how to evade a question he didn't want to answer. "Tell me about Corey!" She practically yelled into the phone.

"He's not good, Erin," he said barely above a whisper. "They're taking him into surgery now. He's bleeding internally."

"Where are they at? I'm coming."

"You can't. We're in St. Paul, and the freeway is closed. The roads are impassible."

She gritted her teeth. "I have to be there. For Mik. For Corey. I need to show him what it's like to be there for the people you love."

"He knows."

A child's cry came over the receiver, waking Erin to reality. Corey didn't need her. He had his replacement wife and daughter.

"You're right, he's got that woman." Erin refused to say the name of her ex-husband's new bride. "But Mik—"

"Lilith didn't make it."

"—does. Wait. What?"

The child's cries became clearer, calling for Mommy.

"It was bad, Erin. The roads were icy. Someone slid into their lane, and they were hit head-on. Mik and Clara are okay. I've got Clara now. Trying to keep her awake."

Erin stared off at the fireplace. She needed to do something. Fix the situation somehow. "Tell me about Corey. Why the surgery? What are his chances?"

"Brain hemorrhage. They're trying to stop it, but they're not optimistic."

Debbie handed her a box of tissues.

But tears weren't even a thought. "Well he better make it. You go tell him he's got two daughters to take care of. An ex-wife who still cares for him. No, change that. I want to tell him myself, so inform him he has to hold on until I get there. He wanted to have a talk with me before I left. You let him know, I'm ready to listen. Got that?"

"I do. And I'm praying. A whole bunch of people are praying. And people from Corey's church are here too."

Erin squeezed her eyes closed. Prayer hadn't even crossed her mind. She caught a glimpse of Debbie beside her, her head bowed. Even Mr. Horton sat close by, hands folded. What kind of Christian was she?

"I'm praying too." She raised her chin. Or she would be the second they ended the call. "Call me as soon you know something."

"I promise. And I made a promise to Corey too, that I'd give you a message."

"Uh-huh. He can tell me in person."

"I knew you'd say that, but he made me promise. He said he's sorry. For everything."

She scoffed. "I want to hear those words from his lips."

"That's not all."

Erin wiped a tissue beneath her suddenly runny nose but didn't respond. Couldn't respond. How dare he threaten to die on her and get out of the tough job of saying those words face to face? It was just like Corey to take the easy route.

Cries for Mommy became shrill.

"Erin, Corey wants you to raise Clara. It's in his and Lilith's will."

Bouncing little Clara on his lap, Jon Monson listened to silence on Erin's end. He'd made those changes in the will himself just a few months ago after Corey had finally screwed his head on straight.

None of them had imagined that change would be necessary this soon.

Clara released another shrill cry for Mommy, so he tucked her against his shoulder, rubbing a hand over her back. This was why he never wanted to become a parent. He had no parenting skills whatsoever.

Silence still echoed from Erin's end of the phone. Knowing her past, that scared the Dickens out of him. "Erin. Talk to me. Hand the phone to Debbie. Are you there?"

"Jon?"

Debbie. Whew. "Is she okay? Do I need to come up there?" He'd saved her life once and would commandeer a snowmobile and race to her now if he had to.

"I think she's in shock. What did you tell her?"

"I was afraid of that. I told her that Corey listed her as guardian, should something happen to him and Lilith."

"You've got to be kidding me. No wonder she's in shock."

"Giving her custody made sense. She knows Clara better than anyone else."

"As a babysitter."

"Yes. Clara's *only* babysitter." With Corey working on his art at home, Clara didn't have to go to daycare, and Erin had volunteered for infrequent babysitting duties so the sisters would have more time together. With Erin, it had always been about what was best for family. "Besides, Erin's a great mom, and Mik is Clara's sister. This is all about what's best for the child, and Erin is who's best."

"Right. But is Clara best for Erin?"

That was the million-dollar question. "I don't know." Would custody of her ex-husband's child, the one who triggered his divorce and remarriage, send Erin over the edge again?

"Stay with her." Jon bounced Clara, who was calming down again.

"She won't leave my sight. Mr. Horton has offered us the spare bedroom for the night."

"Perfect." Just the assurance he needed. Clara squawked again.

"Sounds like you have your hands full."

"Guess I do. This child-sitting thing isn't for sissies." Give him his child-free, bachelor life any day. As a divorce attorney, working with so many broken families affirmed that decision, in spite of Corey's last words before heading into surgery.

"No. No it's not. Let Corey know we're praying and not to give up. We'll be down as soon as the roads allow."

"And I'll keep you posted if there are any updates." He hit End Call then stood and bounced Clara on his hip. He was on the same page as Debbie. Corey better not give up. Not when he'd finally learned what living was about. Not when their friendship was back on track. Not when his daughters desperately needed a father.

"You hear that, God?" He looked up and spoke in a whisper, even though Clara's cries would cover anything said. "You can't have him yet."

And then there was Erin.

Oh, he'd hated dropping that bombshell on her, especially when the news could affect her mental health, but the sooner she realized the responsibility that lay ahead of her, the better.

If Corey didn't make it.

"It's okay, sweetie." He kissed the screaming child's forehead and paced the waiting room. "Uncle Jon has you."

"Jon?"

He turned to the familiar voice and heaved a sigh. "Mr. and Mrs. Belden. So glad you could make it safely."

"It's Joyce to you." Mrs. Belden relieved him of the girl, thank goodness. "Come to Grandma, sweetie."

And just like that, Clara hushed. Proof that he should never marry or have kids.

"How's Corbin doing?" Henry Belden gestured to a pair of open chairs across from where Mik had fallen asleep sitting up. Or she was faking it well. Being a teenager was tough enough, but with the mess her dad left her in, Jon did not envy the job Erin had.

He gladly joined Corey's dad. "Not good, Mr. B—"

"Henry."

"Henry." Jon looked down the hallway from where he expected the surgeon to come. "Not good. He's got an intracerebral hemorrhage—"

"What's that in English?"

"It means the brain tissue is bleeding. That on top of other injuries. It's not good, Henry. It's a miracle he's alive."

"Then we'll expect another miracle." Joyce sat beside him, cradling a now-sleeping Clara on her lap. How did she do that? "You get in touch with Erin?"

He nodded. "She said she has a thing or two to tell Corey."

"I'm sure she does." Henry picked at some imaginary spot on his jeans. "And I'll be backing her up. What our boy put her through. What he's still putting us through."

What he put Mik through. He better live so he could make it up to all his family. Corey had apologized to nearly everyone he'd hurt over the last years, but apologies didn't undo the havoc he'd created.

Besides, Jon needed his best friend. Corey was all he had.

Well, except for Erin.

Speaking of righting a wrong, how was Jon going to make it up to Erin for his disappearing act these past three-plus years? He'd find a way. He had to. He'd promised Corey before going into surgery that he'd watch out for—no, those weren't Corey's words. He'd said, "Care for Erin, Mik, and Clara." That Erin needed a man like him, and the girls needed a father. If only he hadn't promised Corey that he would be that man.

Chapter Three

Erin awoke and sat up in a panic. Where was she?

"You okay?" Debbie's voice drew her attention to a rocking chair to her left.

Oh, that's right. They were at Mr. Horton's. Debbie had slept in the other twin bed in his guestroom.

And Corey was in the hospital.

Sunlight bled through the curtain. Morning? What time was it? Why hadn't they heard anything more about Corey? If the sun was shining, that meant the roads were likely open, and they had to leave. Now.

She threw off the covers and realized she had no spare clothes with her.

Debbie got up and set something on the bed. Her suitcase. "Mr. Horton and I retrieved all our things last night. You were out cold. I was just going to wake you up."

"Any news?" Erin threw open the suitcase and grabbed jeans and a sweatshirt.

"He came through surgery but isn't out of the woods."

"So, he's going to live."

"That's not what I said, hon. Things aren't looking good. He lost a lot of blood. His body is banged up. He . . ." Debbie sniffled and wiped her eyes. "Let's get you to the hospital. Maybe hearing your voice will make a difference."

"Or maybe it'll make him worse." She drew on her jeans.

"I don't believe that, and neither do you. He's not the same person who messed up with you."

"But I'm still the same person he walked out on." Erin pulled the sweatshirt over her head then secured her hair in a ponytail. "I'm ready."

A couple hours later, Debbie pulled up outside the emergency room door of Grace Hospital in St. Paul. "Are you sure you don't want me to come in with you?"

Erin nodded and got out. She held onto the vehicle door and looked inside. "But keep your phone close. I have a feeling I'm going to need to vent."

"I'll be available."

Erin turned to go.

"One more thing."

Erin glanced over her shoulder at her friend leaning across the seat.

"It's okay to feel."

Feel? The only thing she felt was numb. No, not true. She was angry at Corey. Again.

"And feelings aren't bad, it's what you choose to do with the feelings that matters."

Yeah, yeah, yeah, she got it. "So, don't go giving Corey an earful for hurting my daughter and Clara." Which she'd really love to do.

Debbie shrugged. "Probably not the best idea."

"But it would make me feel better."

"Until it made you feel worse."

Right.

"And it's okay to share what you're feeling with others. They'll get it."

No, they won't. That was one lesson she'd learned over the years. No one cared one iota about her feelings, when she understood what they were. No one but Debbie.

"You sure you don't want me to come in with you?"

Erin shook her head, snapping back to reality. "I'm good. Really." She could be strong for Mik. She always had been.

"Erin, go find your daughter."

Her daughter.

"I'm going." She shut the SUV door and aimed for the hospital. What about her ex-husband's daughter? Would she be here, too? Corey wouldn't dare abandon another daughter. And if he did, how could he possibly expect Erin to raise and love the child that he left her and Mik for?

Mik and Clara deserved better, so Corey had better live, the jerk.

She hurried through the revolving doors and navigated a maze of corridors to an elevator. She rode that up a couple of floors, then wound down a few more hallways scented with antiseptic.

There was Corey's mom.

And Clara.

But where was—

"Mom!"

"Mik!" She spun around and her daughter bowled into her. "Oh, honey, are you okay?" Erin cradled her daughter's face between her hands and lifted up her chin. A few scrapes and bruises were the only indicators that a tragedy had taken place.

"Daddy." Mik sniffled and tears streamed down her daughter's cheeks. Like her father, Mik displayed her emotions for all to see.

"Oh, honey." Erin drew her daughter tight against her, absorbing her child's heaving sobs. This girl needed her father.

"Erin?"

Without releasing Mik, Erin looked to her left. And up. And blinked. "Jon?" No glasses. Styled hair. And a fancy suit, minus the jacket. Not at all the Jon she remembered. Somehow, he seemed taller too. This man was a head-turner, and no longer a geek. It had been well over three years since they'd seen each other, but this was a big change even for that.

He shrugged a single shoulder. "Came from a date."

Erin looked around the waiting room occupied only by her ex-mother-in-law.

And that child.

"She went home." The dark bags beneath his eyes gave away his lack of sleep. He gestured to a chair.

She ignored it. She'd just sat for two hours in a SUV. Now she needed to stand. Walk. Pace.

Pray.

"I'd offer you a coffee . . ." He shrugged. This incident might just induce her to drink the nasty stuff.

"I'll take one." Mik managed to lift her head, her gaze seeking approval from Erin, as if her never-stand-still daughter needed caffeine.

That wasn't a battle worth fighting today. "Fine." If her daughter wanted to drink coffee, she could go right ahead.

Jon headed down a hallway.

"Wait up." Erin led Mik to a chair, promised to be right back, then caught up to her former best buddy. "How's he doing? Can I see him?"

He kept walking.

"I need an answer, Jon."

He finally stopped and leaned against a wall, bracing his forehead on spread fingers as if trying to pull out emotions, or stuff them back in. "It's not good," he said, barely above a whisper. Even with his head down, she could see tears staining his cheeks. "He lost too much blood. His organs are shutting down." Sniffling, he glanced up at her with eyes veined in red. "They're waiting for family to withdraw care."

"No." Erin shook her head and looked back toward the waiting room. "He's too young. Mik needs him. *Clara* needs him. He'll pull through."

Jon took her hand and looked her in the eye. Then nodded. "You should go tell him that yourself. I believe in miracles."

And she was claiming one today. "Where is he?"

"I'll take you. Henry's with him right now."

"Then let's go wake him up so Clara and Mik have a daddy." Erin strode down the hall then stopped and looked back at Jon. He nodded to the hallway to his right. "Oh." She hurried back and walked alongside her childhood best buddy, one of the 3 Sixlets. Corey hadn't liked calling themselves the Three Musketeers. That wasn't colorful enough for him. The fact that their little group consisted of only three friends, not six, hadn't mattered. Even after she and Corey had started dating, Jon had hung around. Even in their marriage, Jon remained best friends with both of them. But when Corey abandoned her, Jon had too. That had hurt almost as much as Corey's actions.

He steered her down another hallway, then stopped by a closed door.

"This is it?" She reached for the knob.

He gripped her hand. "It's not pretty, Erin. He's beat up badly, then there's all these wires and tubes . . . You won't recognize him."

Erin clenched her fists and her jaw. "Doesn't matter."

"Just wanted you to be prepared."

She nodded and opened the door.

And couldn't move. Jon's warning wasn't sufficient at all. That man lying in the bed was as pale as the snow outside and had to be twenty-five years older than her ex-husband. "That can't be Corey. Are you sure?"

Jon didn't answer. He didn't have to.

She forced her feet to move to the side of the bed and took his hand. It felt cold, lifeless, so she braced it with both her hands, hoping to warm it, let Corey know she was there.

"Hey Red Sixlet, this is one heckuva way to demand attention. You do know I had to cut my retreat short. You owe me, so you better get your behind up out of this bed soon and pay me back." She rubbed a finger beneath her nose. "And your daughters need you, too. You think I want to handle Mik alone during her teen years? Uh-uh. And Clara. She's a mini-Lilith with all that blonde curly hair, and a mini-you with her love for art. Who's going to teach her if you're not around, huh? You know I can't even draw a stick figure. So, you need to fight this, Red, got it?"

"She's right, Red." Jon had somehow moved to the other side of the bed without her noticing. "With Clara, the Sixlets have almost completed our six-pack, so you've gotta stick around. If you don't, I'll sue you, man. And if you go, who am I going to pick on?" His gaze lifted to Erin. "Who'll look out for Pearl?"

Her Sixlet nickname. She hadn't heard it in years, and hearing it now almost made her want to cry.

But she wasn't a crier.

She regained her voice. "Exactly. And who'll keep Purple in line?" She speared Jon with her gaze. "The guy sniffs out trouble faster than snow falls in April."

"True." Jon quirked a smile. "Trouble always seems to find me, and I need you to bail me out, Red."

Silence overtook the room, then Jon was praying out loud, begging for a miracle. Asking for wisdom and guidance, back to begging.

She added a soft "Amen" to his, then just stood there holding

Corey's cold, limp hand.

She'd expected something more. Maybe a twitch of an eye or movement in a finger, something to indicate that her Corey was still in there.

Jon gestured toward the door, but she couldn't leave yet, not when she had more to say. Debbie had told her not to be afraid to express her feelings, and rare feelings were bubbling to the surface. Now wasn't the time to hide them.

She leaned over, close to his ear, planning to tell him how angry she was, but other, foreign words spilled from her mouth, and once they started gushing, she couldn't stop. "I'm so sorry about us, Corey. I'm sorry for not trying harder. I shouldn't have given up so easily. I . . ." Forgive? Even now, the word wouldn't break free from her mouth. Instead, she braced a hand on his cold, paper-like cheek. "You were always my first love." She kissed his cheek. "And I still do love you."

She'd never stopped, even though he'd been a Class-A jerk. Yeah, feelings were stupid. No wonder she avoided them.

Then in a fog, she followed Jon out the door. This couldn't be happening. Corey couldn't die now, not when so many things were left unsaid. Why hadn't she taken a moment to listen to what he had to say earlier? Even listening for a few minutes could have changed the timeline of his life.

An arm circled her shoulders, then Jon drew her in close to his chest. A normal person would cry, but she couldn't even pretend to summon tears.

"We're not getting our miracle, are we?" She whispered into his shirt. "We have to say goodbye."

He stroked her back and mumbled, "I think we do. It's not fair to him to keep him from going home. You do know, he's a believer now."

Erin nodded. Corey had told her as much several months ago,

not that she'd cared then, but it mattered now. She stepped back, took Jon's hand, and led him to the waiting room where Corey's parents and Mik still awaited. All three looked up at the couple.

"It's time?" Jon graciously spoke the words for her.

Henry and Joyce nodded their consent. Mik, sitting uncharacteristically still, looked to the wall, maybe hoping to hide more tears. Then Jon informed the medical staff of the family's decision.

But first they had to say goodbye.

Keeping one hand in Jon's and the other in Mik's, they led the small group to Corey's room. Nothing had changed. Just the beep, beep, beep of some machine that said his heart was still pumping, probably with the help of another machine. Corey hadn't miraculously opened his eyes. Wasn't sitting up. Wasn't talking up a stream or asking for a paintbrush.

He just lay there.

God wasn't giving them a miracle.

His parents approached him first.

And Henry grasped his son's hand. "Hey Corbin, looks like Jesus wants you to come home. Who are we to argue with that? Don't forget to put in a good word for me, okay? I know I don't always make it to church, but He and I commune up at the cabin a lot. Had a talk or two about you, and He just said to trust Him. Guess I'm still doing that. Love you, son."

Joyce adjusted the sheets, pulling them up to her son's chin. "You always were the dramatic one, Corbin. I'm going to miss that. You added so much color to our lives. Everything's going to seem a bit grayer now." She sniffled and Erin handed her a tissue. "And Heaven's going to be that much more colorful. I can see you standing at the easel, Jesus at your side, painting with colors we never imagined. Make certain you save one of those pieces of artwork for your father and me.

"Oh, and your brother's still out galivanting around the world. He wanted to make it home, but the airport's been closed. Always an excuse with him, right? He sends his love. I know I didn't say it enough, but I do love you, Corbin. With all my heart, I love you. Now, go help God paint a sunset."

Gripping Erin's hand, Mik also took her dad's hand. "I'm sorry I've been such a brat lately. I didn't mean it, I just . . . I wanted you and Mom to be back together like it used to be, and I know that was selfish."

"No, sweetie, it wasn't selfish at all." Erin squeezed her daughter's hand. She wouldn't allow her daughter to feel any guilt for wanting their family to be whole.

"I promise to be a better daughter for Mom. Maybe I'll even take out that paint set you gave me. Maybe I could paint the softball field, with you in the stands. What do you think of that? I'll miss seeing you there. You were my biggest fan." She kissed his cheek. "Love you, Daddy."

"Hey, Red." Jon pretended to punch Corey in the shoulder. "You've got a lot of people loving on you here. Not one of us would object, though, if you sat up and said, 'April Fools!' Yeah, we'd freak out a bit, but then we'd all have a good laugh. But hey, if that's not in your plans, I get it. You've got a chance to walk through those pearly gates, and man, you need to take it. There's no more pain there. No mistakes. No heartbreak. I envy you, Red. Oh, and would you do me a favor? Check out all the hamburger joints. When I join you, we'll share a Juicy Lucy together like old times. Love you, Red."

Oh, dear Jesus, how was she going to make it? By these tributes, one would think Corey was the best dad, son, friend out there. But he hadn't been. Not at all. And now she was supposed to give him a glowing farewell? With everyone watching? Yeah, she meant what she'd told him a few minutes back, that she still loved him, but those words had exited and fled and new feelings had taken their place.

"Just be honest, Pearl." Jon whispered in her ear.

She looked back at him, and he nodded. The family gathered in the room all gave their affirmation.

"Well then." She gripped Corey's lifeless hand again. "What I said earlier about you being my best friend, and that I still love you. True. I've been bitter, and this new thing you dumped on me? Raising Clara?" She shook her head. "I don't know what you're thinking. How can I love her when all I'll see is you? With Lilith. That's not fair, Corey, and you know it. I'll do my best, that's all I can promise. I'm still going to miss you, you jerk. I've always missed you."

That was it. She couldn't take it anymore. Couldn't watch the doctors remove life support.

She hurried from the room and strode down the hallway in search of a restroom, a place where she could have privacy to sort through her thoughts and try to figure out what she was feeling. All she knew was that her desire to start over again, to maybe have time for romance, had been squashed by her ex and his will. Sure, she was being selfish, but raising a child wasn't like adopting a cat or a dog. It was a lifetime commitment she had no choice in, thrust on her.

She found a restroom and locked herself inside a stall where no one could find her. She had to figure out a way around receiving custody of Clara. In their sixties, Corey's folks wouldn't want to raise a three-and-a-half-year-old, and his brother was too busy traveling the world to settle down with a child.

What about Lilith's parents? They came from money. They could easily afford a nanny and college and all that came with raising a child. And they were in their early fifties.

Yes, they could do it.

The only other option would be adoption, and that didn't sit right with her. The sisters shouldn't be separated that much.

All she really knew was that she could not, she would not raise her ex-husband's love-child. Clara deserved to be loved, and Erin couldn't promise that.

Once the funerals were over, she'd ask Jon how to sort through custody issues legally.

Chapter Four

Jon couldn't remain in the room as medical personnel removed life support from his best friend. They'd said it could take hours or days before Corey finally went home. And there was no doubt anymore where Corey was headed. He'd become on fire for Christ in his last months.

So why would God take him just as Corey had come to know Jesus? With his art, he could have made such an impact on the world.

Jon wiped an arm over his eyes and nose. Now who would he have to shoot the bull with? The two of them could talk about anything, but then, they had been friends for over twenty years, almost two thirds of his life.

Along with Erin. The 3 Sixlets. Jon shook his head. They'd made a great team until Corey messed everything up.

Wait. Where was Erin? He looked up and down the empty halls, then jogged to the waiting room. Empty. She'd left the hospital room before him. Where would she go? He dug out his phone and scrolled through the numbers until he found one he hadn't called in too long, and pressed Call.

It went to voice mail.

A curse word flitted through his head as memories from nearly four years ago replayed like a movie in his brain. He had to find her. Now.

He hurried back toward the hospital room and found Corey's folks and his daughters in the hallway. There wasn't a dry eye among them. The last thing he wanted to do was worry them more, but he had to find Erin.

Panting, he blurted out, "Do you know where Erin went?"

The Beldens exchanged a look, then both shook their heads.

"Haven't seen her since she said goodbye to Corey." Henry's eyes narrowed. "You don't suppose . . ."

Jon gulped, grateful Henry didn't finish the sentence. Jon knew what he referred to. "I hope not."

Mik mumbled something.

"What was that, dumpling?" Henry placed a meaty hand on his granddaughter's shoulder.

"Bath. Room." She enunciated between sniffles. "She always hides in the bathroom when she wants to be alone."

He should have known. That was exactly where he'd found her almost four years ago. He looked up and down the hallways checking for signage, but saw nothing, so he ran to the nearest nurses' station. "Where's the nearest restroom?"

A young man in scrubs laughed. "Gotta go that bad, huh?"

He growled back. "Just tell me where it is."

"Down the hallway and take a left." He gestured to his right. "Some people have no sense of humor."

Jon barely heard the words as he took off. He turned the corner and found a restroom. For men. He almost swore out loud this time. Where . . . ? He turned in a circle.

Behind him. Duh!

He banged on the women's room door.

No answer, not that he expected one.

He banged again. "Erin, if you're in there, please answer me."

Still quiet.

This time, the curse word slipped past his lips. God would

forgive him. Just as He'd forgive Jon barging into the ladies' room.

"Then I'm coming in." He pushed open the door. There were three stalls, and only the door to the handicap stall was closed. "Erin, you better speak now or I'm—"

"I'm here, all right? Can't a women pee in peace?"

Whew.

"I was . . . worried."

The toilet flushed over his declaration, then the door flung open. "No need to worry." She stepped past him to the sink.

No surprise, Erin's eyes weren't wet. Her face wasn't flushed red with grief, although he knew she felt it. She just felt it deeper than most and couldn't always identify what she was feeling, not until it spewed out like a volcano releasing pent-up gasses and lava. Her release was just as volatile and dangerous.

"You're okay?" He looked over her shoulder, into the mirror, as she washed her hands.

"Do you make a habit of entering women's bathrooms?" She brushed past him to the self-starting dryer.

Same obstinate woman she'd always been.

"Only when I'm concerned about you," he said once the dryer shut off.

"Concerned about me?" She slapped a hand to her forehead. "Now you're concerned about me? Then where have you been the last four years when I've needed you?"

"I . . ." He couldn't answer. Not here. Not this way.

"Yeah. Just as I thought." She fled from the room, leaving him standing there, wanting to chase after her, tell her he'd wanted to be there for her, but he couldn't. Not on that day almost four years ago. Since then, avoiding her had become easy.

But now, with Corey about to meet Jesus, with this crazy—but correct—change in custody for Clara and his promise to Corey, he couldn't avoid Erin any longer. They'd be working together tightly for the next months as they straightened out the matters of Corey and Lilith's estate. The will was straightforward, but when it came to legal matters, the cogs turned slower than a sloth at the DMV.

In the meantime, he had something even less fun to worry about: meeting with the social worker and Erin to send Clara home.

The door to the bathroom opened, tearing him from his reverie. His gaze collided with a twenty-something woman whose eyes grew round as quarters.

"Uh, I'm s . . . sorry." She backed out.

Idiot. He hurried from the restroom, threw a hasty apology to the young woman, and retreated to the waiting room where he found Clara clinging to Joyce, Mik slumping, Henry probably in with Corey. No sight of Erin. Why wasn't he surprised?

Sophie, his date from last night, had also arrived, but in the capacity of county social worker here to relay the "good news" to Erin that Clara would get to go home with her. He'd already cleared that with Sophie, but not Erin. Oh, that was going to go over like turkeys dropped from a helicopter.

Now to convince her that Clara living with her was the best thing for all involved.

Especially Erin.

Once he found her. Again.

At times like this, Erin wished she liked coffee. She sipped at her Pepsi, willing the caffeine to kick in and wake her up from this nightmare, but the antiseptic sterility of the hospital hallways told her otherwise. So, since this was her new reality, she'd better figure out how she was going to deal with Clara.

No. She'd worry about Clara tomorrow. Or the next day. Right now, she needed to take her daughter home and hold her and hopefully get some sleep. Mik was so much like her father in that she needed that touch to show she was loved, where touch only added to Erin's stress.

No doubt, that was one of the things that had driven Corey away.

Tomorrow she'd give Debbie a call to help unpack her feelings. And then she could find a solution for Clara.

The hallway spilled into the waiting room, and she immediately searched for Mik, but her gaze slid to Jon having an intimate conversation with an elegant-looking woman. His date from last night, maybe? She'd love to see Jon find someone, even though he'd long ago claimed the life-long bachelor title. That could always change. Or, as far as she knew, maybe it had already changed. While Corey had often mentioned Jon in casual conversation over the years, he hadn't expounded on their friend's love life.

She hurried past the couple, sat by Mik, and wrapped an arm around her daughter's back. Mik leaned into her, and Erin felt tiny shudders from silent tears. Corey never really knew how much his little girl loved him, how she looked up to him, how she'd desperately longed to have him back in her life full time.

"I'm so sorry, Sixlet."

Mik's shuddering stopped, her head angled toward her shuffling feet. "I always liked that nickname." She sounded like Erin's baby girl again, not the angst-ridden, anger-driven teenager.

"I know, baby, I know." Erin stroked her daughter's silky chestnut-brown hair.

She sniffled. "But I was such a brat to him, and now . . ."

Erin kissed Mik's forehead. "And he loved you regardless. You were so precious to him."

"Then why . . ." Mik shook her head. "Forget it."

No, she wouldn't forget it. Mik deserved an answer to her question. Assuming her daughter was wondering why her father left them, Erin explained as best she could without putting Corey down. That had always been her goal, but she'd failed too often. "Remember that just because we're adults, doesn't mean we don't act stupid or childish or selfish. I hope you'll forgive your daddy . . . and me. We both should have been better examples. I promise to try harder."

"I do too. Pinky swear?" She held out her right-hand pinky, and Erin hooked her own pinky around it.

"Pinky swear." In Mik's book, that carried more weight than swearing on the Bible. Erin sealed the promise with another kiss to the forehead. "What do you say about going home and getting some sleep? It's going to be a long few days coming up."

"That's a good idea." Jon suddenly hovered above them, alongside the elegant woman who now held a sleeping Clara in her arms. Erin had been so immersed in her conversation with Mik, she'd completely shut out the rest of the world. Something she excelled at doing. Another thing Corey had disliked about her.

Had Jon and this woman been a thing for a while? Clara looked awfully cozy with them.

Wait. Maybe that was her answer! Maybe Jon was going to marry Miss Elegant, and they could adopt Clara and live happily ever after! Jon would make certain that Mik and Clara spent lots of sister time together. They could even have barbeques together and act like one big family. Yeah, that would work.

Maybe they were already officially a thing. Erin glanced at the woman's ring finger. Empty, but that didn't mean anything nowadays when so many were ignoring long-held traditions.

Erin stood and offered her hand to the woman. "I don't believe we've met. You're a good friend of Jon's?"

The woman smiled up at him, and he shared the glance, one Erin couldn't interpret, not that that was unusual.

"We go way back and have worked together frequently." The woman took Erin's hand. "Sophie Nichols. I'm the social worker assigned to Clara."

Oh. "So, you aren't together?"

The two laughed as if she'd told the funniest joke.

And that awoke Clara. The child looked up at Sophie and her lower lip started to tremble. A crying child was the last thing this tired group of people needed, so Erin reached out for the child who eagerly came to her and wrapped her arms around Erin's neck.

The couple shared a glance that communicated something else Erin couldn't understand.

Then Sophie gave Jon's hand a quick squeeze. "I allow him a sympathy date now and then when he needs a plus-one, but I've known him long enough to realize the two of us wouldn't last any longer than a Minnesota summer."

Jon shrugged. "She's right."

Well there went that plan.

Sophie gave Jon a side hug, like a sister would, darn it. "Unfortunately, there's only one woman for this guy, but she's clueless."

Interesting. Erin tapped her chin while lightly swaying with Clara on her hip. Maybe her plan wasn't foiled yet. "Then maybe you and I need to get together for a cocoa date to discuss this mystery woman."

"Don't you dare." He skewered Sophie with another indecipherable look. It almost felt like people were talking behind her back. "I'll have you both know that my bachelorhood remains firmly intact, and I plan to keep it that way."

Both women laughed. Oh, it felt good to do that.

But now it was time to go home and let Mik cry on her shoulder. She adjusted Clara to the other hip and then reached down to touch her daughter's arm. "Let's get going, Sixlet."

"Actually, Michaela." Jon set a hand on Mik's shoulder. "Sophie and I need to talk privately with your mom for a moment, then I'll bring you all home."

Oh, that's right. She hadn't even considered that she didn't have transportation home. Her brain was still on retreat.

And what did Jon and the social worker need from her at this moment? "Can't it wait?" Her gaze slid from Jon to Sophie. "It's been a really long day."

Sophie touched Erin, who flinched. "I'm afraid it can't wait. It's about Clara."

Now that woke her up. Taking care of Clara was priority number one. Keeping the awake-one-moment-and-sleeping-the-next child on her hip, she followed the couple down a hallway to an empty waiting room. They weren't sending Clara to some foster home, were they? She hugged Clara tighter. Henry and Joyce may not want permanent custody of their granddaughter, but they would be glad to take her in until custody was established.

Jon and Sophie sat side by side, and Erin took a chair kitty-corner to them. She'd voice her opinion before they had a chance to offer something foolish. "If your thoughts are about shipping Clara to some foster home, forget it."

Sophie touched her again, and Erin did her best not to react. "I was hoping you'd say that."

Oh, good. "She'll be staying with Henry and Joyce, then?"

"Actually." Sophie folded her hands on her lap. "The number-one priority for us is the well-being of the child."

"Right." Erin kissed the child on her forehead where a single bandage was attached. "And I can't think of anyone better than her grandparents."

"They would be good, yes, but there's someone better." Jon bore his gaze into her so hard that she felt as if he'd pressed her into the chair.

"What do you mean?" Her words came out small, quiet as she clung to the child like a shield. She might not be good at reading non-verbal communication, but she wasn't a dummy.

They wanted her to bring Clara home.

"Erin." His gaze still had her pinned. "You've been her primary babysitter. She knows you better than her grandparents." He nodded to the girl. "Obviously, she feels comfortable with you. Corey always said no one was better with kids than you."

He did, did he? Would have been nice to hear from his lips.

"He and Lilith also agreed that one of the smartest things they'd done was to change their will to give you custody."

Erin certainly wouldn't call it smart. This child needed someone who would love them unconditionally. That could never be Erin.

"And Jon tells me that you already have your home set up for the care of a young child. You've got a crib, toys, food. It's childproofed. You clearly care for her, and she loves you. Erin, you are who's best for her."

"But . . ." But what? She couldn't argue with their logic, but that didn't mean she had to like it. "Don't I have a choice?"

"Of course, you do." Sophie smiled in a way that was probably meant to put her at ease. "But I also know enough about you from talking to Corey's family that you want the best for Clara."

So, everyone had ganged up on her. Erin clamped her lips

shut and glanced from Jon to Sophie and back again. Fine. She'd take Clara home tonight, but she wouldn't like it. Not one little bit. She might even stop in Corey's hospital room and give him another piece of her mind. The jerk deserved it.

Chapter Five

Erin clung to the worn-out child as she hustled away from Jon and Sophie. Instead of hurrying home with Mik to comfort her, she had to go home and prep for a busy three-year-old. Mik was not going to like that and would likely take it out on Erin. Why did it seem she was never in control of her own life? Even on his death bed, Corey was controlling her.

"Erin, wait up." And Jon, the traitor, was in cahoots with him. So much for the belief that childhood buddies are lifelong friends. She didn't slow, but let him catch up, and soon they walked side by side, but she felt a million miles distant from him. Talking from miles away made no sense, so she ignored him.

"I understand this is hard on you."

That she couldn't ignore. She came to a dead stop and glared at him. "Oh, you do? You understand nothing. You weren't abandoned by the two people you'd loved most in the world."

He flinched as if she'd punched him. Good.

"You haven't had others constantly throwing wrenches in your plan. Did you know I'm starting my own bookkeeping business? I'm sure potential clients will understand when I show up with a child in tow."

"I see you haven't lost your sarcasm." He dared to smile.

And that just made her angrier. "Oh, I'm just getting started. I was moving on, Jon. I was finally putting him behind me, maybe planning to date again, and now—"

Clara released a cry for "Mommy," and Erin patted her back. "It's okay, sweetie, I've got you." This poor child. How was Erin going to make her understand that Mommy and Daddy were never coming back?

She hurried away from Jon, but with his long legs, he quickly caught up.

"I'll hire you."

"You? Well, that makes it all better then. I might be able to buy food for the girls with what your account will bring in."

"I'm trying here, Erin."

Yes, he was. And this situation wasn't his fault. She sighed while rubbing her hand in circles on Clara's back. Thank goodness she was a placid child, unlike Mik had been.

"And I'm sorry. I'm just . . . angry." That was a feeling she could easily identify. "But I don't know who I'm mad at, so you get the brunt of it."

"I can take it."

"You always did." Even back when she and Corey were dating, Jon had acted as a buffer between the two. He should have become a diplomat.

She hiked Clara up on her hip again. This child was getting heavy.

"Want me to take her?"

"Could you?" She'd have to redevelop those Mommy muscles.

She passed off the child to Jon. Clara took one frantic look up to see who held her, then snuggled back in as they kept on toward the waiting room.

"She likes you."

"At the moment, yeah, but last night, not so much."

"Last night, she'd just been through pretty severe trauma, and you had a date interrupted." Which reminded her, someone was missing. "Where'd Sophie go?"

"She's getting my car."

"You let someone drive your car?"

"Extenuating circumstances."

"What about a car seat? You can't use the one from the accident."

"Sophie purchased one."

"Are you sure you two aren't a thing?"

"No doubt."

Well, Erin had her doubts. She still believed they'd be good together, then Clara would have two loving parents. The child deserved a mother and a father, not an overly-tired single mom with a teen entering puberty.

The waiting room finally came into view, and Erin immediately sought out Mik. She was bundled up on a double-wide bench, eyes closed. But was she sleeping? At home, she would sleep, probably not well, but definitely better than here.

Erin squatted beside her daughter and pushed hair from her eyes. "Hey, Sixlet, how about we get you home to bed?"

Mik blinked her eyes open and then sat up quickly. She looked down the hallway that led to her father's room. "Is he . . ."

She looked to Joyce for affirmation, then said, "Not yet."

"I have to stay with Daddy."

"But . . ." But what?

What was the right thing to do? Make Mik go home? Should Erin stay here with Mik and Clara? Should she take Clara home where she could sleep and eat? A normal person would apply common sense and know what to do.

Erin had never been normal. Anxiety, that too-familiar foe, zinged through her nerves, and heat flashed through her bones.

"We'll stay with her." Joyce approached Erin and knelt beside her but thankfully did not touch her as so many others would do.

"You take Clara home. She doesn't need to be here."

"Thank you." Erin heaved out a breath, grateful for this woman who'd demonstrated the true meaning of mom, unlike her own mother. Joyce not only understood Erin's eccentricities, she accepted them as part of who Erin was.

"You ready?"

Erin looked up and back at Jon carrying not only Clara, but the diaper bag. He didn't realize it, but he was a natural.

If not Sophie, some other woman out there would be lucky to snag this bachelor and the cuddly child. Erin had every intention of playing matchmaker until he broke down and realized he was marriage and father material.

And then she'd be free of Corey forever.

This kid-sitting thing wasn't for sissies. Clara was a small child, but she was still a dead weight, and whatever was in this diaper bag had to weigh fifty pounds. Jon would never look at a mom the same way again. They were superheroes, just without a cape and a spangly uniform.

He walked beside Erin, whose bluster had finally worn down. Her feet shuffled on the unforgiving hospital floors as if they didn't want to take another step. Not that he blamed her one bit. Corey had dumped on her big time.

Corey wasn't the only one; Jon was just as culpable. His exodus from Erin's life wasn't that easy to explain. He did have his reasons, but looking back now, they'd simply been excuses to avoid heartache again.

If she only had a clue what he'd once felt for her.

Corey would advise him to stop living in the past. Yeah, Corey had somehow become wise in his last months of life. Just in time for God to call him home.

A rogue tear slipped from Jon's eye. He thought he'd shed them all over the past twenty-four hours. Man, he was going to miss that guy.

They exited the hospital through large revolving doors, and Sophie was waiting out front. Sophie. Always reliable. Intelligent. Big-hearted. Beautiful Sophie. If things were different, they could have been a couple. Friendship would suffice.

Jon may not be marriage material, but maybe that would make him a better friend going forward. Erin had needed him when Corey left her, and he hadn't a clue how much until today. Things would be different now. He'd be there for her in whatever capacity she needed. He wasn't going to fail her again. He'd keep his promise to Corey. And to himself, no matter how much Erin tried pushing him away.

Half in a stupor, Erin walked up the now snow-free sidewalk to her home. Yesterday's April blizzard only showed remnants of what it had been. Apparently, the temps had reached sixty today. Not that she'd known, having been cooped up in the hospital half the day. What she needed now was a good long sleep so her brain would function tomorrow.

She dug through her purse searching for keys. Naturally, they'd found their way to the very bottom. She finally grasped them and pulled them out, only to send them flying into a patch of snow. Seriously?

She tromped toward them, but Jon held out an arm.

"I'll find them." He smoothly handed over Clara, who was just beginning to wake up, and set down the diaper bag, then waded into ankle-deep snow, with expensive shoes. And to think he used to brag that he'd be known as the tennis-shoe wearing lawyer. Apparently not for dates, though. Sophie had to mean more to him than he realized.

"Found them!" He held up her key chain and hurried back. He kicked off the snow from his shoes as he inserted the key then turned the doorknob. "Home, sweet home." He gestured inside.

"I play!" And just like that, Clara seemed wide awake. She squirmed from Erin's arms and toddled toward the box of toys Erin stored in her living room.

"Uh-oh." Jon grimaced as he stepped inside.

"Is that official attorney-speak?" Erin elbowed him. "For 'It's time for me to leave.'?"

"Would you like me to stay?" He began closing her front door.

She shook her head. "Nah. I'll feed her and wear her out." Hopefully. "Are you heading back to the hospital?"

"As soon as I drop off Sophie." He shrugged. "I need to be there with him."

"I know. I'm glad you remained friends." Even if it was at her expense.

"I'd like for you and me to remain friends."

She chuckled at the absurdity. Yeah, he'd helped her today, but that was one day out of a thousand. "Well, it's a little late for that, don't you think?"

"Erin . . ."

"And I won't hold you to bringing your business to me. I don't want your pity. I'll survive. I always do." She gestured toward the door. "But I do appreciate your help today. And Sophie's." She nodded to the car. "She's waiting."

"Right." He took a step toward the car, then turned back. "I messed up, Erin. I shouldn't have abandoned you when Corey left, and I'm not going to make that same mistake again. You won't go through this alone. And that's a pinky-swear promise."

With that, he turned and hustled toward his car. A rare feeling nudged its way past her emotional defenses. Hope. But she quickly forced it back down because when the things she hoped for didn't come through, it hurt a lot more than if she hadn't hoped at all.

Instead, she'd focus on reality that could be tangibly grasped. Like that curly-haired blondie sitting amongst her toys on the carpet, playing quietly. She was so very different from Mik, who'd been a whirlwind since she was born. Seeing her so quiet and still in the hospital had been like watching someone else's daughter.

The child would now be going through puberty while dealing with her father's death. Oy! How was Erin supposed to parent that?

She looked up at the ceiling. "Really, God? I choose to start living again, and this is what You give me? I can't do it. You know I can't. What do I do now?"

Her gaze flicked to the child playing peacefully, clueless that her world had just tilted beyond repair, and sat down and played with her.

Then sang with her.

And read her books.

And after the tenth reading of *Go, Dog, Go*, Clara fell asleep, and Erin tucked her into the portable crib.

Then it was time for research. This child lost both parents at once. Erin had no clue how to talk about death to a teenager, much less a three-year-old, so she turned on her computer and started searching. There was a lot of advice online, but the common thread was, keep it simple and honest. Don't try to sugarcoat it with euphemisms. Don't be afraid to use emotion.

Ha!

And respond to whatever the child's emotions were with comfort and reassurance.

In the morning, she'd call Debbie and ask her advice as well.

Ding! Dong! Propelled Erin upright. Where? What? Erin blinked her eyes to focus and took in her surroundings. Office. Research. She'd fallen asleep in her office chair?

Turning her sleep-stiffened body, she glanced at the clock to the left of her desk. Ten a.m. already, and not a peep from Clara? What if the accident had done more harm than the doctors thought?

She heard what sounded like a doorknob turning and bolted from the chair. Someone was breaking in!

Grab something!

She snatched a book from the desktop and peeked out the office door toward the front door. It was opening. Clutching the book in her right hand, she raised an arm above her head and shouted, "Get out!"

A dark-haired head peeked around the open door. "Erin?"

"Jon! You almost gave me a heart attack." She lowered the book to her side as Jon stepped in followed by Mik, who hurled past Erin to her bedroom. Oh, no. "Is he gone?"

Jon didn't answer. He didn't need to. The red-blotched face and swollen eyes told her what she needed to know. Even she could decipher those mannerisms. And even she knew that her old friend needed a hug, so she forced open her arms and let Jon in.

He gripped her tightly and heaved sobs, and Jon wasn't a sobber. He wasn't even a crier. She'd never seen him with his heart so broken. Finally, he stepped back and rubbed an arm over his eyes and his nose. "I'm gonna miss the jerk."

But was she? Shouldn't she feel sadness right now? Shouldn't she be hurting like Jon? Corey'd been her friend long before they married, and then they'd been married for nine years. Shouldn't she feel something for him? Debbie would tell her not to force the feelings, they would come naturally. Easy for her to say. She wasn't the ice queen, as Corey once called Erin.

She may not feel but was aware enough to know her daughter needed her right now, so she gestured toward the couch. Jon silently sat and stared out a sunlight-infused window showcasing weather they expected in April.

Jon peeked from the corners of his eyes and managed a weak smile. "Planning to take me out with your Bible?"

"What?"

He nodded toward her right hand that still carried the book she'd picked up in self-defense.

Her Bible.

She shrugged. "Can you think of a better weapon?"

He laughed, then quickly sobered. "How can I laugh when Corey's gone?"

"It's okay. Healthy even." Advice she could give because she'd read it in her research last night.

On the way to Mik's room, she heard happy babbles coming from the master where Erin had temporarily placed the porta crib. Clara was okay. Whew. Hopefully, the happiness would last.

She then knocked on Mik's door. No answer. She knocked again.

"Go away!"

That wasn't happening. Yes, her daughter needed alone time to process her father's death, but more so, she needed to know her mother wasn't going to abandon her.

She knocked again. "I'm coming in." And she slowly opened the door. Her teenager was reclining against her headboard, looking far younger than her thirteen years, clutching Luna, a multi-colored stuffed dragon, to her chest. A gift from Corey when Mik was Clara's age.

"Oh, honey." Erin joined her daughter on the bed and pulled her in tight. Mik didn't resist.

She stroked her hair, something Corey had always done that Mik loved. "I'm so sorry."

"No, you're not." Mik sniffled. "You're glad he's gone. He treated you rotten."

Not untrue, but also not the memory Erin wanted to leave with Mik. She borrowed from what Jon had told her. "But he'd changed. He was sorry. And besides, he always, always loved you and would have done anything for you."

"Right. Everything except keep our family together. And now he's abandoned Clara too."

What was it she'd read last night? She searched through the files of her brain until she found something that would fit. Don't argue. Let the child feel. Let them get out their emotions, tell their story. It wasn't wrong. It just was.

She continued stroking Mik's hair, wishing she had tears to share. "I'm sorry, sweetheart. So, so sorry." And then she quieted, letting her daughter cry until the sobs turned to infrequent shudders and finally silence. She lay her daughter back in her bed, tucked Luna in the crook of her arm, then covered up both daughter and dragon.

This was only the beginning.

How was Mik going to feel about Clara—whom she heard chatting in the room next door—staying here temporarily? And about Corey wanting Erin to be her legal guardian? Erin couldn't predict her daughter's feelings, so she'd have to wing it.

Oh, she hated winging it.

Which meant now was a good time to get some answers from Jon.

Chapter Six

Jon sat on Erin's living room couch, staring out her front window at the now snow-free lawn. How could Corey be gone?

One second, he'd taken a deep breath—and Jon swore he saw Corey grin—and then his earthly heart stilled. Now he was painting sunrises and sunsets alongside Jesus. Jon couldn't wait to take in tonight's sunset!

He heard a door close behind him, and another door open, then the happy babble of Clara. She'd been so quiet, and he'd been so self-absorbed, he'd forgotten about her. He drew a hand down his damp face, looked back, and didn't even try to muster a smile.

But then Clara toddled into the room snuggling a stuffed, orange crocodile. Had to be a gift from Corey. Who else would give their child a crocodile?

She rounded the couch and held up the pet to him. "Chomper's hungwy."

"Chomper's hungry?" He set the animal on his lap and petted its soft fur. "We better feed him, then."

"Her." Erin said behind him.

"Her?" He looked back.

"Chomper is a her." Erin nudged Clara toward the hallway. "It's potty time."

"That's good to know."

"That it's potty time or that Chomper is a girl?" Erin asked with a snide grin.

He couldn't stop a chuckle. "I guess both are valuable pieces of information."

"I thought so."

Holding onto Chomper, he got up and stretched and realized that, yeah, going to the bathroom was a valuable piece of information, because he suddenly needed to go too, and this house had only one restroom. After he waited outside the bathroom door for what seemed like forever, doing an adult version of the potty dance, Erin and Clara finally came out. He handed off Chomper to Clara, then rushed past, ignoring Erin's laughter.

"I said it's good to know."

Her chuckles filtered through the door.

Ha, ha, ha.

When finished, he joined Erin, Clara, and Chomper in the eat-in kitchen. Clara was seated on a booster seat by the table, with a bowl of Cheerios and milk in front of her, along with sliced bananas. No surprise, Chomper was also seated on a booster seat and had a plate of Cheerios in front of her.

"Would you like Cheerios as well?" Erin pulled open a cabinet door and took out two bowls, not waiting for the obvious answer.

"Well, if you don't have Lucky Charms . . ."

"Just ran out. Sorry."

"If I have to suffer." Growing up, he, Corey, and Erin had practically lived on Cheerios. Sometimes plain, other times with milk, and other times Corey had made chocolate bars using them.

She pulled out her chair to sit, then stopped. Her face was unreadable, which wasn't unusual. "One more thing." She opened her pantry door and took out a bag.

Of Sixlets.

"Perfect." She always complained she didn't comprehend things, but she understood far more than she realized.

He filled both his and Erin's bowls with cereal and milk, then they each added a handful of Sixlets.

"Me too, candy!" Clara reached for the bag.

"Of course." Erin gave her a couple.

"Chomper too!"

"Well, duh!" Jon slapped his forehead then handed the girl a couple of candies for the crocodile.

"Would you care to say grace?" Erin reached out her hand.

He gladly grasped it as she took Clara's hand. Clara held Chomper's, as did Jon. He thanked God for the food and for the precious time he'd gotten to spend with Corey. He apologized for not being there for his friends and promised to do better. Then he prayed for wisdom in dealing with Corey's estate and ended by thanking God for Erin's steadfastness. He could always count on her, even when she couldn't count on him or Corey.

Then he raised a spoon filled with milk and cereal and looked at Erin.

She just squinted. Okay, she had no clue what he was suggesting.

"A toast." He raised his spoon. "To Red Sixlet."

"Oh." She raised hers and they clinked the spoons together. "To Red."

"Me, too!" Clara scooped cereal and a Sixlet onto her spoon and shoved it toward Jon. He clinked his spoon against her now empty one, then did the same with Chomper. "Now, we eat."

Trying to eat healthy, he hadn't tasted a bowl of cereal this good in a long time. Well, that was going to end. God gave them food to enjoy it, right?

He had seconds. As did Erin and Clara and Chomper.

And he realized, as Erin organized the bowls and silverware in the dishwasher, he'd just spent an entire meal smiling and laughing. Corey had been gone for barely two hours. Shouldn't he feel more remorse?

Maybe, but a huge part of him was jealous. This morning, Corey had received a hug from Jesus and now they were painting together! How could Jon be sad about that?

Truth was, he wasn't sad for Corey, he was sad for himself, because he'd miss his friend like crazy. And he was angry at the mess Corey left behind for him and Erin to clean up. With him being executor of the will, and Erin caring for Clara, they wouldn't even have time to grieve. And then there was angsty Michaela that Erin would have to deal with. Oh boy. Maybe it was a good thing that Erin was a deep feeler.

But for now, he and Erin needed to—

"We need to talk about Corey's will." Erin pulled back Clara's chair, and she climbed down by herself then grabbed her crocodile.

"Yes. We do." Erin was not going to be happy.

Despite herself, Erin had enjoyed the breakfast with Jon and Clara. And Chomper, of course. In those few moments, life almost felt normal, when she knew her "normal" had shifted dramatically. Oh, she hated change.

She guided Clara to her corner of toys and hoped they would keep her occupied. She also sent up a prayer that Mik would rest well and long or she'd be grumpy for the rest of the day.

Then she sat across from Jon at the kitchen table, where she could keep an eye on Clara, but so the child wouldn't hear their conversation. She steeled herself for what he was going to tell her, much of which she already knew the answer to, but hoped desperately that it had changed or that she'd heard wrong.

She folded her hands on the table, directing her nervous energy their way. "First, what do you know about the accident?"

"Not much." He craned his neck to look out of the kitchen and down the hallway. Looking for Mik maybe? "I just know the roads were super-icy. They'd gone as a family to watch the hockey game."

"Clara, too?"

"Clara too. Corey even texted a cute picture of her at the game wearing noise-cancelling headphones. She looked like she was having fun. Probably more fun than Corey and Lilith, but they wanted to do this for Mik. They wanted to show that her passions were just as valued as theirs."

Corey? Putting someone else first? Again? "Well, that was a change."

"Agreed. But he had changed these past years. He finally stopped running from God."

After he ruined a family.

Man, did every thought of him have to be negative? Shouldn't she be happy that he'd returned to his faith and was now with Jesus?

She shifted in her chair, hoping to shift her attitude along with it. "Okay, so they left the game, and the roads were icy . . ."

"Right. And he was probably going too fast. You know Corey."

She nodded. The guy had loved speed.

"It sounds like they couldn't stop at a red light and slid through the intersection. As did the SUV coming from the other direction, who veered into Corey's lane. They hit head-on."

She shivered at the image painted in her brain.

"Lilith was killed instantly, and Corey . . ." He sniffled again.

"And yet Mik and Clara were okay."

"I guess that's not uncommon. As for Corey, he lived longer than expected. He just kept hanging on. I think he wanted to talk to you. Medical personnel said he mumbled your name."

"He did want to talk." She blew out a breath, recalling some of the last words Corey ever spoke to her. "And I turned him down. Maybe if I would have said yes . . ."

"Uh-uh. You are not going to take the blame for this. Got that? This is on the goofy weather and Corey and . . . and God's crazy timing."

"Crazy is right. When I meet Jesus face to face, we're gonna have a talk."

"You and me both, Erin. You and me both."

"But now . . ." She closed her eyes, trying to script her questions and concerns before speaking aloud. She was far too good at blurting out blunt thoughts that she hadn't realized were insensitive.

"What exactly did their will say?"

"First, I need to let you know the will won't be filed until Monday. As the executor, I'll take care of it. The law can move very slowly, but I'll do what I can to speed it along."

"I'm sure Corey would appreciate that."

He just shrugged. "I wish I didn't have to do it at all." His jaw seemed to tighten. A sign that he was holding back tears, maybe? "But know, it can take months, depending upon the courts."

"Does that mean I could be Clara's temporary guardian for months? And did he provide a way to pay for her care? How am I supposed to grow a business when I have a child with me?"

"As I told you earlier, you can have my business, and I'll pay well."

"I need more than one client."

"Then I'll help find you clients. I have connections."

"You have an answer for everything, don't you?"

"I just want you to know that you're not doing this alone, okay? And once the will has gone through probate, then he's providing for you and for the girls."

"For me?"

"He'd planned to provide more anyway, but yes, once this goes through probate, you won't have to worry about money anymore. His artwork this past year has sold very well."

Now that almost made her tear up. So, someday soon she wouldn't have to count every penny? Being a bookkeeper, she was skilled at counting those pennies, but it would sure be nice to reserve that skill for work. Just the idea of that stressor being gone made her want to hug Corey.

That was good news. Great news, in fact, but it wasn't what she really needed to find out. "Okay. I get it. Corey and his wife were thinking of us in their will. Awesome. But what about Clara? What does the will say about custody?"

"I can't tell you verbatim, and I obviously don't have the will with me, but the gist of it is that they're granting you full custody of Clara. She—and Mik—will be well provided for."

"But . . . me?" She shook her head. She still couldn't wrap her mind around the idea. "They want me to raise the—" She shot a quick look at Clara, who happily played with Chomper knocking down piled blocks, and lowered her voice. "They want *me* to raise the child he had due to his affair." It wasn't a question, but more of a dumbfounded statement. "And they thought *I'm* the best for Clara?"

He dragged both hands through his hair. "Yes. They both— not just Corey—they both believed you were the right person to raise their daughter."

She laughed at the absurdity. "Do I have any choice in this?"

"Of course, you do, but I don't understand what the problem is." He laid his hands palms up on the table. A sign that he was open to new ideas? Or that he wanted her to be open? "I've been watching you all morning with Clara. You're amazing with her, and she loves you. Trusts you."

"But don't you see? That's the problem. She loves me, but there's no way I can ever love her. When I look at her, I see that woman. That child's a mirror image of her mother, so when I look at her, I see lies and betrayal, broken vows and abandonment. I can babysit her, but that doesn't involve losing a piece of my heart."

"I think you're selling yourself short. You have an amazing capacity to love."

She snorted. "Um, remember who you're talking to. The Ice Queen, as Corey put it bluntly when he told me he was filing for a divorce."

"He was an idiot. The thing I've always admired about you is how fiercely you love. No, you don't wear your emotions on your sleeve, but that's not bad. It's just different. A good different, in my opinion. You don't usually overreact. Like you're doing now."

"I'm overreacting?" She slapped a hand to her heart. "You and Sophie said that the goal for Clara was to do what's best for her, and that's not me. Unlike me, children are intuitive, especially that child." She gestured toward the living room. "She will know the truth in here—" she jabbed a finger at her heart "—no matter how I try to fake it. I assure you, I am not the best for her."

"And I disagree."

"Disagree all you want, but I know someone who would be much better."

"I'm sure you do." He crossed his arms, and his mouth formed a line straighter than a ruler. Even she could read that expression. "But let me rule out a few names for you that Corey explicitly said weren't an option."

"Be my guest."

"Obviously not Henry and Joyce." He held up a hand with one finger raised. "They're planning their retirement, and that doesn't include raising another child. Corey was also afraid that they would raise her to take over their business, and he didn't want his artistic child to be stuck in a job she hates."

"I wasn't going to suggest them."

"Well, good. At least we can agree on that."

"It's a miracle," she said drily.

He held up a second finger. "You can also cross Lilith's parents off the list. Both Corey and Lilith said, and I quote, 'No way in blankety-blank will they get custody of Clara!'"

"Oh . . ." Well, there went that idea. Although they didn't top Erin's list, they'd still been an option. She drummed her fingers on the tabletop. "They're that bad?"

"According to Corey and Lilith."

"And Corey actually used the words 'blankety-blank'?" She grinned, hoping to lighten up Jon, prepare him for her suggestion.

And it worked, as his lips lifted into a slow grin. He nodded toward the living room. "Modified for little ears."

"Okay, then." She nodded to his hand. "Who else should I scratch off my list?"

Jon flicked up a third finger. "Zax, of course."

"Agreed." Corey's older brother would hate being tied down with a child, but he made a fantastic uncle.

"Then who do you think would be a better guardian than you?" His raised fingers clenched into a fist. "That's it for family. And you were Clara's main babysitter. You're the obvious, and only, choice, unless you want her to wind up in foster care."

No way was Clara going to foster care. Erin would see to that. The trick was convincing him. Erin raised her pointer finger. "You're forgetting one person."

He sat back in the chair, his lips scrunched, and his gaze toward the ceiling. "I give up. Please enlighten me."

"Well, it's someone who knew Corey and his wife very well. Clara really likes him. He's well off, so he'd be able to support her now and through college. And he definitely wants the best for Clara."

He raised his hands, palms up. "You've got me stumped."

"That's because you're not looking in the mirror."

"What?"

"It's you, Jon. You'd make the perfect guardian for Clara."

Chapter Seven

Good thing he wasn't drinking or eating anything, or it would all have spewed out at Erin. "You've got to be kidding. Me? Raise Clara? I didn't realize you were a comedienne."

"Not joking." She held up a hand and displayed her pointer finger, clearly mimicking—or mocking—him. "You love her, which is more than I can say for myself." The second finger flew up. "You're far better with children than you give yourself credit for. And judging by that pretty black Mercedes you're driving around, money isn't an issue for you."

"That's only three."

"That's all I need."

The woman was going to drive him to drink. "Got a beverage? Preferably something stronger than water."

"Sorry. No alcohol allowed in my house."

"Another reason you should take custody." Not that he drank either, although sometimes his job made losing himself in a drunken stupor sound enticing. But he refused to become his father.

She got up and took two bottles of Pepsi from the fridge. "Strong enough for you?"

"Perfect." He unscrewed the cap and swigged down half the bottle. The caffeine rush should help him get through this ridiculous debate. He recapped the drink then laid out his next point. "You're forgetting, I'm not mentioned in the will."

"You're an attorney. Change it."

"It's not that easy."

"But not impossible."

Dang, the woman had an answer for everything. "Listen, Pearl." He used her nickname to soften her up. Hopefully. "I'm not father material."

"I disagree. You're great with kids."

"Yeah, like an uncle. Like Zax."

"Nope." She shook her head. "Zax buys them spendy gifts then flits around the world. You play with them, read to them, hug and care for them. Like a father."

"A child needs a mother."

"Oh, I agree. Which is why you and Sophie—or whoever you're dating—need to get serious. I like Sophie. She'd be good for you and Clara."

"Nothing's ever going to happen between me and Sophie, so don't go there." He took another long swig of pop.

"Why? Are you gay?"

Pop sprayed from his mouth, dousing Erin. "Oh, man, I'm sorry."

She dabbed a napkin at her shirt and started laughing.

He joined in until tears streamed down his face. "You can't be serious."

"I'm dead serious. Listen to this evidence. You never dated in high school. Never had a girlfriend in college, that you mentioned. You just hung around with me and Corey. Maybe I didn't comprehend that you were attracted to him. Now, you go on non-committal dates with an amazing woman like Sophie and tell me nothing will ever happen between you. I'm not stupid, Jon Boy."

Wow. Sometimes he was truly amazed at how poorly she read

people. "Are you finished?"

"I think I made my case." She licked a finger and drew an imaginary line on an invisible chalkboard. "I'd gladly take it before a judge."

"Oh, now you've stepped into my territory." He rubbed his hands together and stood up, intentionally hovering over her. He glared down at her hard enough to make her flinch. "There's an important piece of evidence you missed, Counselor."

She sat up straight, and fire sparked in her eyes. "Oh, yeah? Let's hear it."

He leaned closer to her, but this time she didn't back away. "Miss Sophie Gardner is the one who's gay." He licked his finger and drew on the chalkboard.

"Oh." Erin seemed to wilt. "Rats. And here I thought I'd made some good points."

"Good surface points but lacking proper evidence. Sophie's been dating the same woman for the past four years. Believe me, I tried convincing her that she'd rather date a man, but no go. Besides, I've had my eye on a particular woman for some time now, but I'm pretty much invisible to her." He returned to his seat and threw a satisfied smirk at Erin. "Case closed."

"Mystery woman?"

He knew he'd gone too far with that statement. Of course, she latched onto it. "And that's all you're going to get from me."

"We'll see about—"

Something crashed, and a cry from the living room pierced the air.

"Clara!" Faster than he could blink, Erin was up and to the child's rescue.

She'd simply knocked books off a shelf. No cuts. No blood. Just startled, and quickly calmed by Erin's hug and soothing words. More evidence in his favor. Erin might believe she couldn't love, but he knew better. He'd witnessed it, just now.

The trick was getting Erin to dig deep enough into her gut for her to recognize what she really felt.

Erin breathed in and out slowly, calming down her heart as she cuddled Clara against her chest. Getting used to a child's curiosity was going to take some doing, and it looked like she really didn't have a choice. Not when an attorney was on Clara's side. How could she convince Jon that she wasn't the right person? By persuading him that he was not only fit to be a father, but the best choice for Clara?

Maybe if he met the right woman. She tapped a finger against her chin. Who did she know that would be good enough for Jon? And who was this mystery woman Jon and Sophie had alluded to?

"I want Mommy." Clara's declaration followed by soft sobs broke into her musing and snuck into a normally unreachable part in her heart, nearly splintering it. Sure, she'd done a lot of research last night, but every situation was nuanced. She had to let Clara know her mommy and daddy weren't coming back, and the sooner she told her the better.

But how?

She looked up to Jon, who was lurking at the kitchen entrance, hoping he could read the desperation in her eyes, but he just shrugged and shook his head. Big help he was.

What was it she'd read? Be honest. Understanding the concept of death will be difficult, so try to relate it to another loss. Had Clara experienced any other losses? Erin closed her eyes, searching her brain files, while Clara's cries for Mommy, and then Daddy, grew stronger.

"What's going on . . . ?"

Erin turned to Mik. When had she snuck into the room?

"Why is she here?" A hard edge took over Mik's voice while Clara's cries escalated.

Really, God? You're going to throw this at me all at once? Then You better give me some words and a whole bunch of grace.

Erin picked up Clara, sat on the couch, keeping the child tucked close, and gestured with her head to the spot beside her.

Naturally, Mik sat across the room on the cushioned rocker instead. That was where Erin should have sat, if she'd been thinking straight.

"So?" Mik crossed her arms.

Erin slowly inhaled a breath, to calm herself and to give herself a moment to corral her thoughts. "So." Erin circled her hand on Clara's back. "Clara will be staying with us for the time being." Be honest, Erin, tell her the rest. "And possibly until she grows up."

"She what?" Mik bounded off her chair. "First, she takes away my dad, and now she's taking over my home?"

"Mik, honey . . ." What else? Her daughter had spoken Erin's sentiments exactly. Maybe if she explained Corey's reasoning, even if she disagreed. "This way the two of you can grow up together. As sisters should."

"And." Jon sat beside Erin on the couch. "Your father and Lilith felt that your mom was the best choice as guardian."

"But it's not fair." The waterworks started then, and every nerve in Erin's body went on high alert as Mik and Clara cried in tandem. The phrase, "Quit crying, or I'll give you something to cry about" flitted through her head, but she refused to use it like her mom had, and damage these girls.

"You're right, Michaela, it's not fair. I agree. But I also agree that Clara staying with us right now is in her best interest." Oh, it hurt her to say that, and she refused to look at Jon. He probably wore an I-told-you-so smirk. She couldn't resist adding. "As for the future, we'll see."

"Fine." Which Erin knew meant "I don't like it, but know I don't have a choice, so I'll live with it."

"In the meantime, though, I need your help with—"

A standard ringtone chirped beside her.

"I've got to take this." Jon leaped up from the couch and spoke as he hurried down the hall. "This is Jonathan . . ."

Erin waited until she heard the click of a door closing before continuing. "As I was saying—"

"Spill it, Mom. Now you can say whatever you were holding back with Mr. Lawyerman in here."

"What?"

"Come on, it's obvious that you're as thrilled about having her here as I am. So, what's the problem?"

Annoyed with how transparent she was, and how intuitive Mik was, Erin drew the crying girl even closer. Clara finally started calming down, thank goodness. "Your father and his wife named me guardian of Clara."

"Seriously?"

"Dead."

Mik began laughing.

"What's so funny?"

"One last dig from good ol' Dad, right?"

Erin pinched the bridge of her nose, holding back her agreement, and not liking the stench of her lie. "Not a dig. Just the best for his daughter." Whose cries for Mommy and Daddy became hysteric. She had to know something was wrong. This child never threw fits.

"So, what do we do then? What's your plan?"

"How do you know I have a plan?"

"Mom, you always have a plan."

True. It was how she coped. "My plan is to play matchmaker with Mr. Lawyerman. Clara knows him, he's good with her, and he'd be able to provide. All he needs is a wife."

"Good luck with that. The dude loves his bachelor status."

"Oh, I know. I tried convincing him how good Sophie was—"

"Sophie? You mean the gay social worker chick?"

"You knew?"

"Well, duh. It's obvious."

To everyone but her, apparently. "Is it also obvious that Jon isn't gay? Serious question." She hated that Mik could read people better than her, but she wasn't afraid to use her daughter's expertise.

"Very."

"Oh," she said mostly to herself. "So, I should have checked with you before I asked him."

"You didn't." Mik laughed so hard she started coughing and crying. At least it wasn't sad crying anymore. There would be enough of that over the next few days, months. Year, probably.

"Oh, I certainly did, and he quickly put me in my place."

"Mom, you crack me up. Daddy and I used to laugh at your goof-ups all the time."

Erin looked away from her daughter and stared at the wall. Once upon a time, Corey had laughed with her, not at her. He'd once been attracted to her lack of social awareness. Until he'd decided that wasn't cool anymore, and he found someone her exact opposite.

"I'm sorry." She heard Mik mumble.

"It's okay." She set the now-quiet and sucking-her-thumb child onto her lap. Corey had tried to wean her off the thumb. Right now, Erin didn't care. If that was where the child found comfort, so be it.

"I'll help you."

Erin jerked her gaze toward Mik. "Help me?"

"You know, find someone for Mr. Lawyerman, so it can be just the two of us again."

"And so I don't make any more orientation faux pas?"

"That too."

"Thank you." Erin drew her fingers through the Clara's hair. "And I have one important question for you."

"What's that?"

"Did Clara ever have a pet that, uh . . ." How to say it so the child didn't realize what they were talking about. Guess in this case using euphemisms was okay. "A pet that passed away? I need to tell her . . ."

"There was that clown fish."

"What was its name?"

"How about I talk to her?"

What a mess. Jon hung up after getting an update from Corey's parents. That Corey and Lil didn't have a funeral plan already wasn't a surprise. What twenty- and thirty-somethings did? But it sure would have made dealing with Lilith's domineering parents a lot easier. The Caldwells hadn't asked the Beldens their opinions regarding funeral planning. No, they *told* the Beldens what was going to happen, including plans to "rescue" Clara from Corey's "mentally unstable" ex-wife.

Bring it, had been his first thought. Yeah, they had expensive lawyers at the end of their purse-strings, but they didn't have him, and he was good. But then, winning came with being smarter than them, not more arrogant. Besides, the last thing he wanted for Clara and Erin was a strung-out court battle fighting for the child's best interests. Clara's best interests were for her to remain at Erin's.

His biggest challenge was convincing her of that, especially since his abandonment of her lost him any cred with her. What he needed to do was find time to share why he'd . . . run. That was exactly what he'd done.

He wasn't going away this time. Never again. No matter how hard she pushed, and he knew she'd shove with every muscle she had. He pocketed his phone and left the office, probably soon to be a nursery, to relay what the Beldens had told him.

Needing to awaken over-tired muscles, he stretched in the hallway, then peeked into the living room. And froze.

Mik lay belly-down on the floor, drawing pictures on an unlined notebook in front of her as Clara lay beside her watching, listening, captivated.

Clara wasn't the only one.

"Remember Kalee Kaleidescope?" Mik pointed to a simple fish she'd sketched. Clearly, she hadn't inherited her father's artistic talent, but art was something Clara understood.

"Uh-huh. Kalee go to fish heaven." Her lower lip protruded out.

"Do you remember why?"

Clara shook her head.

"What did Daddy say about Kalee's heart?"

"It stopped burping."

Jon had to slap a hand over his mouth to contain a laugh. He watched Erin do the same.

To her credit, Mik just smiled. She may not have wanted this little sister, but she sure was good with her.

"That's right. Kalee stopped burping and her heart stopped pumping."

"She go to fish heaven."

"That's right. She went to fish heaven, to God's big lake in the sky."

"I go see that big lake?"

"Someday you will." Mik drew a picture of a car. "Remember when Daddy's car crashed?"

Clara's lip stuck out further, and she pointed to a bandage on her forehead. "I got owie." She pointed to bruises on Mik's legs and arms and a bandage on her neck. "You got owies too."

"That's right. We both got owies, and so did Daddy and your mommy."

"Are they at hopsital?"

Mik shook her head and pointed to the picture of the fish. "Remember how Kalee's heart stopped working?"

"Uh-huh." Her lip trembled. "Did Daddy, Mommy hearts stop too?"

Mik nodded and wiped a tear from her cheek.

Jon wiped away a tear as well. Erin did not, but that wasn't because she was unfeeling or unconcerned.

"Did they go to fish heaven too?"

"They went to people heaven."

"I go see them in people heaven?"

Mik sat up and gathered her sister on her lap. "Not for a long time. Only when your heart stops working here. Then God fixes it in heaven."

"But I don't want Mommy, Daddy in heaven." Her little chin quivered, and tears trailed down her chubby cheeks.

"I don't either, sweetie, I don't either."

The two of them sat on the floor, rocking. Then Erin joined them, holding both children. Oh, she might claim she couldn't love Clara, but he knew otherwise. She already loved the girl—it showed in her actions. After all, love was far more than a feeling.

The trick was getting her to realize that loving was exactly what she was doing.

In the meantime, though, he had to take care of dirty work that couldn't wait. He cleared his throat, and the huddle of females all looked at him. "Mik, would you mind watching Clara for a bit? I need to talk with your mom."

Erin got up quickly, as if ready to be free of the group hug. She probably was eager. While she knew most people loved hugs, she tolerated touch. She followed him into the office, closed the door, and then slumped into her office chair, crossing her arms on the desk and resting her head there. "The phone call had to do with me?"

Jon leaned against the desk and looked to the left to see Erin. "You, Corey, Lilith." He crossed his arms. "That was Henry. He wanted to get funeral plans done, but the Caldwells are being sticklers. Henry thinks Corey and Lilith would have liked their service together. Lilith's parents want them separate. Honestly, I think they want to wash their hands of their daughter's involvement with an artist."

Not that he'd be too upset if he never had contact with them again, but the last bit of news he had for Erin informed him they weren't out of his life by a long shot.

"Will the funerals be separate?"

"Yes. Henry gave in and said he wants the service soon. Zax should be home tomorrow and needs to return to wherever he was in a week. So, Corey's funeral is planned for Tuesday."

"That soon?"

"Why wait?" Had been Henry's response, and Jon couldn't say he disagreed. Why put it off? "Lilith's folks want to finish their vacation first."

Her head jerked upward. "You can't be serious."

"Completely serious. That's what Henry told me right after he called Belinda Caldwell a very, not-nice name."

"Like mother, like daughter."

He couldn't argue with that. Although Lilith had undergone a change of her own these past months.

This next bit of information needed to be stressed to Erin, so he wheeled her chair to face him and he squatted to be at eye level with her.

"Oh, I can read that body language." She sat up straight, crossed her arms, and lasered her gaze directly into his eyes. "What is mine telling you?"

"That you're miffed at me for taking charge instead of asking."

"Bingo."

He plopped down on the floor and raised up his hands, palms skyward. "I'm sorry."

She relaxed and drew a hand down her face. "Me too. What do you need me to know?"

"That the Caldwells aren't happy that you have custody right now."

"When they're off on a vacation that's more important than their daughter's funeral?"

He shrugged. "I didn't say it made sense. Now they have some money backing them, but you and Clara have me."

"Wait. You're assuming I won't gladly hand over Clara."

"You would do that? Against Corey and Lilith's wishes?"

"Oh, so sorry. I forgot that they bent over backwards for me."

"Still wielding sarcasm like a sword."

"It's a useful weapon."

"It's a shield. There's a difference."

Erin clamped her mouth shut.

He got up into a squat again to look at Erin equally. "Do you really want her to go to the Caldwells? Think about it, Erin. I know you want what's best for Clara."

She kicked at the carpeted floor. "I wish you'd use lawyer-speak. I can combat that."

"So . . . ?"

"Fine." She flung up her arms. "Clara can—should stay with me for now. But there are things I need from Corey's place. Mik has belongings there as well. Can we get in?"

"Not a problem." He drew a keychain from his pocket.

"Corey gave you a key?"

"He stuck it in with the will. I'm assuming Mik has access too."

Erin shrugged. "Possibly, but you never knew with that woman."

"True." He stood up and re-pocketed the keys. His knees couldn't take the squatting. Guess he wasn't young anymore either. "Want to head over today? Joyce said she'd be glad to watch Clara."

"Not really, but it's best to get it over with."

"Just warning you, it won't be over until we go through probate." And that could take as little as a month, but rarely did it go that smoothly.

"Fine. Whatever." She drew her phone from her pocket and quick-dialed someone. "Joyce? Yeah, Jon, Mik, and I need to head to Corey's place, and I don't want to bring along Clara . . . Thanks. See you soon."

She set her phone on the desk. "Done. And now there's something else important you need to understand."

He spread his arms wide, hoping she'd see that as him being open. "I'm listening."

She stood up and crossed her arms again, telling him she wasn't open to other ideas. Had to be one of her favorite postures, maybe because she knew he wouldn't mistake it. "This is not a permanent situation, understand?"

"Completely." He comprehended that was what Erin thought

she wanted at this juncture. But once the cogs of probate had finally spun through, she'd change her mind. No matter what it took from him.

Chapter Eight

Eerie was the word Erin would use to describe stepping into Corey's home. Less than forty-eight hours ago, the couple had left home with plans of returning later that night or the next day. Random lights were on throughout the house, and the TV was on in the living room. Safety measures Erin had instilled in Corey. One would think upon entering that not only did people live in the house, but that they were there this very moment.

Mik stood in the foyer, shivering. Cold? Or also sensing her father's lack of presence?

Erin decided it was the latter and rested a hand on her daughter's shoulder. "If you'd like to go wait in the SUV, Jon and I will get what you need."

"Feel free." Jon held out the keys to his Mercedes. Erin was almost tempted to grab them and go for a joyride herself. Would Mik? Erin hoped she'd raised her daughter better than that, but she'd suffered so many losses, that would wreak havoc with anyone's parenting.

"N . . . no. I have to do this." Mik picked up a copy paper box and aimed for the stairs leading to her bedroom. But she still trembled.

Erin removed her sweater and draped it over Mik's shoulders.

Such maturity from her daughter, though Erin realized it would be fleeting.

Erin looked around the opulent home she'd been in one time. No wonder Corey had chosen that woman over her. He'd moved onto Easy Street and hadn't had to worry about responsibilities.

Artwork covered many walls. Corey's? She studied a colorful, textured painting above the sofa, of a waterfall pouring onto rocks. The water reflected light like a prism. Beautiful. Yep, there was Corey's signature at the bottom.

Something else glinted from the picture, and Erin did a double take. Not all of the rocks at the bottom were painted, but a handful were real rocks inserted into the canvas. She touched them just to make certain they were real.

"Genius, isn't it?" Jon seemed to materialize beside her. "That's what his patrons look for in his work. What has he hidden among the paint? And the fact that his work is so real, and almost three-D-like, sometimes it takes a while to find the actual object."

"Patrons? Was he popular?"

"Very much so, and with a wealthy clientele." He looked down at her. "You didn't know?"

"Not when he always claimed he was too poor to increase child support. I pretty much ignored anything spoken about him the last years." Suddenly cold, she hugged herself. "Just the mention of his name would make me angry."

"I don't blame you."

She glared up at Jon. "His wasn't the only name I hated hearing. If I'd had a lawyer on my side, maybe I wouldn't have had to struggle all this time." Before he could respond, she grabbed a couple of empty plastic containers and headed for the stairs. The nursery was likely up there. She'd come solely to get necessities for Clara, not to join Corey's fan club.

At the top of the stairway, she glanced both ways and spied a myriad of doors. More doors than she had in her entire house.

He hadn't been able to afford an increase in his support. Ha! What a jerk. Maybe with his death, he'd finally support his child properly.

More of his paintings lined the hallway walls. If she were vindictive, she'd take a spray paint can to each one, but if they were as desirable as Jon claimed, then they meant more support for the girls. She had to keep reminding herself, it was all about what was best for them, not about her seeking vengeance. Even though that would feel really good—for the moment. She knew better than to believe that feeling would last.

Now where would the nursery be? She would have put it next to the master—wherever that was—but she and Corey had rarely thought alike. Hard to believe that was what once attracted her to him.

She took a left, just because one door was actually open that way. Mik's room? The thick, padded carpet absorbed the sound of her footsteps as she approached the open door. Yes, Mik's room. Mik sat on her bed, holding a framed picture in her hand. Her box was empty still, no surprise.

She didn't have posters of rock stars or teen idols, but of sports figures, both male and female. Where their daughter had gotten her athletic prowess from was a mystery.

Neither she nor Corey had a speck of athletic ability, which was what had brought them together in the first place. She, Jon, and Corey. As non-athletes in a school where athleticism was highly regarded, the three had been outcasts. Two nerds and an artist. They'd formed their own clique Jon initially coined Two Nerds and an Artist, or 2NA. Somewhere along the line that changed into the Three Musketeers and then the 3 Sixlets. They'd remained that until Corey irreparably tore them all apart.

Erin took a deep breath and silently asked God for forgiveness. Would bitterness ever leave her? She needed to show a united front for Mik and for Clara if she wanted them to grow up without resentment, probably directed at her.

"How's it going?" Erin sat beside her daughter and glanced at the picture. Mik dressed in her softball uniform and Corey with an arm around her, looking very proud.

"He started liking my games." Mik drew a finger over her dad's face. "He used to come just because that's what dads are supposed to do, but lately he enjoyed it. I could hear him yelling his support."

"I noticed that too." He used to only attend when convenient, but lately, Mik's games had taken priority. Maybe everyone was right about his change of heart. "Listen, if this is too hard—"

"I need to do it, Mom, okay? Just let me be."

"You're right. I'll leave you alone, if you point me toward the nursery."

Without taking her gaze off the photo, Mik said, "Out the door, take a left. Almost to the end of the hallway, the door on the right."

"Thanks." Erin stroked her daughter's hair. "Just let us know when you're ready."

Mik didn't answer, not that Erin expected her to, so Erin found the nursery and packed up necessities, clothes, a few toys. She even took a picture of a colorful fish off the wall, something Corey painted, and couldn't resist searching for the hidden object. There it was, among the scales, a small gemstone. Clara's birthstone maybe?

Yeah, Corey really had been gifted. Why hadn't she noticed that when they were married? Probably because they were too busy working and trying to keep their finances above-board.

That's what happens when you head into a marriage already pregnant. One of many life-altering mistakes she'd made with Corey. The hard part now was going to be teaching Mik not to follow her parents' example. Erin had grown up watching her mom's self-destructive behaviors, some brought on by mental illness she'd chosen not to treat, and had sworn not to repeat them. But then Erin had done exactly what she'd promised herself not to do. How was she to break that cycle with her daughter?

She filled the containers with Clara's items, then carried them downstairs, one at a time. All the stuff would overflow in Erin's office-turned-nursery, but it would suffice. It had to.

What sounded like glass shattering came from the kitchen, and Erin followed the noise. Sure enough, Jon stood amidst what had once been a glass bowl filled with strawberries.

He spotted her and shook his head. "Just trying to clean out the fridge and my usual butterfingers took over."

"I always told Corey we should call ourselves the Three Butterfingers."

He smiled at that. "Though I have improved. Racquetball once a week helps."

"You play racquetball?"

"A lot of colleagues did, so I forked out for a bunch for lessons. Gotta take advantage of networking opportunities. Turns out all I needed was a new eyeglass prescription, a whole lot of training, and mostly determination."

"Oh, that's all."

"Yeah." He stepped out of the mess he'd made on the floor. "But I'm still a work in progress. And to be honest, I like that I've added muscle to my bones. Opponents can't call me Swizzle Stick anymore."

Yeah, she had noticed he'd filled out, and certainly not in a bad way, which meant it shouldn't be too difficult finding women for him to date. Intelligence and good looks were very attractive. And he used to be kind. Maybe his selfishness these past years were solely for her. Yeah, she'd go with that. Now to start paying attention at church, the only place she knew of that would have plenty of single women. Well, other than bars, and Jon never drank. Or at least he didn't used to drink. Four years ago, he hadn't played racquetball either. Regardless, *she* would not be entering any bars to find a life partner for Jon.

"What are you thinking?"

She startled at Jon's question, waking her from her musing. "I, uh …" Certainly was not telling him what she'd been thinking! "How can I help you, besides cleaning up the mess on the floor? I've got what I need from the nursery, and I'm letting Mik have space."

"Good plan." He gestured to copy paper boxes he must have brought in from his SUV. "I figure we can donate dry goods to a food shelf, and I know a shelter that will gladly take fridge or frozen goods. If you empty the pantry, I'll take care of this mess I made and the fridge."

They worked quietly side by side for the next few hours, emptying the refrigerator and the pantry, long enough so that the moon and stars had taken over the light duties for the day. And no sign of Mik the entire time.

"I need to check on Mik." Erin wanted to give her daughter space, but now her absence was concerning. Up until now she hadn't shown symptoms of depression, but it did run in Erin's family, and Corey's death could very well be a trigger.

She hurried upstairs to Mik's room. Neither her daughter nor the box were there. She checked all the bedrooms and bathrooms upstairs, but nothing. Then she did the same downstairs

Where was she? And where was Jon?

Her breaths coming in quick puffs, she rushed to the living room and found Jon on the couch, snoring. How had fallen asleep so quickly? She shook him, and his eyes shot open. "I can't find her."

He jolted to a sitting position, and blinked. "What?"

"Mik." She clenched her fists tightly. Anxiety was a feeling she understood all too well. "She's gone, Jon. Mik is gone."

Chapter Nine

Panic squeezed Erin's heart, and she barely registered what was happening as Jon helped her sit on the couch.

"Take slow, deep breaths, Erin. One, two, three, four . . ."

Yeah, she knew the drill, but she didn't have time for a panic attack. She had to find her daughter. Suddenly sweating, she got up and wished she could shed her T-shirt. "Help me find her. Now."

"Let's talk this through, okay?"

"Talk through what? I searched the entire house, and there was no sign of her!"

"What about outside?"

"Why would she go outside? She hates the dark." Had since she was a toddler. That was why Corey had given her a stuffed dragon so that it would breathe fire into the darkness for her.

"Maybe, but she spent a lot of time with Corey in his art studio."

"He had an art studio?"

Jon didn't reply. He obviously knew that anything he said would torque her off. Instead, he jogged down a hallway, toward the back of the house, and out into a yard lit with stringed lights, leading directly to a cottage-like building.

Lights shone through the curtains. Mik had to be there.

Jon reached the cottage first and tried the door.

Locked.

"Michaela." He pounded on the door. "If you're in there, let us in."

No response.

Erin checked a window to see if she could see through the curtains.

Not a thing.

She joined Jon at the front door and summoned her caring-mom voice. "Mik, honey, I know you're upset. I get it. I am too. Please, let us in." Erin put her ear to the door but heard nothing.

"Mik, please."

Jon echoed her words.

Still nothing.

Well, forget trying to be nice. Time to bring on the don't-you-dare-cross-me-mom voice. "Fine. You don't open this door by the count of three, I'm kicking it open, and you know I will." She'd actually done it once before, shortly after Corey had left them. She wasn't beyond doing it now.

"Okay." Mik!

Erin's knees nearly buckled. Oh, thank you, Jesus.

The sound of a lock turning was followed by the door slowly opening. It took every muscle Erin had to hold back and allow Mik to invite them in.

Her daughter walked away from the door and plopped down on a chaise.

Erin pushed open the door, and her eyes grew wide at the array of canvases and paintings and art supplies she couldn't name.

"This was Daddy's favorite place." Mik kicked at the paint-splattered concrete floor.

Erin had no doubt this was where Corey had come to escape. It looked like a piece of heaven for him.

Did he have his own art studio in Heaven? If he did, it would be a lot more magnificent than this, and this was pretty good.

Erin sat by Mik, and brushed hair back from her face. "How are you doing?"

Mik's gaze went to her lap, to a book clutched in her hands. A book Erin knew very well. She'd given Corey that journal about five years ago when they first recognized that they needed help to save their marriage, and he'd gone to a counselor who recommended journaling.

She'd rarely seen him write in it, and she'd long blamed his lack of effort for their demise.

"May I see that book?" Erin touched the leather cover.

Mik shook her head, and tears leaked from her eyes, landing on the journal. "It's proof that Daddy didn't love me."

———————

Erin
April 9, 2019

Dear God,

I'm angry.

Yeah, I know that comes as no surprise to you, but I need someone to pour out my thoughts to, and you always listen. And you love me in spite of myself.

It's rather ironic, isn't it, that I begin writing in a journal after Mik found Corey's? After venting to Debbie, she recommended I pour my thoughts out on paper as well, that it's cathartic. Burning Corey's journal would be cathartic as well, but Debbie said I might regret that. Usually, I agree with Debbie, but this time . . .

Anyway, I said I'd give journaling a shot, see if it helps, but instead I'd write my thoughts to you, as a prayer of sorts.

Right now, I'm trying to decide on what to wear to Corey's funeral today. I know, I know, with all the problems in the *world*, that's what I'm focused on. Selfish, right? Debbie would probably tell me it's a coping mechanism. Regardless, what I wear today is what's on my mind.

Black would tell others that I'm in mourning, but at the moment, I am not at all sad. I'm angry. Even in death, he keeps complicating my life. What the heck did he write that made Mik feel she wasn't loved? I'd always defended him to her. I've hidden his journal for now. With all of Mik's mixed emotions, I can't afford to have her heart broken any more. With mental illness running in the family, it scares me.

So now today, I get to go to Jerk's funeral—yeah, I know, you're not keen on me calling him that, but I could call him a lot worse. You've heard me use worse.

I have no desire to go to the funeral, and if not for Mik, I wouldn't attend at all, but she needs me there.

Back to what I should wear. Do you really care? Maybe you do, after all you clothed the birds and the flowers, right?

I don't want to wear black because that would be a lie. Red would reflect my feelings but would be disrespectful. Maybe just khakis and that boring, beige blouse Joyce gave me a while back that I've never worn. I love Joyce, but not her taste in clothes. At least she'll be happy to see me wear it.

There, my first journal entry is complete.

And I still feel angry. Guess I shouldn't expect a one-and-done, though, should I, Lord?

Sorry for griping so much, but thanks for listening.

———

Erin held Clara's hand and Mik slogged alongside as they walked to the church Corey had attended with his new wife. That they'd even gone to church had surprised Erin. Back when he turned away from her, he'd also shut out God.

But then, she hadn't been much more than a go-to-church-on-Sunday person, either. It had been tradition more than faith, and her mom had set a poor example for even attending. Corey's folks though, they lived what they believed. One positive aspect from the divorce was that it had ignited her faith. God had become real to her, and she'd learned to depend on Him rather than think of Him as a Santa Claus figure who gave you gifts when you behaved.

If only she could rid herself of the bitterness toward Corey. Every time she thought she'd moved on, something would remind her why she resented him. Resentment was the one feeling she fully recognized—God probably had something to do with that, because He did want her to change. And she'd begun . . .

But then Corey had to die and leave her his love child.

Clara tugged on her hand, yanking Erin out of her pity party. These unwelcome parties had to come to an end, or these two girls would join in.

Chin up. Walk confident. Don't let stares and gossip bother you. Start acting like the adult you are.

They walked inside the building that looked more like a warehouse than a church, and Jon was right there greeting people. When had he become so adept at being social? The two of them had connected as children because of their ineptitude with social skills.

Admittedly, he'd taken over well on Sunday after Mik had found Corey's journal. He'd packed his car while Erin tried to reassure her daughter of her father's love, and then he'd carried all of Clara's belongings into Erin's house while Erin did more damage control with her daughter. She couldn't have handled the evening without him. And she told him so again now as he wrapped her in a brief hug.

Mik took the opportunity to break away, probably to the restroom. Like mother, like daughter.

"Just doing what I should have done long ago." He stepped back and wiped a handkerchief across his nose.

"If you're hoping for forgiveness, it might be working." She nodded to more people entering, strangers to her. "You're busy. We'll catch up later." She continued through the church's concrete block wall lobby that was softened by easel after easel of what she presumed were Corey's paintings. A portrait of a toddler finger-painting drew her in. Clara.

"That's me! Daddy make this!" Clara reached up and touched the painting, and Erin didn't try to stop her even if art critics would be upset. This was more about Clara learning what death really meant.

Clara raised her arms to Erin. "Up, please?" The child was polite, too.

Erin lifted her so they could both study the piece better. She searched for the hidden item Jon said had become Corey's trademark—it shouldn't be that hard to find!—but Corey was good.

There it was. A button. She touched the third button down on Clara's dress. Was it a memento of some kind? Had it fallen off one of her pieces of clothing?

How could a man who'd been so awful to her and Mik paint such beauty?

"Brilliant work, don't you agree?"

Erin turned toward an older couple who dressed impeccably. No doubt, they didn't purchase their wardrobe from the local big box like she did. "Yes. It is."

"You must be Erin." The woman extended her hand. "Belinda Caldwell. And this is my husband, Charles."

"Nice to meet you." The man thrust out his hand.

Erin accepted his offer. Corey's wife's parents? "I thought . . ." That they weren't coming. She clamped her mouth shut before something insulting snuck out.

A silent exchange that Erin couldn't decipher passed between the couple before Belinda responded. "You are correct. Once we got over the shock that Lilith was gone, we came to our senses." The woman broke eye contact and her gaze went to the portrait of Clara. "An amazing likeness, wouldn't you agree?"

"Yes. Amazing."

"Gramama." Clara reached out her arms for the woman.

Recalling what Jon had said about Corey and *that woman* not wanting these two to have custody, Erin reluctantly handed over the child then looked around for Jon. He remained at the door, greeting mourners. A very pretty mourner at that. She and Jon seemed quite familiar with each other. A possible match? Perhaps Jon's mystery woman.

"My daddy, mommy go be with Jesus." Clara's comment jerked back Erin's attention.

Mrs. Caldwell's jaw trembled as she clung tightly to her granddaughter, and the silent Mr. Caldwell looked away. Hiding tears maybe?

"Yes, dear, your mommy and daddy are with Jesus." Belinda drew her granddaughter closer.

"And Daddy's painting sunsets with Jesus!"

"Amazing sunsets." The woman offered a sad smile to Erin. "You've already done a masterful job with Clara."

"I'm doing what I can."

"And under very difficult circumstances, I'm sure. Thank you."

"You're welcome." Her gaze flitted to Jon again, hoping he'd get the signal and come help her out. That pretty woman remained at his side. Interesting.

Not the time for that. She needed to know if this couple was safe. They were being very pleasant. But were they too nice? Not in Erin's perception, but Jon might interpret something else.

"Would you mind if Clara stayed with us through the service?" Mrs. Caldwell kissed her granddaughter's forehead.

"I, uh . . ." What would Jon recommend?

"Dear." Belinda laid a hand on Erin's shoulder, and Erin's muscles tensed. "Charles and I wish to assure you that our threats of fighting the will were made in haste and out of grief for our daughter. If Lilith and Corey felt you were the best caregiver for our granddaughter, who are we to argue? We're certainly not young anymore and couldn't keep up with her. But we would appreciate the opportunity to spend time with her while we're in town."

Erin shrugged, not certain if her next words would fit the legality of the situation. "I'm sure it can be arranged." Jon would have to dictate the circumstances.

"Thank you, dear, and we are very sorry for your loss."

Erin just nodded as the two walked away with Clara, though she wanted to heave a relieved sigh. Caring for this child, much less trying to love her, took far more energy than Erin had to extend.

"Pearl?"

Erin whirled toward the familiar voice, and in spite of being at a funeral, she couldn't stop the smile from spreading across her face. "Zax!" She hadn't seen Corey's brother, Zachary, in over a year. No surprise, though, the man looked as roguish as ever with that thick mop of hair as unruly as he was, and the mischievous dark eyes to match. Erin had always thought the man should be in front of a camera, not standing behind one as a photojournalist.

"I'm so sorry, Zax." She let him draw her into his arms for a hug she embraced. Zax was one of the few who could get away with it.

"Me too." He hugged her tighter.

She absorbed the tears he was now shedding. The two brothers may have fought a lot, but they were also fiercely loyal to each other.

He finally stepped back and wiped his hand over his nose. "The brat just had to go and grab more attention, didn't he?"

"Yeah, you know Corey. Always wanted the spotlight." Which was not at all who Corey had been. That was more Zachary's personality, but he'd constantly ribbed Corey about it.

"Come with me." Zax took Erin by the elbow and led her to a classroom. He pulled out a child-sized chair for her, and he sat opposite, his piercing eyes boring into hers. "I want the truth. How are you doing?"

She shrugged. He didn't need to be dragged into her drama.

"Truth, Pearl."

She slumped and studied the low-napped carpeting. Why could she never say "no" to him? Tell him it wasn't any of his business? "I'm angry," she muttered the words. "He keeps screwing up my life."

"Clara?"

"You know?"

"Jon told me."

"Why would Corey do that to me?" Her gaze riveted on Zax. "To her?"

"I can't tell you exactly what my brother was thinking, but I'm pretty sure he wanted the best for Clara, and I agree that would be you."

"Did you, Corey, and Jon team up and say, 'let's mess with Erin'?"

"I'm sure it looks that way."

"Smells like it, too."

"I suppose it does." He ran a hand over his Tony Stark-like facial hair. "Know that I'm just a phone call away."

"That, and an ocean."

"Technology brings us a lot closer."

"Well, maybe I want the real thing, not an image on the screen."

With a sigh, he kneaded the back of his neck. "Exactly what the folks said." He looked out the classroom door, then at Erin. "One more thing. Mom asked me to put together a video for the service. She called it a photo eulogy."

"Lovely." Her sarcasm snuck out again. A video that would likely ignore the years she and Corey had together and spotlight his fabulous new marriage and family. And probably make Mik feel worse than she already did.

Zax touched her hand, prompting her to look him in the eye. "I'm narrating as it plays. It's honest, Erin, just like the stories I tell overseas, I'm telling Corey's life story. The 3 Sixlets. Your marriage. Mik. Him messing up. Him finally growing up. Faith became a big part of his life. I want people to see how it changed him, and they can't see that unless they see the bad parts as well as the good. I told Mom I wouldn't do one of those glossed-over pieces that shows how *perfect* Corey was, and she agreed. It will not be your typical tribute."

And Zax was just the person to get away with it. "Thank you."

"I suppose I should join the family." He stood up and offered his hand. "Will you sit with us?"

She shook her head. Being here was awkward enough without mourners seeing her as part of the Belden family. "I plan to stay in the back. Mik's fine with being with you guys. The Caldwells have—"

"Mo-om—Uncle Zax!" Mik's voice went from a whine to a squeal behind her.

"Hey, Sixlet. I was wondering where you were."

She practically bowled him over with a hug. "I've missed you."

"Nowhere near as much as I've missed you, Six."

"Are you gonna stick around now?"

"I'll be here for a week, but then I've got to go back."

Mik's whole body slouched as if a sudden weight had dropped on her, and she shook away from his hug.

"Hey. I'll be back more often. I promise. Someone's gotta keep the boys away from you." He bopped her nose. "You're getting as pretty as your mom."

Mik looked back at Erin, and her nose wrinkled.

Zax winked at Erin. "Believe me, Six, guys are going to be fighting over you."

"Please don't encourage her, Zax." Mik was unhappy enough about not being able to date until she was sixteen and had a job.

"You're right." Zax raised his hands in surrender. "Off to join the folks. You coming with, Six?"

"I can sit by you?"

"Gotta have my best girl beside me."

Her daughter beamed as the two headed toward the door, Zachary's arm around Mik's shoulder. The man still hadn't lost his charm.

"Oh, Mom?" Mik stopped and looked back, her eyes narrowed. "Do you realize who has Clara?"

Apparently, Mik didn't care for that woman's parents either. Erin didn't care. "Yes. Clara's grandparents. And they're just holding her during the service."

"Dad didn't like them."

"No, he didn't," Zax said.

"Well, he didn't like me much either, so I have something in common with them."

Mik let out a huge sigh then kicked at the carpet. "Guess he didn't like me much either." Her chin quivered, which meant tears were on the way again.

"Oh, honey." Erin mentally slapped herself for stepping into that one, as she drew Mik tight to her body and held the now-sniffling child.

Zax squinted at Erin. Maybe asking what Mik's drama was about?

She mouthed, "I'll explain later."

He rolled his eyes and formed his hands into a circle, like he wanted to strangle something. That was body language she recognized as Zax had used that very same motion in regard to his younger brother many times as they were growing up.

At least Erin wasn't alone in that thought.

Tonight, after the funeral, Erin planned to dig into the journal and find something that would reassure her daughter that Corey did love her. Even if she had to forge a few new words.

———

Corey
May 9, 2014

Counseling was Erin's idea. It usually worked for her, so I promised I'd give it a try.

Writing in this stupid journal, though, was my counselor's idea, as if putting my thoughts on paper will help me feel less anxiety. Of course, Erin jumped at the idea and gave me this journal. A boring, brown leather book with blank pages inside. I know, she just wants me to get better. I want me to get better. I promised to try.

Anyway, the doc said to write whatever comes to mind, and I don't ever have to share it with anyone. I do like the idea of having a secret from everyone. From Erin, my parents, Jon. It almost seems prodigal. Sometimes I envy my brother.

So, here it goes, my big secret.

I hate my job.

No, I can do better than that.

I HATE MY JOB!

Yeah, that's it.

I hate accounting. I hate numbers, how they never vary. One plus one always equals two. They have no color or melody or scent. They always stay in their boundaries. Like me. Boring. Wish I wasn't so good at it. Maybe if I start messing up, Mom and Pop will fire me.

Now there's a fantasy. With a wife and eight-year-old to support, that'll never happen. Some days I hate being tied down to them.

You know what? The doc was right. Getting my feelings down on paper is freeing.

The problem is, how do I free myself from my family and the family business?

Chapter Ten

Oh, boy. Erin hid Corey's journal inside her nightstand and slammed the drawer shut. No wonder Mik felt her dad didn't like her. Not that it made Erin feel any better either. He'd felt tied down to them as if he had nothing to do with it? Maybe if he hadn't pressed her for sex before they were married . . .

She pounded her pillow to refrain from screaming.

No, that was unfair. Yeah, Corey had pressed her on their college break, but she'd instigated it, flirting, hoping to wear him down. Yet, he was the Christian. He'd been raised to wait until marriage, whereas her mom had only told her to use protection. They'd both failed miserably at obeying their parents, and look where they ended up. Married with a child far too early. Was it any surprise that their marriage had ended in divorce?

Raising Mik was going to be difficult enough, but raising Clara too? When she got to be Mik's far-too-wise and inquisitive age, what would Erin tell her then about her father's behavior?

Erin re-opened the tableside drawer and took out her own journal. The way she was going, she'd need another journal by the end of the week.

She started writing out a prayer . . .

April 9, 2019

Hey God, me again.

Corey's funeral was . . . odd. I saw so many old friends that either ignored me or avoided me. People think that when you divorce, you just divide up family and belongings. But that's far from true. I got physical custody of Mik, and we shared legal custody with her spending a weekend a month at his place and the rest at mine, with her having no true home. Yet, I'm supposed to assure people that Mik will be so much better off because Corey and I couldn't get along and were making our home a tense place to live.

What a bunch of drivel.

So yeah, our family and home were divided—I got the house, which also meant I got the mortgage and barely enough support to keep us afloat—but so were our friendships. After the divorce, people acted weird toward me. I guess I acted weird toward them too. The divorce embarrassed me. I was a failure, just like my mom and her mom and . . .

Telling close friends (of which I had few. My time was spent raising our daughter and we didn't have the money to go out, so friendships deteriorated) was hard enough, but how do you inform acquaintances? Like the women in my Bible study group who all have perfect marriages and were quick to point out what I should have done to save my marriage. I found a new Bible study group, one with real people who had messy lives, just like me.

How was I supposed to inform people on social media? I just changed my status from "Married" to "Single" and hoped that people didn't notice. Ha! People I barely knew were suddenly messaging me, trying to dig into my personal life. A lot of people judged me, threw Bible verses at me. How dare they! I deleted all my accounts shortly afterwards. I didn't need "friends" like that.

Then there were gossips at church I barely know, but who noticed right away that I was worshiping alone. Some, who knew about Corey, had the audacity to blame me for him cheating! Said if I'd paid him more attention, he wouldn't have had to look elsewhere. I found a new church, too.

How do you send out a joyful Christmas card when your big news is that your husband got another woman pregnant and asked for a divorce? Some people I know who've gotten a divorce just sent a family picture minus the spouse. All that would do was raise more questions, so I stopped sending Christmas cards.

Oh, but Corey's "lovely" new wife, she mailed out a beauty of her new family, which sent Mik into another tailspin. I'm not ashamed to say that I pegged that card to my bulletin board and mutilated it with stick pins. Should I apologize for that, God?

Jon, who, as you know, handled the divorce, convinced us to craft an explanation (AKA, "a lie") to appease the nosy and gossips. I'd summon a not-so-convincing smile and say, "We drifted apart, but we're still friends. We stand together in raising our daughter who is adjusting well. We'd appreciate it if you'd respect our privacy." Blah, blah, blah. I nearly choked every time I told that lie, when I really wanted to say, "The scumbag chose a new family over me and Mik. She's very upset that her daddy doesn't live at home anymore and that he doesn't make time for her ball games."

But I digress. I was going to talk about the funeral, but my feelings—my anger—took over. Why is that the only feeling I recognize?

Anyway, Zax was right about the video story he crafted. It showed Corey as a baby, of course. Lots of pics with the two brothers. Then there were a lot of the 3 Sixlets, too. I even smiled at some of those. He also included a wedding photo—our wedding may have been small and rushed, but we'd been happy that day. And, of course, Zax included some of our Christmas card photos. The happy ones showing Mik growing from a baby to a nine-year-old.

Then the cards stopped.

And Zax literally said, "My brother messed up big time." That almost made me cry. I loved seeing someone acknowledge the truth.

From there, I tuned out a lot. I didn't want to see him happily remarried. I didn't want to see Mik glowering in her new family photos. I didn't want to hear about the success Corey found with his mixed-media artwork.

Because he found that happiness without me, and I wanted— I want to be happy too, and now he's ruined that for me. Again.

Yeah, I shed a few tears this afternoon, but not out of grief, rather, out of pity.

The video ended with a stained-glass-like mosaic of Corey's life. The good. The sad. And the faith filled. Including a verse from Ephesians that said we are Your masterpiece.

That final frame was beautiful, and it promised good things. Not a bad video created by a non-believer.

Am I really your masterpiece, God? Have you made me new to do good things for you? It sure doesn't feel like it.

Still, I hope.

Erin dropped her pen at a shrill cry that made the hair on her arms stand up straight. What? Oh, Clara! She threw off her covers and hurried to the room next door, the office-turned-nursery.

Clara held up her chubby little arms, her body shaking in sync with her sniffles.

"Hey, Lollipop, what's the matter?" Erin withdrew Clara from the foldable crib, using the nickname Zax had given her early on when her hair started growing out in ringlets like Shirley Temple. He'd been a sucker for her old movies and loved "On the Good Ship Lollipop." So, with that, Clara's nickname had been born. Hopefully, using the name now would help settle the child.

Erin sat with her in the office chair.

"I go home." Clara snuggled in, and her body quivered.

"Oh, Lolli . . ." She drew the child in closer. "You have a new home now, with me and Mik." At least until a better home could be found.

"I no wike your house. I wike mine."

Erin did her best to hold in a sigh. As it was, Clara likely sensed Erin's feelings. "I know, Lolli, I know. It's okay to be sad when you have a new home."

That was what Debbie would tell her. It was okay to be sad. To be happy. Angry. To feel. What you chose to do with those feelings is what mattered. Like in that Pixar movie, *Inside Out*.

"I be sad?"

"You can absolutely be sad. You can cry, if that's how you feel."

If only Erin had heard those words when she was young, instead of, "Cry and I'll give you something to cry about." Her mom had never hurt her physically, though.

She shook off her self-pity and settled the now mostly calm child on her lap. "You can come to me any time and tell me how you feel, understand?" No one would invalidate this child's feelings.

Clara nodded, and rubbed her fists over her eyes. "I 'stand."

"Good. Now I have a question for you. If I get you a big girl bed, will that help?"

"A big girl bed?" Clara sat up straight, her blue eyes round as Tootsie Pops, fitting her nickname.

"Mm, hmm. Like Mik's but one just your size." When they'd gone to Corey's house, Erin had noticed that the crib had been converted into a toddler bed. It was too large for this room, or she would have asked Jon if they could move it here. But she'd seen other toddler beds online that would fit.

"My size?"

"Special for you." Erin bopped her nose. "After you sleep tonight, we'll go shopping tomorrow."

"I wike shopping." Clara's face lit up as bright as the streetlight.

I'll bet you do. Her mother had loved shopping, too, but she'd also had plenty of money to spend. Erin carried Clara over to the bed and laid her down. "Goodnight, Lollipop."

"Ni' night, wowwipop."

Erin smothered a warm grin as she left the room. No, she would not let that child worm her way into her heart. She couldn't. That would only end up with two more broken hearts.

Chapter Eleven

Corey

June 5, 2014

I discovered something today, something that made me feel alive again.

After work, I didn't want to go home. I couldn't smile and tell Erin everything was okay. I couldn't face her after work, so I lied. Told her I was going to a ballgame with Jon.

Instead, I went to the new art gallery in Brainerd. I used to dream about having my paintings on the gallery wall, but then Erin got pregnant, we got married, and I had to grow up and be a husband and father.

Don't get me wrong, I love Erin and Mik, and couldn't imagine life without them in it, but being a parent does force you to change priorities. Since paint supplies cost a lot of money, it had to go. I didn't realize until today how much I missed it.

Today I spent more than three hours soaking up the displays, and it felt like only one had passed.

I should tell Erin the truth. She'd probably join me. But I like having this to myself.

I also like, maybe a little too much, this prodigal rush. It must be what Zax feels when he's doing something Mom and Pop don't approve of. But it's not like I'm doing something bad. I'm not going to bars and getting drunk. I'm not cheating on Erin. I'm not doing drugs. I'm going to an art gallery! What's wrong with that?

He lied to me!

No doubt, that was how the affair started. Numb, Erin tucked Corey's journal into its drawer. *That woman* had worked at that gallery.

Erin got out of bed and drew on a robe. The truth of Corey's words frosted her veins. He'd hated his job. He didn't or couldn't tell her. Why hadn't she seen it? Why did she have to be this ice queen who couldn't read people's feelings and gestures? Shouldn't a wife be able to tell when her husband was unhappy?

The doorbell rang as she shuffled toward the kitchen. Who would be stopping by this early? She glanced at the clock on the microwave. Whoa. Eleven thirty already? Way past time to be up and dressed and in her office.

More importantly, was Clara okay? She never slept this long. Whereas Mik would sleep all day if Erin allowed.

If it was Joyce or Debbie, she'd answer. They could deal with her just-out-of-bed look. She tightened the belt around her robe and looked through the peephole.

Jon? What was he doing here? No way could she answer the door looking like Cruella de Vil's ugly stepsister. She stepped back a few feet then yelled, "Be there in a moment."

First, she checked on Clara. Sound asleep still, with her stuffed crocodile, Chomper, cuddled in one arm and her thumb in her mouth. Whew.

Then she hustled to the bathroom and tugged a brush through her tangles and ran a toothbrush over her teeth. Finally, she threw on a pair of jogging pants and a long shirt. For Jon, she didn't need to be fancy, but she did need to be out of her pajamas. Finally set, she answered the door, and warm air rushed in ahead of Jon.

Hard to believe that less than a week ago, a blizzard had taken Corey's life.

"You okay?" Jon squeezed past her, a thick file folder in his hands, glasses on his face, and his signature bowtie attached to his shirt. All business and giving off a slight Clark Kent vibe. This was the Jon she remembered.

"I uh . . ." She stared out the door. "It's spring."

"Yeah," he said quietly. "I noticed that too."

In other words, he was mourning. At least that was what she thought he meant. She shut the front door and gestured to her couch. "Are you okay?"

He shrugged. "Mostly. I figure diving into work will help me deal with stuff."

"Or bury it."

"So, you're a psychologist now?" He quirked a smile.

"When you've talked to them as often as I have, you pick up on a few things."

He pointed to the spot beside him, but she chose the rocker kitty-corner to the couch. A psychologist may have something to say about that as well.

"What brings you here?" She eyed the file on his lap.

"I promised you work." He pulled a page out of the front of the file. "Mine plus a bunch of other recommendations. I know my account alone won't keep you afloat, but getting a few of us should keep bread and butter on the table." He handed over the page.

She scanned through the list. All attorneys, no surprise, but many would have deep pockets. Jon certainly did. "Thank you for this."

"It's the least I can do."

That didn't make sense. She shook her head. "You owe me nothing." He hadn't made promises that he'd broken. He'd just . . . disappeared when she needed him.

"But I do owe you." With his pointer finger, he nudged his glasses into place. One would think with his income he could afford glasses that wouldn't slide down. "I shouldn't have been your divorce attorney. It didn't feel right at the time and it feels slimy to this day. I shouldn't have made it easy for him to go away, but I did, and I can never repay you for my part in your break-up."

Erin just sat there, stunned. Not once had she blamed Jon, rather she'd been grateful that he'd offered his services pro bono during the divorce. And now this.

Maybe a Clark Kent comparison wasn't so far off.

Jon grabbed his leather briefcase from his car and slung it over his shoulder before crossing the busy street to his office. Objective number one had been met for the day: he'd passed his bookkeeping tasks on to Erin and given her several more recommendations. Hopefully, a few of them would pan out for her. She deserved to have something positive happen.

Objective number two was to inform his current bookkeeper that his services were no longer required. Not easy, as Taskforce Accounting had done a superb job for him over the years, but making it up to Erin, and making certain Mik and Clara had a good life, took precedence.

He entered the front door of the nearly hundred-year-old office building, a reminder that not everything ended in ruin, even though that was the message he'd learned much of his life and throughout his career. He hadn't planned on thriving as a divorce attorney—he also handled family law and estate planning—but divorce was where he made his money. And sometimes that ate at his gut, that he was so good at bringing marriages to a legal end.

"Hey, Jon, you in the clouds?"

Jon shook his head and slammed on his brakes before walking right into Zax in the wide-open foyer. "Man, I'm sorry. Just waxing nostalgic. Wondering how I became known as the Divorce Authority. Not exactly the moniker I would have chosen for myself."

"Yeah, but from what I hear you end up keeping more families together, and those that split do so as amicably as possible."

Jon shifted the briefcase to his other shoulder. "Like Corey and Erin? On the outside, it looked amicable, but you and I know differently."

"Well, in that case, you stood up for Erin. Considering that witch Corey married, if not for you, Erin could have found herself on the street."

Jon pushed past his friend. He didn't appreciate someone speaking ill of the deceased, but he also couldn't argue with Zax's statement. If Lilith and her money had had a say, Erin and Mik would have had to find a new home. With prodding from Jon, Corey had stood up to her.

But like Corey, Lilith had changed these past months as well, proving that God was a God of miracles.

Time to change the subject away from Corey and his issues. "What brings you here? Looks like you were heading out."

Zax leaned against the brick wall and showed that grin women seemed to swoon over. "Your secretary—"

"Legal assistant."

"—and I hit it off yesterday—"

"At the funeral?"

"—and I told Gina I'd drop by today so we could plan something. She promised to show me her hot-pink pickup."

Naturally. Jon should have anticipated they'd get together when he saw the two seated across from each other during the post-funeral meal.

"Gina's engaged. Leave her alone."

"Said she broke it off. They're no longer together."

"Oh." Well that was the best news he'd heard all day. Why an intelligent woman would choose to date someone who treated her like mud, he'd never know. But then to move on to a player like Zax? "Just treat her with respect."

"Hey, I respect every woman I go out with."

Right. "Somehow I think you and I have a different meaning for respect."

"Coming from the thirty-year-old virgin." Zax smirked and put his hand on the metal door plate. "I'll take that into consideration."

"If you want a way to kill some time, I know a couple of adorable females who would love to see you."

"They wouldn't happen to go by the names of Sixlet and Lollipop?"

"They're the ones."

"Not a bad idea." With a wink, Zax left the building.

And Jon stood there shaking his head. How Zax and Corey were the sons of the Beldens, the most upright couple he knew, Jon would never comprehend. The Beldens had been more parental toward him than his own father, who hadn't given a rip about his son. If not for the Beldens, Jon wouldn't be where he was today. More importantly, he wouldn't have his faith to lean on. They'd done the same for Erin. Somehow, their faith hadn't spread to Corey and Zax.

Speaking of which, he handed both Zax and Gina over to God and prayed for wisdom in dealing with them.

He entered his office space where Gina had on a headset and was engrossed in typing something on her computer.

"Morning, Counselor," she said without slowing. How she spoke, listened, and typed at the same time and maintained nearly a hundred percent accuracy, he'd never know. She was the queen of multi-tasking.

"Good morning." He set his briefcase down on a visitor chair and motioned for her to remove her headset. "Got a moment?"

"Sure thing." She pulled her hands away from the keyboard, circled her headset around her neck, and swiveled toward him. "Let me guess, you ran into Zax on your way in." She was also clairvoyant, it seemed.

"Sure did. Told me you and what's-his-face broke up."

"Yep." She wriggled the fingers on her engagement ring-free hand. "I finally listened to you."

"Good to hear."

"And don't worry about Zax. We're just going to have some fun while he's in town. He needs something to take the edge off of losing his brother, so we're gonna go dancing."

It was the kind of dancing Jon worried about, the kind that included heavy drinking, and could find her pregnant, with Zax an ocean away.

"I see those cogs turning in your head, Counselor." She wagged a finger at him. "Don't worry about me. I'm a big girl. I can handle myself. Besides, why are you concerned with my love life when you have issues of your own?"

He fiddled with his tie. "I don't have issues."

"You don't? Then why is a kind, wealthy, good-looking man like you single, huh?"

He leaned his head back, bonking it on the wall. This again. He wasn't going to rehash it with her. "None of your business." He started to stand.

"True. Corey's ex-wife is none of my business, but someday you're going to deal with your feelings for her."

"She's a friend." This time he did stand.

"Uh-huh. You just keep telling yourself that." She put on her headset and resumed typing. Conversation over.

He would keep telling himself that he didn't have feelings for Erin until he believed it. He'd witnessed the destruction of far too many families in his short career. Many were Christian couples, good couples, some who had been together for fifty years! He couldn't promise Erin that would never happen to them. Yes, he'd promised Corey he'd care for Erin and the girls, but "care for" was a long way from marriage. Besides, he could not bear hurting her again.

Erin bounced Clara on her lap, trying to stop the child from crying, as she brought up the first name on the list of potential contacts Jon had given her. She located their website. Learned their specialties. Checked their Google rating, everything she could think of to show that she'd done her research before calling them. Marketing herself wasn't her gift, but she realized that if she wanted to have a successful home-based bookkeeping business, selling her services would now be part of her job description.

But making the sale couldn't be done with a small child in tow. It was time to wake up her teenager and put her to work babysitting. Oh, Mik was going to love that. Not! The fact that Erin had let her sleep in this long should buy Erin some cred, but pubescent teenagers weren't exactly logical.

She set Clara on the floor, which brought on another wail. Yah. This was going to be one fun day. Rather than pick her up and spoil her, she took Clara's hand. "Want to help me wake up Mik?"

And just like that, the tears stopped. Clara adored her big sister, even if big sis didn't return the feeling. Clara led the way to Mik's room and knocked on the door.

"Wissa, wake up! Time to pway!"

"Go away!"

Not happening, dear child. Erin knocked on the door this time and summoned her compassionate voice. "Honey, I realize this is a tough week for you, but I'm going to need your help."

Mik hurled a word Erin did not allow.

"Lord, You have to help me here, because my temper is about to erupt," she prayed under her breath. Reacting to that word was exactly what Mik wanted, and it would catch Clara's attention, so Erin would ignore it. For now. And remove Clara from the situation so she wouldn't be privy to more colorful words from her sister.

"Lollipop. It's nap time." Technically, it wasn't, but she needed the child out of earshot.

"I no wike naps."

"I know, Lolli. Just a little one will make you feel better, and you get to sleep in your new bed!"

"I no wike it."

"But Chomper does." Erin picked up the child struggling to be released, and carried her into the nursery. She set her down in the toddler bed she'd purchased that morning with Clara's approval, and tucked her in beside her pet crocodile. Clara stayed put but unleashed a torrent of tears and screams.

Yippee.

Not that Erin didn't expect it, but she'd hoped the bed and Chomper would ease the naptime routine.

She left the nursery and shut the door, muting the screams slightly. Then she returned to Mik's door. Maybe her daughter was doing the right thing. Hiding away to grieve, where Erin was just trying to move on, one slow step at a time.

Perhaps trying a Debbie-like tactic would work. She knocked on the door. "Want to talk about it?"

There came that ugly word again. Erin couldn't not say something, right? Silence would be giving Mik permission to speak like that. Erin would rather confront her face to face than with the door in between them, so she tried the knob. Locked, naturally. Now what? How was she supposed to deal with a thirteen-year-old who'd just lost her father? For the second time?

Erin couldn't relate to that. Her father had never been around.

God, what do I do?

Debbie would probably tell Erin that Mik was dealing with her grief by lashing out at the person closest to her, and that Erin should love her in return.

But how do you do that?

There was one way to find out. She leaned her back against the door and slid down until she was sitting. With silence from Mik behind her and screams from Clara in front, she spread out her arms and opened up her hands, opening herself up to hearing from God.

"I don't know what to do." She whispered so Mik wouldn't hear. Probably wouldn't anyway, over Clara's cries. "I'm trying to be the best mom I can, but I don't know how. My mom never taught me. I know I'm supposed to love them, but what does that look like? Does it look like discipline? Does it look like wrapping them in a hug they try to fight out of? Should I be selective with the battles I choose to fight? Is letting Mik get away with that behavior loving or damaging? I. Don't. Know! And I really, really need Your wisdom."

That wisdom usually came from the Bible. She dug out her phone from her front pocket, brought up a Bible app, and searched for verses on grief. No surprise, many of the verses were found in the Psalms. They talked about turning your burdens over to God, that He's near to the brokenhearted, that joy will eventually come.

Then she turned to Matthew 5:4

"Blessed are those who mourn, for they shall be comforted."

They shall be comforted . . . How true! Simply reading His word was a comfort. It calmed her heart and her thoughts, if not Clara's cries. For her, it was better than a hug. Well, to her, most anything was better than a hug.

But for Mik, that was different. Unlike her mother, and so much like her father, Mik yearned for hugs, so that was exactly what Erin would give her, assuming the old credit card trick would work on Mik's door.

She retrieved a card from her wallet then slid the card between the door and the jamb and pushed on the deadlatch, forcing it back inside the knob mechanism. Keeping the card in place, she tried the knob. Yes! It turned.

She knocked again before pushing open the door.

Mik sat on the bed wide-eyed and stunned into silence. "How . . . ?"

"My secret." Erin hid the card in her pocket. No doubt, Mik would learn tricks of her own soon. "Because you need this." Erin waded across the clothes-strewn room, sat on her daughter's bed, and enveloped Mik in her arms.

The teen stiffened, probably surprised that her mom was the one initiating the hug, then melted into it. Followed by sniffles and heaving sobs.

Erin remained silent and just stroked her daughter's chestnut-colored hair that was similar to her own. The cries from across the hall also quieted.

"I miss him." Mik said between sobs.

"I know, baby, I know."

"And I'm angry at him."

Me, too.

"I feel like my life is falling apart."

Exactly.

"And I don't have anyone anymore."

Now that one hurt, probably an intentional arrow to the heart, but Erin held tight to her daughter trying not to show the arrow had hit its mark.

The doorbell rang and, startled, Erin dropped her arms to her side.

Mik started laughing amid sniffles and wiped a hand over her eyes and nose. "You should see your face."

Erin smiled and tapped her daughter's chin. "I love you, Sixlet." Then she got up and hurried to the door. She peeked through the spy hole. Zax! Not caring what she looked like, she threw open the door.

"Hey, Pearl."

"Come on in."

"Uncle Zax!" Mik sped into her uncle's arms, nearly knocking him over.

"Hey, Six, ever think of trying out for football?"

"Yeah."

And she had. She wasn't happy that it was a boys-only sport at her school.

"Of course." He put an arm on her shoulder but looked at Erin. "How about I take my favorite nieces out for ice cream?"

"Yes!"

Erin could have kissed him for that offer. "That would be lovely."

"But Clara's asleep. You should just take me."

Not happening. "Clara's in her bed, but not sleeping. I'll get her." A twinge of guilt gnawed at her for that lie as she hurried to the nursery, while listening to Mik try to barter with her uncle. Yes, Clara was in the toddler bed, but Erin had no idea if the child was asleep or not. In another minute, she wouldn't be because Erin was not going to turn down this opportunity for alone time.

She opened the door and was relieved to see Clara sitting up, her thumb firmly ensconced in her mouth, while hugging Chomper. She didn't move when Erin entered, likely her way of showing she was angry. That would change in roughly two seconds.

"Lolli, how would you like to go out with Uncle Zax for ice cream?"

"I wuv ice cream!" The child jumped up and held her arms in the air.

Erin took Clara's hand, and the child leaped from the bed. "Uncle Zax must have known you like ice cream. He's taking you and Mik out."

"Yippee!" The child skipped from the room, and ran to her uncle, who scooped her up in his arms, then threw her in the air.

"How's my favorite Lollipop?"

"I yummy!"

"You are? Let me see?" He kissed her cheek. "Why, yes you are. You're the yummiest niece I have."

The child beamed with the praise. "I wike ice cream."

"Well, isn't that a coincidence? Mik and I like ice cream, too. You want to come with us?"

"Uh-huh."

"Well, you've just made my day." He kissed her cheek again. "But I'm guessing you probably should go potty before we go." He set her down and patted her bum as she scurried off toward the bathroom.

His ease with his nieces made Erin a wee bit jealous. "You are so good with them."

"What can I say?" He blew on his fist and rubbed it over his heart. "Women adore me."

"And your humility astounds me."

"As does your sarcastic wit, Pearl. Glad to hear you've still got it."

"Ha ha."

He grinned and it was easy to see why women adored him. Growing up, she'd had a massive crush on him as well until she realized that his arrogance was just a cover for his insecurities. He was more like a big brother to her now.

He laid a hand on Mik's shoulder. "Is it okay if I treat Six to a movie afterwards?"

"Depends on the movie." She eyed her daughter, who begged to see shows inappropriate for her.

He named the title, and Erin gave approval. "I think that's just what Mik needs."

And just what I need, too.

"Thank you," she said, as gently as possible, hoping to convey her true gratitude.

"I'll always be here for you, Pearl."

"I know." *Except for when you're across the ocean,* she wanted to add, but didn't want to wreck the moment, grateful that he was here today. She'd take what she could get.

And with both girls gone, maybe she'd actually get some calling done and add to her client list.

Chapter Twelve

After making seven calls that ended with "No, thank you," she finally got a "Maybe." Tomorrow afternoon, she'd meet with Attorney Vanessa Martin. Hopefully, a face-to-face would sell the service. Hopefully, the fact that they were both women would help. She made three more calls, and on the third got another, "Meet with me on Monday."

Yes! She pumped a fist, celebrating the small victories.

But now she had to find a babysitter for tomorrow. That wasn't something she wanted to force on Mik right now. She tried the Beldens, but they had a commitment. She thought about trying the Caldwells, but they were busy planning a funeral for Friday. She tried Debbie, but she was working. That left Zax. But she was already leaning on him today. Maybe Jon? Nah, he definitely was too busy.

It wasn't as if she had a slew of babysitters in her contacts. *She* was Clara's babysitter.

When Zax dropped off the girls, she'd ask him, plead with him.

She yawned and realized how exhausted she felt. It seemed she'd been going non-stop for days. With the girls still gone, maybe she could sneak in a short nap. What a luxury that would be!

Her soft bed called to her, and she listened, covering up with an afghan Joyce had crocheted for her after Corey left. She closed her eyes and waited for sleep to come, but her mind kept drifting to her nightstand and the journal hiding there.

Don't do it, Erin. You're having a good day, and this could ruin it.

Erin shoved away the voice, drew out the journal, and dove into Corey's thoughts:

July 10, 2014

I met someone today. No, it's not what you're thinking. I'm not having an affair. I wouldn't do that to Erin or Mik. I'm not that kind of man.

Sure, things aren't great right now. Erin's always nagging. Wants more free time. Wants me to do more to help her around the house. Make a meal now and then. Really? What does she do all day? How hard can it be to watch an eight-year-old? And Mik is well behaved. The house should sparkle when I get home. I shouldn't have to support the family and cook supper too. My dad never had to cook.

So, yeah, I told Erin I was taking an accounting class every Thursday night, so I can go to the gallery. Told my folks too, just in case Erin brings it up to them. Just as long as they don't find out the truth. Honesty was always stressed in our family, especially being accountants, and I've never been a liar. Besides, my attitude is always better after a trip to the gallery. That should count for something, shouldn't it?

Anyway, back to meeting someone. Lilith's the education coordinator for the gallery, so she helps educate the community about art. How cool is that? Our area needs more teaching about art. More appreciation so we creatives don't feel ashamed for using our gifts.

She's the first person in a long time I talked to about my desire to paint. She didn't put me down or roll her eyes when I told her about a mixed-medium idea I've been envisioning. No, Lilith got excited about the idea and encouraged me to follow through, to follow my heart. She can't wait to see what I create.

Erin used to love what I created.

She will again.

And that will get our marriage back to where it belongs.

———

Erin returned the book to its hiding spot and sat numbly on the bed.

She'd been nagging.

Hadn't listened to his dreams.

Had stopped loving his art.

Had the affair been her fault?

The home's front door opening shook Erin from her thoughts. She'd played the I-blame-myself game when Corey had first left her, but Debbie had convinced her the only person to blame for cheating was the cheater.

She massaged her wrist over the tattooed word, Lulu, as she hurried to the living room that was suddenly filled with laughter. When was the last time she'd heard that amazing sound in her home?

She entered the living room in time to see the two girls hog pile their uncle, with his face to the ground. To much of the world, Zax came across as vain, but the world didn't see this side of him. He loved his nieces, would do anything for them, and they adored him. To be honest, she could add herself to the adorers list, especially right now.

"I give! Uncle!" He feigned pain as he raised his head and caught her watching them. A single eyebrow raised.

What did he mean by that?

The two girls seemed to notice her at the same time, and the giggling stopped. They slid off their uncle's back and onto the floor, keeping their gaze on her as if they were expecting a reprimand. Was she that harsh of a mother?

"Hey, ladies." Zax pushed himself up into a sitting position and nodded toward Erin. "How about the two of you give us adults a moment?"

"Then you and I go to a movie?" Mik stood and clasped Clara's hand.

"Only if it's still okay with your mother."

Mik did an eye roll that other teens would be jealous of. Even Erin knew what that meant. Mom was a fun-assassin.

Tension returned to her wrist, and she rubbed.

"You okay?" Zax stood, his gaze anchored on her wrist, and nodded to the couch.

"I'm fine." She dropped her arms to the side, but his gaze didn't lose its intensity. "I said I'm fine." She plopped down on the rocker and glared at him as he sat on the edge of the couch.

"Just making sure. I know this isn't easy for you."

He's concerned, Erin, and he just lost a brother. Give him some slack. "For you, either."

"No, it's not. I wish I hadn't been so awful to him the last few years, that I would have attempted to forgive him, reconcile. And now, I'll never have the chance." He looked away but couldn't hide his sniffle.

This was where emotive people would instinctively reach out and offer a hug. The action certainly wasn't natural to Erin, but she got up and sat by him on the couch and spread an arm around his back. He quickly turned into her arms and gave her a full hug as tears wet her shoulder.

"I was so awful to him, Pearl, after he . . ."

Cheated on her and left her. She'd filled in that blank enough over the last years that it came naturally.

"I should have forgiven him." He released the hug and looked at the floor. "He's my brother, and I treated him like dirt. Even when he reached out and apologized, I treated him like he was a pariah." He squeezed the back of his neck with both hands, a stress trait he shared with Corey. "And now, I can never make it right. How do I live with myself?"

As she would have done for Corey, she pulled down on one of his arms and then massaged his neck for him. "As you showed in the video at the funeral, Corey reaffirmed his faith." Faith that had gotten buried beneath work and parenting and money woes during the marriage. Had that been her fault, too? "You'll see him again, and you can tell him how much you love him."

Zax released a nervous laugh. "Only if Jesus lets me in."

"You believe, Zax, I know you do."

"I guess." He shrugged, followed by a sniffle. "I'm just not a fan of His restrictions."

"Those *restrictions* are there for a reason," she said far more sharply than she intended.

"Oh, man, I'm sorry, Pearl. Yeah, you're right, of course. Corey wasn't a fan either and that ended up hurting everyone."

"And I didn't mean to snap."

"Right now, we're all out of sorts." He slapped his knees then drew an arm across his nose. "Well, I promised Six I'd take her to a movie. That still okay with you?"

"She's expecting it. As long as you take her to the movie you mentioned earlier, you're good. She loves spending time with you." Which reminded Erin she needed to ask another favor of Zax. "Speaking of which, I really need a babysitter for tomorrow afternoon. I have a potential client interview."

"Oh, man, I would, but I have to work on my upcoming story tomorrow—I'm going to Israel for Holy week."

"Israel? That should be interesting."

"It is. It's part of a year-long series I'm working on, Walking Through the New Testament. I'm presenting it through a secular lens. The boss is getting after me to get him my plans for the week. Then tomorrow night I have a date."

"A date." Why wasn't she surprised? "Anyone I know?"

"Jon's assistant, Gina Holmquist. I met her at the funeral, and we hit it off."

Erin shook her head. Only Zax would find romance at a funeral. "Let me guess, tall, blonde, and leggy?" She described the woman she'd seen beside Jon at the funeral.

"So, you do know her?" He grinned.

"No, but I was hoping maybe she and Jon were together."

He laughed. "First thing I asked her, and she laughed at me. Said Jon has one love, and that's the law. Anyone who can break through that will be a miracle maker."

"Don't you know anyone you could set him up with?"

He raised both hands. A stop sign.

That she understood. "But you have to know someone who would be—"

"I don't like getting set up, and I don't do matchmaking. End of subject."

Fine. "Well, someone will nab him. He's a good catch."

Zax raised his brows. What did he mean by that? That was a gesture she never could decipher because it always seemed to mean something different.

Maybe Law was the mystery woman in Jon's life. That would

make sense, as he did love his work more than anything else, it seemed.

She wasn't about to ask Zax for clarification, though. It was better to move on to another subject. "I need a miracle for tomorrow, or I'll be taking a child with me to my appointment." Or she could only hope that since the appointment was with a female attorney, the woman would be compassionate toward Erin if Clara did come with her.

Chapter Thirteen

Erin jabbed at the End Call button on her phone. No one could watch Clara while she talked to a potential client. No one. Out of desperation, she'd even tried Gina, Jon's legal assistant.

They both laughed over that.

So that left her with two lousy choices: postpone the appointment or take Clara with her. As she was dealing with a female attorney, someone who might understand and empathize with the plight of a single parent, she chose the latter.

While Clara fussed in her room, Erin prepared for her appointment, dressing in a charcoal gray suit with a pencil skirt and light-grey, pullover satin blouse. Professional, yet flattering. She hoped, anyway. It wouldn't be enough to cover up the fact that she'd have a three-year-old child in tow, but that couldn't be helped.

She just prayed that Clara would get over her whininess and play quietly like she used to do before her entire life was uprooted. Erin would fuss, too. Oh, who was she kidding? She was whining!

Time to pull up her big-girl panties and deal with what life threw at her, stop fretting about what she couldn't change, and work at making a difference where she could.

She filled the diaper bag with treats and toys then went to retrieve Clara from the nursery. Naturally, she was now sleeping, with her mouth feverishly sucking on her thumb. The poor thing needed some stability in her life.

Erin bent over and picked up the child who immediately wound her arms around Erin's neck. Little sniffles shook her body. Even that dug into Erin's feelings and made her heart ache for the child. After this meeting was over, Erin would devote the rest of the day to Clara, like she used to do with Mik.

Erin helped her dress in clothes warm enough to wear outside without adding a jacket. It was hard to believe that just a few days ago, the deadly blizzard had blanketed the area. Now today, temperatures were supposed to be in the fifties. If only the weather had been like this last Friday.

It seemed so much longer ago than that already.

She shook off that thought. Wishing for the past to change was a waste of time and emotion that she didn't have. All she could do was move forward.

With plenty of time remaining before her meeting, Erin threw her messenger bag and the diaper bag over her free shoulder and, with Clara skipping by her side, carried it all outside to the detached garage. She'd only cared for Clara a few days but was already adjusting to this mom gig.

She opened the side door to the garage, hit the button, and the garage door cranked up as if begging for some WD-40. Of course, it had been begging for months. Someday, she'd get to it. She opened the back door of her car, threw in the bags, then picked up Clara to set in her car seat.

Clara screeched and tightened her grip on Erin's neck. Her tears came down hard. "I no go bye-bye."

"It's okay, Lolli." Erin did her best to sound soothing, while speaking through clenched teeth. Couldn't one thing go smoothly today? "It's just a short drive."

"I no wike cars. They go boom."

Oh. The sentence punched the air from Erin's gut. Oh boy.

She stroked Clara's hair, gently untangling curls. "I'll be very careful. I promise."

"Daddy careful, too."

You poor child. Erin hugged her tightly, hoping to reassure her. "My car doesn't go boom. I promise." Again, Erin tried to lower the child, who only held on tighter.

Well, this wasn't going to work, and she was using up all her margin time. Would a distraction work? If so, what kind of distraction?

Come on, Erin, think! What does Clara love to do?

Art.

Yes! That was it!

"Come on, Lolli." She set her down and took her hand. "I have a special surprise just for you." Well, years ago it had been a gift from Corey to Mik, who had no interest in it whatsoever.

"For me?"

"Yes. From your daddy."

"My daddy?"

"Yep. Special from him." Now to find it. Quickly.

She hurried into the house, into her office, and folded open the closet doors. Thankfully, the pile of belongings hidden there didn't avalanche toward her. She did a quick scan and moved a few boxes around.

There! At the bottom of a pile of boxes, of course, but she'd found it. She removed the top boxes and finally got to Corey's gift to Mik, back when she was Clara's age: an art activity box. He'd made it himself out of a tin, Scooby-Doo lunchbox. Inside, he included a blank notebook, fat crayons, markers, and an all-white smock. Corey had wanted to paint the smock alongside Mik and was sorely disappointed when she showed no interest.

Had that been another factor in his eventual desertion of his family?

Nope. He was not allowed to intrude on her day.

Erin gave the box to Clara, whose eyes grew as big as suckers. "This is for the car only."

The child's lip protruded out and quivered.

"It's okay, Lolli." Erin knelt and held out her hands. "Can I show you something in the box?"

Clara nodded and handed it back.

"Thank you." Erin unclasped the lid, opened it, and removed the apron. "This is a special car apron. You wear it anytime you're in the car and it'll protect you. Let me help you put it on."

"Okay." Came out tentatively.

Erin unfolded the apron that even had pockets. She looped the strap over Clara's neck, then tied it in the back. "How's that?"

A smile bloomed on Clara's face. "We go bye-bye now." She grabbed the handle of the art box and everything inside tumbled out.

Murphy's Law was trying to beat her down today, that was for sure, but she had no plans to let it. "Help me pick this up, and we'll go."

"Okay." Clara filled the lunchbox.

And Erin clasped it shut before handing it to her. "Time to go."

Clara practically skipped to the car. Could it really be this easy?

Erin opened her car door but didn't pick up Clara. Hopefully, letting the child climb in by herself would help her face her fears.

But her feet suddenly grew roots. "I no go."

"Okay. But then you can't have the art kit. It's for going bye-bye only."

Clara looked down at the lunchbox, up at her seat, and back to Erin who nodded toward the car.

With an adult-like sigh, Clara climbed into the car and into her seat. Tears rolled down her pudgy cheeks, and Erin kissed them away.

"You're a brave girl. Your mommy and daddy would be proud of you."

"I want Mommy, Daddy."

"I know, Lolli. I do too." *I really do want them back.* But that wasn't happening, so Erin buckled in Clara then hurried around to the driver's side. By now, all her time margin had been eaten up, and she had a short fifteen minutes to get to a place thirteen minutes away. And that was with no more speedbumps.

Okay, God, I need Your help here. It was a bit late to ask for help—that should have been her first reaction—but at least she was asking now.

Fourteen minutes later, her hand clutching onto Clara's, she strode into the swankiest building in the Brainerd area, and stood outside a door that had Law Office of Vanessa Martin, Attorney at Law, etched into the glass. Erin inhaled a deep breath and released it to the count of ten before entering, all while praying that the counselor would be understanding of Erin's need to have Clara along.

She directed Clara to a seat in the waiting room, then approached the receptionist and handed her a business card. "I have an appointment with Vanessa Martin."

The woman's gaze flicked to Clara then back to Erin. Scowling, she made the interoffice call. "Erin Belden is here to see you. And she's not alone."

Oh, thanks a bunch, lady. She summoned a confident smile and said, "Thank you" before sitting beside Clara. Well, Clara wouldn't be a complete surprise to the attorney, at least.

A shortish, round-faced woman appeared from down a hall. She looked jolly, really. Definitely more like a pastry chef than an attorney.

Relief filled her. Certainly, this woman would understand.

"Erin?"

"Yes." She stood up and offered her hand.

The woman clasped it in a tight grip. "Vanessa Martin." Her head turned toward Clara. "And this is?"

Erin summoned the speech she'd prepared in the car. "This is Clara. Her parents . . ." Erin shot a glance at Clara who was busy with her art kit. "They passed away over a week ago, and I've been assigned as her temporary guardian."

"Hmm." The woman's lips pinched. "Just how temporary?"

"Until the probate hearing determines who is to be legal guardian." Wouldn't an attorney know that?

"I see." She clasped her hands in front of her ample stomach. Did that mean she was relaxed? "Then you and I should waste no more time today. While I have no problem with my employees and contractors having families, I do expect professionalism at all times. And this . . ." She nodded to Clara. "Is far from professional. I wish you the best in your endeavors, Ms. Belden."

"But I—"

The attorney spun around before Erin could finish her plea and puttered back down the hallway.

Erin glanced at the receptionist, who looked away.

Well, if that was how they were going to be, Erin didn't want to work for them anyway.

"Come on, Clara, it's time to go."

The child placed her crayons back into the tin. Erin clasped it closed and handed it back. "You can be a big girl just like me." She showed the girl her messenger bag slung from her shoulder.

"I big wike you." Clara gripped the box handle tightly and smiled.

Side by side, they strode from the office. Erin rubbed her feet outside the door as if wiping off the dust. Yes, she needed business, but not from people like Vanessa Martin.

The problem was, she was afraid that many of the references from Jon would be the same as Vanessa.

"She said what?" Jon closed his office door then hit the speaker on his phone so he could work while talking to Erin.

"She said I was unprofessional, and she refuses to work with anyone like me."

A bunch of nasty descriptions much worse than *unprofessional* flitted through his mind regarding Ms. Vanessa Martin. In the courtroom, she was a bulldog disguised as a jolly grandma, but he'd thought, maybe, the woman would have a soft place for Erin.

"I'm sorry." He removed his bowtie and flung it onto his desk. "I'd hoped she was different outside the courtroom, but apparently not."

"Any more bulldogs on the list? Just so I can be prepared for them."

On his computer, he brought up the list he'd given to Erin and ran through the names. "I'd be lying if I said there weren't any bulldogs, but Martin's probably the worst."

"What's your opinion of Lawrence Portsmouth?"

"Lurch? I mean, Larry? Why?"

"Did you say Lurch?"

"Could be." That was what everyone called the man behind his back.

"Well, I have an appointment with him on Monday. Do I need to put on my armor before going?"

He laughed but pictured the Frankenstein lookalike

glowering down at Erin, and balled his fists. "Not a bad idea. Yeah, he's tough, I'm not going to lie." If only he could be there to shield her. Life shouldn't be this tough for her, and he hated that she was going through it alone. Hated that once again Corey had stuck it to her. If his friend were still alive, he'd give him a piece of his mind. Not that it had helped in the past.

"What if I can't find a sitter for Clara again? It's not like I have a list of available sitters at my ready. I'd thought I was past that stage."

He imagined her slouching onto her couch, a bowl of Sixlets in front of her, her go-to for stress relief. "I wish I could help you." He brought up his calendar and double-checked the date. No surprise, he was booked, if not overbooked, for the day. "If I think of anyone, I'll pass it along." Not that he had a list of babysitters lying around either, but he'd ask.

"Much appreciated. And I'll put out feelers as well. But right now, with Clara napping and Mik hunkered down in her room listening to who-knows-what, I'm going to pretend my bathtub is jetted and pamper myself."

"You deserve it, Pearl." He scratched out a note to himself to gift her with a weekend at a posh hotel, all by herself. First, he had to find out when the Beldens could watch the girls.

"Yeah, right."

"You do." She had to believe it somewhat. After all, he'd noticed the tattoo across her wrist that spelled out, "Lulu." His research showed that Lulu was Arabic for Pearl. Interesting. Somehow, he had to make Erin really believe that the nickname fit her perfectly, that she was a treasure hidden inside a hard-to-crack shell.

He intended to crack that shell, no matter what it took.

Chapter Fourteen

Was it wrong to relish the fact that both Mik and Clara were gone today for *that woman's* funeral? Zax had picked up Mik this morning, and the Caldwells had picked up Clara shortly thereafter. They'd asked if they could keep Clara all day, and Erin had to hold back her glee as she'd said, "Of course." Chances were, Zax and Mik would make a day of it as well, before he flew off to Israel.

For the first time in a week, she could make real progress on her job, the initial task being moving her office furniture into her already-crowded living room, then some of her living room furniture into the nursery. Erin loved the times when she could turn off her brain and do physical work, although an extra pair of hands would be nice.

She opened all the windows in her home, letting in fresh air. Rather than turn on music, she listened to God's music outside her windows as spring was slowly pushing aside winter. She even hummed along with the birdsong.

This was how she'd imagined her life being when she'd quit at Belden's Accounting and started her own business. Free. No longer shackled to someone else's rules and schedule. Able to take a day off just because. Open her heart to romance again.

Ha! Any intelligent male would take one look at her as a single mom, raising her ex-husband's child, and they'd run far, far away. She wouldn't blame them. But, oh, it would be nice to be special to someone again. Someone who wouldn't abandon her. Life had taught her that fairy tales and happily-ever-afters didn't exist in reality.

After dressing in old jeans and a T-shirt, Erin stood inside the doorway to her former office and mentally planned out the move. The computer desk would have to go in the living room, as would her file cabinet. Her bookshelves could stay in here. Even so, there was plenty of room for the toddler bed and Clara's dresser. She'd enlist Jon to help move that from Corey's place.

She inserted furniture sliders beneath the desk legs and slowly pushed it through the doorway and down the short hall to the living room where she left it in the middle of the room. Next came the file cabinet.

Now what to put in Clara's room . . .

The rocker, naturally, but moving that would be trickier as it didn't have feet for the sliders. A second pair of hands would be most helpful as the chair wasn't heavy, just awkward, but she could do this. Maybe a blanket would work.

After running a vacuum over the carpet in the nursery, she retrieved an old blanket from the unfinished attic and secured it beneath the chair, leaving a long tail in front. She grabbed the tail and pulled. It worked! She pulled again.

Ding-dong.

The doorbell surprised her, and she immediately looked to the clock. The funeral was at one, and it was now two thirty. Neither Zax nor the Caldwells would be home yet, would they?

She wiped her hands on her jeans and checked the peephole.

Jon?

She opened the door.

And he held out a casserole dish covered in tin foil. "Thought you deserved some funeral food too."

She peeked beneath the foil. Tater Tot hot dish. Yeah, it was funeral food, but it would sure taste good. "Thank you. Did you make it?" She asked in jest because the Jon she remembered didn't know the difference between a cookie sheet and a skillet.

"Actually, I did."

"Really?" She studied his face, looking for signs of deception like a little smirk or darting eyes but detected nothing out of the ordinary.

He shrugged. "I was tired of wasting money on eating out all the time."

"Huh." Jon was full of surprises since he'd come back into her life. She took the hot dish to the kitchen then returned to the living room to find him removing his jacket and tie.

"Need a hand?" He rolled up his sleeves.

"You're going to work in your suit?"

"When I left home this morning, I didn't anticipate helping move furniture. Mik told me your plans for the day, so I figured I should pitch in. If my suit gets dirty, I bring it to the cleaners."

"Suit yourself."

"Or unsuit myself." He grinned.

She rolled her eyes. "Very punny."

"I couldn't resist." He nodded to the office furniture in the middle of the room. "I see you've made a lot of headway already."

"I get by. It's amazing what a single mom can do by herself." She gestured toward the rocking chair and glanced back at him. "If you could . . ."

His slumped shoulders and face toward the ground stopped her. Signs of contrition? What did he have to be sorry for?

"Are you all right?"

Shaking his head, he looked up but avoided connecting with her eyes. "You should never have been left to deal with . . ." He spread his arms, motioning toward the living room, the kitchen, the hallway. "With this all by yourself. I should have been here for you."

"Uh-huh. That's Corey's guilt to claim, not yours."

"I know, but . . ."

"But what? Did you encourage Corey to have an affair?"

He shifted his feet. Guilt? "No. I warned him away from her."

"So, you knew."

"I suspected."

She shook her head. "And I had no idea until he dropped the D and P words on me. 'I want a divorce. She's pregnant.' Completely took me by surprise. I hate that I can't read people, that I'm so clueless. I made it so easy for Corey, didn't I?" She balled her fists, really wanting to punch something.

"Don't." He closed the gap between them, took her fists in his hands, and gently uncurled her fingers while looking down at her so intently it made her want to back away, but she couldn't. "Like you said, this is on Corey. His choices weren't my fault. They definitely weren't yours."

She swallowed and pulled away, trying to slow her accelerating heartbeat. What just happened there? What was she feeling now? She had to redirect toward something she did understand. Anger.

"So why did you abandon me, too?"

He looked to the left. Was he about to lie? "It's complicated."

Not a lie, really, but not an answer either. "I'm the queen of complicated lives. Whatever it is, you won't surprise me."

"But it might hurt you."

"You really think I can be hurt more than I've already been?" She spread out her arms.

And he nodded toward her wrist that had the tattoo. "Maybe."

"Okay. Fine. I can see you're not going to be forthright, so let's can the discussion. You can lend me your muscles, I'll say 'Thank you,' then you can leave. Capisce?"

"Erin." He stepped toward her again.

She extended her arms, stopping him. "I can't deal with your . . . your weird emotions on top of Mik's and Clara's. But I will appreciate your muscle and your hot dish, and we'll leave it at that."

"Yeah." He watched his foot draw an imaginary line on the floor, then he stood up straight. "Good plan. Tell me what you need me to do."

"I'm your boss?" She could deal with this surface connection much easier and was happy not to delve into his misplaced guilt.

"For this afternoon."

She rubbed her hands together and gave a maniacal laugh. "You're in for it now."

He helped her carry the rocker to the nursery, along with a floor lamp. Then after vacuuming and moving other furniture around, he helped create an office nook in one corner of the living room. It wasn't perfect, but it would suffice until Clara moved in with her forever family, whoever that might be.

They dusted and vacuumed and washed windows, and in short order the living room was ready for life.

Jon put on his jacket over his no-longer-white shirt. "Want to go out for ice cream? I've worked up an appetite."

"I'd love to, but . . ." She glanced at the clock hung on the kitchen wall. "I don't know when Zax will be bringing home Mik or when Clara will get home. I have to stay here."

"Then I'll go get some. Still like chocolate with cookie dough?"

"Oh." She moaned and patted her chest. "You know the way to a woman's heart."

"I try." He grinned and took off.

And she collapsed on the couch. Today had been a good, productive day, thanks to Jon. And in spite of the weird vibe he gave off earlier. Why he'd disappeared from her life, then reappeared didn't matter as long as she got her work done today. Now she was ready to hang her shingle, so to speak.

But only after she sat and relaxed for a moment.

Surprising joy—yes, she definitely felt joy and peace as she plopped down on the couch, and for that she needed to give thanks. She splayed her hands, palms up, and began her heartfelt prayer with a simple, "Thank You, Jesus . . ."

A BMW sat in Erin's driveway as Jon drove up to her house with several pints of ice cream, all different flavors. He'd assumed he and Erin wouldn't be alone, though he'd hoped.

He carried the treats up the steps to her tiny rambler and rang the doorbell. He heard laughter inside before Erin opened the door. Smiling.

He'd forgotten how pretty she was when she smiled because it was so rare. She tended to shove down feelings while she pushed through life as if not daring to enjoy what was going on around her. Not that she didn't have an excuse.

"Do you plan to stand there gawking with your ice cream, or would you like to share?"

He shook his head, dispersing his thoughts, and carried the bag filled with ice cream inside. The Caldwells sat in the living room, Charles in the recliner and Belinda kneeling on the floor picking up toys, looking like she was completely invested in her granddaughter's life. His gut told him otherwise.

Still he smiled at Erin's guests and held up the ice cream? "Kitchen?"

"Be my guest." Erin followed him in and pulled bowls from the cupboard. The same dishware she and Corey had purchased from a secondhand store when they'd first married. The spoons she took out had been purchased at the same place, same time. And here Corey had been living a life of luxury. Made Jon want to ream out his friend one more time. How he had been so careless with other's lives, Jon would never understand.

And now, the Caldwells were here, and he sensed more destruction on the way.

"You keep disappearing." Erin waved a hand in front of his face.

"Oh. Sorry." He scooped mint chocolate chip ice cream into a bowl. "These brought back memories."

She smiled again as she examined the scratched-up spoon's surface with the tip of her finger. "Good memories. These weren't new, but we purchased them together. We treated it like it was fine china, and we were royalty. We were happy." Her smile faded. "Then."

Oh, man. He wanted to wrap her in a hug and tell her she could be happy again, but she'd quickly reject the hug. Not knowing what to say, he picked up the bowls of ice cream and brought them to the living room for her guests. Zax and Mik, no surprise, hadn't shown up yet. No sign of Clara. She must be taking a nap.

"Anyone for mint chocolate chip?" He held up the bowl.

Mrs. Caldwell got up off the floor and stretched out her hand. "Nothing would be better right now."

"What else have you got there, son?" Mr. Caldwell sat up in the tattered recliner, a piece of furniture Corey had refused to take with him because it was too used. He angled his neck toward the bowls remaining in Jon's hands.

"I have one cherry cheesecake and one butter pecan." Mik's favorite. "I have cookie dough in the kitchen."

"Uh, no you don't." Erin came out of the kitchen eating directly out of the cookie dough ice cream container. "This is all mine."

The couple laughed, but he could tell it was strained. He couldn't imagine how tough a day this had been for them. He'd never been a father, but still knew that losing a child would be the worst kind of hurt. Perhaps his thoughts had been too rough on the couple.

"I guess I'll take the cherry cheesecake." Mr. Caldwell held out his hand. "Our Lilith loved cherries, so it's very appropriate."

Jon gave him the bowl and offered his condolences once again. "I'm very sorry for your loss."

"Much appreciated, son." The man patted Jon's hand. "But at least we have Clara. She's a carbon copy of Lilith at that age."

Jon froze at the man's words. Was he insinuating that they'd changed their mind, again, about contesting the will?

"And we're grateful that Erin has been kind enough to allow us babysitting opportunities." Mrs. Caldwell reached across the couch and patted Erin's arm. No surprise, Erin flinched at the touch.

Babysitting. Okay. That he could deal with. He pulled a chair from the kitchen and sat across from the couch.

"We've cancelled our vacation, as well." Mr. Caldwell shook his head. "We just can't imagine trying to enjoy ourselves while our hearts have been shattered."

"And they've offered to watch Clara on Monday for me." Erin dug her spoon into the pint. "So, I can be 'professional' at my appointment." She made the quotation marks with her fingers.

"That's great." He smiled. The Caldwells would likely see through it, but Erin, probably not. He hoped. This couple was saying and doing all the right things, but in the past year, Corey had confessed to him that Lilith didn't fall far from the family tree. She'd learned manipulation well from them.

Jon would not allow Erin to be manipulated too. With her lack of skill in reading people, she would be a far too compliant target.

Chapter Fifteen

The Caldwells arrived an hour before Erin had to leave for her appointment with Lurch, er, Lawrence Portsmouth. She was so grateful for that as Clara was being fussy once again. Thankfully, Mik was back in school, so there wasn't whining in stereo today. Suffering through it this past weekend had been tough enough, and she'd been tempted to add a different type of wine to her day.

But now, she was getting away from the noise, and Clara did love her grandparents. Why Corey and that woman didn't want her parents to be legal guardians made no sense. She found them very down to earth and loving. How they'd parented a witch like . . . that woman, she'd never know.

With Clara occupied, Erin dressed in the same suit from last week. The only good interviewing suit she owned. Even while working for the Beldens, the dress code had been more casual. Erin wanted to step it up a notch, maybe bring in a higher bracket of businesses. Attorneys were definitely in a higher bracket than the machine shop owners the Beldens typically worked with.

After dressing, she pulled her hair back in a bun and sprayed it with a stiff hairspray. Hopefully, it looked business enough. She touched up her make-up, keeping it light, then put on low-heeled grey pumps.

She studied herself in the mirror hung on her closet door. No wrinkles. On her clothes or her face. No random dirty spots. No hair trying to escape the bun, although by the time she arrived at her appointment, that would probably change.

Satisfied, she went to the living room where Clara played on the floor with her grandparents. Belinda Caldwell looked up at her and smiled. "You look fabulous dear, ready to change the world."

"I don't really need to change the world, just my own little corner."

"You never know how changing that one corner will affect everyone else." Belinda nodded and directed her attention back to Clara.

"Well, wish me luck." Keys in her hand, Erin aimed for the side door.

"Auntie Erin, me, hug!" Clara jumped up, raced to Erin, and hugged her knees.

Erin's heart pinged. Nope. She wasn't going to fall for this child. No way. She patted the child's hair while saying a silent prayer that her skirt remained clean. "Thank you for the hug, Lolli. You have a fun day with Gramama and Grandpops."

"I wuv them."

"And they love you, too." Which was why they could be Clara's guardians, if she couldn't find Jon's mystery woman. They were youngish, probably early fifties. Their daughter had only been twenty-five. The problem was getting Jon to see that they would be good for Clara. He seemed to have a chip on his shoulder where they were concerned. She'd been searching for a reason to affirm that chip but hadn't found it. Truthfully, she liked the couple. And today, they were her saving grace.

Erin headed out the door with her proposal while double checking that her skirt didn't have Clara fingerprints all over the bottom. Thankfully, it remained clean, not a guarantee with that child who loved finger painting with whatever she could get her hands on.

She got in her car, and her whole body seemed to relax. Caring for a young child was a twenty-four-hour-a-day job she didn't have time or energy for. So even getting away for paying work seemed like a vacation.

The forty-minute drive to Lawrence Portsmouth's office was uneventful, just what she needed. She'd rehearsed her spiel while trying to erase the image of Lurch from her brain, and failed.

Her GPS led her down a street filled with beautiful historic homes but had her stop by a house that could easily have been owned by The Addams Family, with its peeling paint and sagging balcony on the side of the building. Just looking at it gave her the shimmies. This couldn't be the right place, could it?

A newly-laid sidewalk led to a side door that had writing on the window. She got out of her car to read it: Law Office of Lawrence Portsmouth. So, this was the place. Yay . . .

Well, she was an adult, she could certainly handle entering a spooky law office and facing creepy lawyer.

Proposal in hand, she strode up the sidewalk and climbed the steps to the heavy wood door. She tugged it open and blinked to adjust her eyes to the dark interior.

"Good afternoon," a male voice in front of her spoke and she blinked him into view, her gaze climbing upward. All six foot seven of him, if not taller. The man offered a skeletal hand. "I apologize for the dismal lighting. My electricians are working on it. If I'd known the troubles this old house would bring me, I never would have made the purchase. But someday it will be grand, and I'll be the envy of Little Falls."

Her vision adjusted, she glanced around the room, taking in beautiful hardwood floors, trim, doors. Yes, it could be grand someday. A desk as ancient as the house sat in the middle of the lobby. It was filled with office-looking equipment, but no one sat behind it.

"Erin Belden, I presume?" He gestured to a door off the lobby.

"I am." She walked alongside him. "And you must be Lur . . . I mean Lawrence." If she could've melted into the floor, she would have. She may as well just head home right now.

But booming laughter came from the giant beside her. "Ah, I see Jon Boy has been enlightening you of my colleagues' nickname for me. It serves me well in court." He pushed open a heavy door, revealing a well-lit conference room that seemed out of place in this old building. Everything appeared to be new. The table, chairs, artwork. Although the table looked to be higher than normal.

He gestured to a chair with longer-than-average legs, and he sat across from her, on a lower seat, bringing his face in direct line with hers. Huh. Maybe to not be as intimidating? It definitely worked. Behind him on the wall was a plaque with the headline, "A Lawyer's Prayer" by St. Thomas More. It should help her relax, but she'd let her guard down with attorney Vanessa Martin, and look how that turned out.

"Now, Ms. Belden." He folded his spindly fingers together and leaned toward her. "Why should I take my business from my established accountant and give it to you?"

This is what you came for, Erin. You can do it. She sat up as tall as she could. Didn't smile, but didn't frown either, and handed her proposal across the table. She spoke of her education and experience and pointed out her references. Then flattered him—hopefully—with his positive online reviews and closed with her selling point.

"I plan to keep my clientele list small so that I'm able to provide you with personal and immediate attention. You won't have to go through a secretary to reach me, and I promise to return calls within twenty-four hours. As my references point out, I'm quick and I'm accurate."

"Hmmm." Was all he said as he drummed his fingers together. "You make some very big promises."

"I do. And I know how important it is to keep promises."

"Ah, yes." He leaned toward her as if interrogating her. "But sometimes life intervenes."

She squirmed then forced herself to sit still. "Yes, it does. And should something come up, Belden Accounting has promised to back me up."

"Hmm."

Would he stop saying that, please?

"As you observed from my vacant lobby, my assistant wasn't there. Her toddler came down with the flu, and I encouraged her to stay home. As a prosecutor, I too often see the results of broken families, fatherless families, and I've come to the conclusion that no business is worth sacrificing family over. With me, family always takes precedence. Do you agree, Ms. Belden?"

She raised her chin and looked him square in the eye. This guy should be a counselor. Guys wouldn't dare cheat on their spouses if they had him to report to. "Family should always come first, which is why I'm opening a business at home. This way I can spend more time with my teenager."

"A very vulnerable time." He reclined back and spread his hand on her proposal. "Your credentials are . . . adequate."

Adequate? True, she didn't have the years of experience others had, so she didn't respond. Rather, she waited for him to add to his statement.

"But I appreciate your attentiveness to your family. If more parents cared as you do, I'd be out of a job."

She blinked, trying to figure out if that was a "Yes, I want to hire you," or just a random statement.

"So, I would be pleased to transfer my business to you." He

stretched his arm across the table.

A smile snuck out as she gripped his hand. "Thank you. I won't let you down."

"I don't expect you will." He sat back and smiled, and suddenly he wasn't so menacing. If she had to face him in court, though, that would be another story. "Truthfully, you called at the right time. My accountant will be retiring, so I was about to begin the search. You made my search very easy."

He gestured toward the door.

Guess they were finished. She got up and walked from the building, Lawrence at her side until she got into her car.

She waited until he was back inside his office before she did a little victory dance. Finally, something went right for her! If only she had someone to celebrate with. More importantly, time to celebrate with someone. The Caldwells would be expecting her home soon, or she'd stop by Debbie's on the way home and share a pint of ice cream. Yeah, she'd just had some the other day with Jon, but you can't have too much ice cream, right?

Cravings for ice cream meant one thing: she was feeling something. Debbie would remind her to identify that feeling.

Happy.

Yeah, she felt happy, like when she and Debbie were driving up to the cabin. Had that really only been a week and a half ago? It seemed like forever.

Maybe after the girls went to sleep tonight, she'd celebrate with that pint anyway. She deserved it. She drove toward home, singing along with the radio. Once back in Brainerd, she stopped at the local grocer to pick up a few pints of ice cream then hurried home.

She turned onto her street, and her happiness fled. The garage door was wide open. Her heartbeat ramped up speed as she neared her home, and it nearly burst from her chest when she saw why the door was open.

In these few hours she'd been gone, her single-car garage had been turned into an art studio. Two easels sat in the middle of the garage, and paint-splattered sheets draped the walls. Clara and her grandma stood at the easels, painting, while Charles Caldwell sat on a lawn chair, reading a book. No one seemed to notice her. Tension tingled down her arms, to her fingers, and she clenched her fingernails into her palms.

What gave them the right to take over her garage?

She got out of her car, slammed the door, and ran to the house, not caring if anyone noticed her or not. She hurried to the bathroom, shut the door and locked it, then collapsed onto the floor, hugging her knees tight to her chest. It had been a year since she'd had a panic attack like this. Why now?

She tugged her phone from her front pocket and dialed Debbie's number. She was the only one who could talk her through this.

Erin

April 15, 2019

Oh, God,

I'm sorry I imploded today. And thank you for Debbie's friendship. I'm so grateful for someone who's able to piece me back together.

I know you saw me as I sat on the floor of the bathroom, not wanting to face the world ever again. Then Debbie came and listened as all my frustrations from the past week boiled out.

I'll ask you the same thing I asked her: why? Why now? The Caldwells and Clara weren't doing anything wrong this afternoon.

They just put up sheets in the garage—my dirty garage—and painted. It was completely innocent.

Belinda even came in after my freak-out, and accepted my apology and explanation about Corey's death finally hitting home. You know that's only partially true. I even tolerated her hug as she said she understood and that she'd had moments like that herself.

I doubt it. No one has moments like mine. Why can't I feel things like a normal person?

Debbie reminded me that my way of coping is by plugging away, just doing the next thing without taking my feelings into consideration, so they keep getting pushed down, one on top of the other, and pretty soon, like a volcano, it all erupts. I told her I hadn't felt anything. She said that was because I didn't take a breather to even consider that I might be feeling something. Is that true?

Maybe the problem is, I don't want to feel. Maybe feeling hurts too much.

Please help me understand, Lord.

Corey
July 12, 2014

I took Erin out to dinner last night and planned to tell her about my dream to paint again. We dropped Mik off at Mom and Pop's for an overnight stay and I took Erin to the new Italian place in St. Paul. I'd forgotten how ~~pretty~~ sexy she was when dressed up. Wow! I couldn't stop staring at her all night and pretty much forgot about art, my work, or anything else besides Erin.

Needless to say, that led to a lot of fireworks once we got home.

It used to be like that all the time. Our first ~~years~~ months of marriage were pretty awesome, if I do say so myself.

And then Mik arrived and we had to grow up.

I want that back.

And there's no reason why we can't.

At lunchtime, before we go pick up Mik, I'll tell her about my

. . .

Whew, that was close. I was writing, Erin snuck up behind me, and I slammed my journal shut. She sat on my lap, wearing that see-through negligee I love, and told me how sexy it was that I was still writing and working hard at getting better.

Well, you can guess what happened next . . .

So, I called my folks and asked them to watch Mik through Sunday. They know I've been stressed, that Erin and I are going through a rough patch, and were glad to have Mik.

I promised Erin a weekend she wouldn't forget. Maybe we'll finally have the second child we've been trying for. Why we got pregnant so easily with Mik and can't again is beyond me. But we keep trying, which really isn't a hardship, you know.

Before we pick up Mik tomorrow night, I'll tell Erin about my art. I'll let her know that's what's made a change in me. I'll ask her about converting the garage into an art studio. I realize my car would have to sit outside in the winter but having a place for my art would be worth the sacrifice.

I'll even tell her about going to the gallery after work. I like going, but the lying sits in my gut as if I've eaten too much pizza. Telling her the truth will get us back on track. I know it.

For the rest of the weekend, I'm tucking this journal away. It's time I give Erin the weekend she deserves. One she'll never forget.

———————

July 13, 2014

Oh, she'll never forget this weekend. That's for sure. Me neither.

And it had been going so well.

Before we picked up Mik, Erin changed. Withdrew. I don't know why or what I did. She stopped talking. Spent a bunch of time in the bathroom, like she always does when she gets in these weird moods. Usually, Erin is really chill. Things don't seem to bother her. I used to love the challenge of trying to get her to show some emotion, didn't matter what kind, and I usually could.

But she's changed since we got married. Getting her to loosen up has gotten harder. I don't even like to try anymore. Now, she stuffs down her emotions, packs them super tight, then they boil over like a kettle cooking noodles.

How am I supposed to deal with that?

Suppose I should ask my counselor.

Like a fool, I thought telling her about wanting to paint again would help. I asked about converting the garage. And she just ragged on me about her working her tail off so I get to play.

Does she think I sit around all day doing nothing? Sheesh! After the weekend I just gave her, she acted like it didn't matter.

I had been planning to tell her about my museum visits, too, but forget that. It's her fault that I have to lie.

It's all her fault.

———————

Numb, Erin returned Corey's journal to her nightstand drawer and clutched a pillow to her roiling stomach. She remembered that weekend, probably about four years ago. She had loved that Corey was writing in his journal. It had made a difference in him and things were improving between the two of them.

No. *That woman* had made the difference.

Erin's fists balled, and she fought the urge to punch something. Anger. Debbie would tell her it was okay to feel angry. Go ahead and pound her pillow. Holding in the emotion was the worst thing she could do. Still, Erin hugged the pillow tighter as the memories of that weekend flowed through.

It had been special. She'd planned to tell Corey exciting news, but before she could, he'd surprised her with a romantic weekend alone. That was the first time in months that she'd felt loved.

Until Sunday afternoon arrived. And blood had filled the toilet.

And the pregnancy—their baby she'd yearned to tell Corey about, died.

Erin punched her pillow. Fury. She punched it again and a tear dropped onto her fist. Followed by more dampening the pillow, and an unknown mass clogging her throat. Grief?

Sure, Corey, it was all her fault that their baby died. That three babies before that didn't make it past her weak womb, and another died after this. With rare tears cascading from her eyes, she punched the pillow until her arms felt as if they'd fall off. *Make your lies, your cheating, all about me, you @$#%.* I will not take the blame for your family-shattering choices!

Chapter Sixteen

Jon stared at the computer screen, knowing he needed to finalize this will today, but he couldn't chase Erin from the forefront of his mind, especially after reading the text from Mik. If he wanted to get anything done today, he better call her now.

He informed Gina to hold all calls for the moment, closed his office door, then dialed Erin on his cell.

"Jon?"

"Hey, how's it going?" His voice cracked like he was nervous or something. This was Erin, his lifelong friend. What did he have to be nervous about?

"Not bad, actually. I got a new client. I'm setting up his account as we speak."

Finally, good news for her. He reclined in his chair. "Lurch?"

She laughed. "Yep. I accidentally called him that, too."

Oh, no. "And his response?"

"He laughed. Called you Jon Boy."

Whew. "I'm happy for you, Erin. Any more prospects?"

"A couple more appointments next week. If I can get two more clients, I'll be happy."

"Just two?"

"Mik is still my number one priority."

But not Clara. Somehow, he had to convince Erin that she was the best choice for guardian. "I don't hear Clara babbling. How is she doing?"

A sigh. "Thankfully, Belinda Caldwell offered to watch her three days a week so I can get work done."

Belinda babysitting sounded like a Trojan Horse to him, which meant he needed to stick closely to Erin, make sure she didn't fall for their so-called kindness. He pulled up his calendar on his computer and penciled in "Erin" on any open dates, which were far too few. One per week at the most, including tonight. But today was Maundy Thursday, and he intended to attend service tonight. Or maybe . . .

"Um, I was wondering if I could join you at church tonight."

"Church? Tonight?"

"For Maundy Thursday service."

Silence blew over the line.

"I forgot." She practically whispered. He could visualize her shaking her head while bringing up a calendar. She prided herself on being organized, but Clara was seriously messing with that. "I forgot about Easter. How . . ."

"Hey, life has thrown you some curveballs lately. I understand if you're busy."

"No. I'm actually not busy. And I need to go to the services. Tonight. Tomorrow. Sunday. I need to be reminded of what Jesus did for us and worship Him, especially now, because I'm not feeling very loving or forgiving. But . . ."

Of course, she had a "but." With Erin, nothing was ever easy. "You can't go?"

"Well, it's not that I can't, but Clara goes to bed at seven, seven thirty. Taking her to church would be a disaster."

"Oh. Yeah." Jon leaned back in his chair and stared at the ceiling. He should have thought of that before he called.

"But we could hold our own service at my place."

He bolted upright. "That's a great idea. Want me to pick up

bread and wine?"

"Make that sparkling grape juice for the kids. And can you make it by six? Then it won't throw off Clara's schedule."

He checked his calendar and calculated the amount of time needed to leave work, go home to change, do a little shopping, and drive to Erin's. I can be there at five thirty."

"Perfect. And Jon?"

"Yeah?"

"Thanks," she said in a hushed tone.

"It's my pleasure, Erin. I need you to know you can count on me from now on."

"I'm beginning to believe that."

Musical words to his tone-deaf ears. "I'll see you in a few hours, Pearl." And he'd do whatever it took to get her to believe she was worthy of that name. Maybe Corey had been right in what he'd asked Jon to do. As time went on, the request wasn't sounding so bad after all.

Erin dressed Clara in footy pajamas for church so she wouldn't have to change her again after the service. Then she stared in her closet at her meager choices. Yes, she was holding the service here at home, but that didn't mean she should make a smaller effort of presenting herself. She'd like to think that when the disciples met with Jesus for the Passover meal, they wanted to be at their best.

"Do I have to go?" Mik's moan came from the bedroom door, raising the hair on Erin's arms.

She took a breath before turning to her daughter wearing shorts that were way too short and a crop top. "Yes, you will join us. And you will change into something appropriate."

"But it's just home."

"That doesn't make this service less important."

"None of my friends have to go to church."

Lord Jesus, give me patience and wisdom! "I'm sorry for your friends. They're missing out."

Mik rolled her eyes, of course.

Don't react. Mik was goading for a reaction, and Erin would not comply. "Please change your outfit, also," Erin said as calmly as she could.

"I have nothing to wear." Mik actually stomped her foot. *Jesus, You need to help me here, or I'll be spending the rest of my days in jail for strangling my child.*

Erin breathed in and out to the count of eight. "If you need me to, I'd be glad to help you choose." For herself, she took a pair of jeans and a long-sleeve blouse from her own closet, hoping to give her daughter an idea.

"Fine." She clomped from the room.

Lord, help me. Honestly, allowing Mik to skip the service would be easier, but her daughter needed this service as much as Erin. They both needed Good Friday, too. And they desperately needed Easter.

If yesterday's breakdown had taught her anything, it was that she remained angry and unforgiving toward Corey and that wom—and Lilith. If Jesus could forgive Erin for all her bad choices, she should be able to extend the same forgiveness to her ex.

She rubbed her wrist. This running and hiding in the bathroom every time something bothered her had to end.

The doorbell rang as Erin finished her hair. Extending forgiveness to Jon would come first. She hurried to the door, flung it open, and stared.

Would she never get used to seeing this trendier, buffer Jon?

No glasses. No bowtie. But a blazer over khakis and a button-down shirt. He'd even spent time on his hair. The man had transformed out of the stodgy lawyer role into normal life very well. Very well indeed. How was it no woman had snatched him up yet?

"Is there a problem?" He looked beyond her.

She looked to the floor, hoping to hide what was certainly a blush. *Get a hold of yourself, Erin.* This was Jon, for Pete's sake. Her forever friend. "I uh, no. You just look . . . really nice."

"I try." He grinned. "You're not so bad yourself."

She shrugged. She couldn't remember the last time she'd received a compliment from a man and had no clue how to respond.

"Are you two gonna stand there ogling each other, or are we gonna do church?" Mik's whine raised hackles up and down her spine and broke whatever spell Jon had placed on her.

Erin turned to her daughter, surprised to see that Mik held Clara's hand and had the diaper bag slung over her shoulder. She waved to the side door directing the family to the garage where she'd set up. "Let's get going."

"The garage?" Jon followed behind.

"Thanks to the Caldwells, my garage has been transformed."

"The Caldwells?" He caught up to her and walked alongside.

She could easily be mistaken, but it sounded like Jon had some contempt in his voice. Erin had found them to be very helpful. She refused to respond to his tone.

He grunted something she couldn't understand. All she knew was that it wasn't complimentary. Well, he could think what he wanted. Belinda's appearance in her life right now was a godsend.

As had been turning the garage into a play area. Erin opened the side door on the garage and flicked on the light.

"Wow." Jon said under his breath. "This is quite the transformation."

Yes, it was. The sheets remained up from the other day. Why take them down? And intersecting brightly colored foam mats were spread over the concrete, providing much-needed cushion for their feet. If paint splattered on the concrete, who cared? It was genius, really. Turning the garage into a play area meant her home and office remained clean, so she could welcome clients at any time.

Corey would have loved it. Maybe he wouldn't have strayed if she'd allowed—

Nope. Debbie warned her over and over not to go there. Rather, she needed to focus on the reason they were out here tonight. "Have a seat." She gestured toward pillows—doggy beds, actually—arranged in a circle on the foam mats, and retrieved a bowl filled with water, her Bible, and a towel from a table she'd set up. She set that in the middle of the circle and sat between Jon and Clara, who'd curled up on the pillow like she wanted to sleep. Erin took Jon's and Clara's hands and, without arguing, Mik took Jon's and Clara's. A minor miracle, but still a miracle.

Erin said a prayer thanking God for the evening and for this time spent with family and prayed a blessing over the evening, and they said "Amen" together.

"Mik asked me earlier what Maundy Thursday meant." She looked out the side of her eyes at Jon while Clara crawled on her lap and began sucking her thumb. "And I had to look it up. I knew what the tradition was, but not what the word 'Maundy' meant. It's from the Latin *mandatum*, which is the origin of the word, mandate."

Mik's eyes were glazing over. Time to speed things up.

"Anyway, it means commandment. In John 13:34, Jesus says, 'A new commandment I give to you, that you love one another;

just as I have loved you, you also are to love one another.'" Erin looked to Jon then Mik. "Just how did Jesus love us? What did He do that showed His love?"

Mik looked to the ground, fidgeting. "He died for us."

Wow. Her daughter went right for the biggie, which would easily make Erin's point. "Exactly."

"So, does that mean to love others, we have to die?"

"Well, John 15 talks about the greatest love mankind has for one another is to lay down their life and live sacrificially." Jon pulled out his phone and read John 15:13.

Erin thanked Jon for providing the perfect segue to her point. "Living sacrificially is exactly what Jesus was doing the night He gathered with His disciples. He knew He was about to be betrayed, by one of the disciples. He even knew who would betray Him, yet Jesus served him anyway. Jesus loved him regardless of that betrayal."

Whoa. Her own words slammed into her heart. *Jesus loved His betrayer.* Period. She swallowed a lump in her throat and decided to use her personal story as a teaching moment. She brushed her fingers through Clara's hair—the child was already fighting sleep after a busy day of play.

Erin looked *toward* Mik, but not *at* her. She couldn't. "When your father left me, I didn't show love. I've even held onto hate." She hugged Clara. "That's not what Jesus would want us to do. It's not what He commanded us to do."

"And when I abandoned your mom . . ." Jon took Erin's hand and squeezed it. She didn't pull away, and he held on. "I was running away. I should have stayed, supported her, served her like Jesus shows."

Why did you run away? The thought flickered through Erin's thoughts. She tucked it away to ask later. Again.

"You grown-ups have issues." Mik even smiled.

"Yes, we do. We're all a work in progress." She squeezed Jon's hand and released it. "Mik, would you mind reading the scripture for tonight?"

"I guess." She shrugged, acting nonchalant, but Erin knew her daughter longed to be included.

Erin turned to John 13 and asked Mik to read verses one through twenty about Jesus washing his disciples' feet.

"I don't get it. What's special about washing feet?"

"I, uh . . ." Erin stammered. Here she thought she'd had it all planned out.

"I've got this one." Jon brought something up on his phone again. "Back in Jesus' day, people walked in sandals on dirty, dusty roads, and they ate at low tables, so when it was time to eat, they all needed to wash their feet first. Usually the lowest of the servants would have that job, so Jesus washing their feet was shocking. He was their Lord, and they thought they should be washing His feet, not the other way around."

"Oh, I get it." Mik's face seemed to light up.

Who knew this makeshift service would be exactly what Mik needed? Erin, too.

She removed her shoes and socks and Clara's too. Jon and Mik quietly followed suit. Erin dipped Clara's feet into the bowl, and the child proceeded to kick and splash and giggle. Erin hugged the child and handed her off to Jon. Then Erin knelt in front of Mik and picked up the bowl. Without saying anything, she guided her daughter's right foot into the bowl, washed it, then dried it, followed by the left foot. When she looked up at Mik, tears had stained her daughter's cheeks. Oh, to be able to feel emotion like that.

Erin turned to Jon, who cuddled a now-sleeping girl in his arms. Growing up with Jon, she never would have guessed he'd be this gentle with a child. Another reason why he should find a wife and adopt Clara. Even she could tell he loved the child.

She reached for his right foot and felt his finger beneath her chin.

He lifted her chin, drawing her gaze to his. "You don't have to."

"Oh, but I do."

He looked toward the ceiling, and a tear leaked from his eyes.

"I forgive you, Jon. Will you forgive me?"

He sighed and whispered. "Of course."

She raised his foot and dipped it into the warm water, then the other while vowing to herself she'd serve him as he'd done for her since Corey died. After drying his feet, she reached for the sleeping child so Jon could wash hers.

"Mom, let me."

Something tugged at her heart, warmed it. Erin struggled to name that emotion as she sat on her pillow and handed Mik the water and towel.

"Will you forgive me for being a brat?" Mik dipped Erin's foot into the water, caressing the water over and around it.

"Seventy times seven, Sixlet." Erin laid her palm on her daughter's cheek. "And please forgive me for being so . . . so hard, so clueless. I try—"

"You succeed, Mom. I know it's hard for you."

There went that warm, fuzzy feeling again. Erin couldn't name it—all she knew was that it felt good.

They closed the evening serving communion to each other. Then Mik went to her room, and Jon tucked Clara into her crib.

Leaving Erin alone with Jon, saying goodbye at the front door. Like any self-respecting Minnesotans, the goodbye had already lasted fifteen minutes. That meant they likely had another fifteen to go before Jon left.

"Thank you for tonight." She hugged herself, warding off the chilly breeze. "I would have forgotten all about Maundy Thursday if not for you. Can you make it tomorrow night, too? I got a text from Zax this afternoon that part of his story on the Holy Week will be live tomorrow night. He's walking the Via Dolorosa with other Christians. It would be a great way to observe the day."

"Zax?"

"Yeah, can you believe it?"

"I've seen God work miracles before. Someday I'll learn to expect them."

What miracles would those be? A question Erin would save for another time.

"So, yeah, I'll be here tomorrow night. Same time?"

"But in the house this time."

"I look forward to it." He aimed for the steps, and then turned back as she was closing the door. "Erin." He took a step toward her. An unreadable look filled his face. His eyes were intently focused on her, his neck angled, lips slightly parted. All she knew was that he scared the bejeebers out of her, and she took a step back.

He shook his head, clearing away whatever that facial expression was. "I'll see you tomorrow night."

"See you then." She nodded, closed the door, and moistened her suddenly dry lips. Whatever this feeling was that Jon stirred in her, she didn't like it. Not one little bit.

Oh, man, he'd almost blown it. "Idiot," Jon mumbled to himself as he got into his Mercedes. If he'd kissed her liked he wanted to, really, really wanted to, that would have sent their relationship into a downward spiral faster than a runaway roller coaster.

All his feelings from years ago, before Corey had managed to break through the walls around Erin's heart, came pouring back. But he'd been a teenager then with a teenage crush. Now he was an adult, a successful one at that, one who'd sworn off relationships. Now, thanks to Corey and his last spoken words, the dam had broken on Jon's heart, and it was too late for repairs.

He slammed the car door and started the engine, hoping its purr would calm his emotions. He drove away from her house, praying distance would work alongside the car's purr.

Then he turned his mind back to work. What was the Caldwells' angle? He pounded his fist on his steering wheel. Erin viewed their help as charitable, kind, but he'd seen Lilith, the queen of manipulation, do a job on Corey, and apples don't fall far from the tree. Chances were, the Caldwells had ulterior motives, and he intended to discover what those motives were before Erin did something she'd forever regret.

Chapter Seventeen

With eyes still sticky with sleep, Erin looked around her usually tidy living room and grimaced. Clara sat among her toys which had somehow taken over the living room. A single child shouldn't be able to create such chaos, but this child excelled at it. And with hosting Easter tomorrow, Erin needed a clean house. Well, the living room, kitchen, and bathroom should be cleaned anyway.

Cleaning it all herself would be easy. There would be no arguments from Mik, no coaxing Clara to pick up her toys. If Erin did it all, though, the girls would learn that they didn't have to clean up after themselves, which would result in bigger messes down the road. But Erin was not beyond bribery.

She pounded on Mik's door, hoping her daughter would hear that over the earbuds she most certainly had in.

"What?" Came out in about five syllables.

Erin conjured up a smile. "I have a proposition for you."

She waited. Counted to ten before she heard movement inside the bedroom. Made it all the way to twenty before the door cracked open and a single eye peeked out. "What?" Only one very sharp syllable this time.

So, her daughter's vocabulary consisted of a single word this morning. Erin would work with that. "We're having company tomorrow."

The door inched open enough so Erin saw two eyes. "Yeah, so?"

Ah, so she did know more words. Nice. "I would appreciate your help preparing."

Her daughter's whole body slumped as if she were being asked to clean the town dump. And to think this was just the beginning of the dramatic teen years. Yay.

"Would you prefer to clean the bathroom or the kitchen?"

Mik's left nostril wrinkled. "Neither?"

Exactly the answer Erin expected, but she was ready with her covert bribe. "Me neither, but the work needs to get done, and we can't decorate Easter eggs until that work is complete."

Mik's body lifted as if tugged up by a puppeteer, and the door flung wide open, revealing a bedroom floor covered in more clothes than the living room had toys. That was a battle for another day.

"*You* want to color eggs?" Dying eggs had always been one of Mik's favorite activities with her father. Erin had never liked the mess but watching father and daughter bond over the activity had been worth it. Now it was one more role she'd be taking over for Corey.

"I learned of a new way to dye eggs. Thought it would be fun to try."

"Is Uncle Jon gonna help?"

"Clean?"

Mik snorted. "Yeah, right. Is he gonna help dye eggs?"

"Why would he help with that?"

"I don't know." Mik shrugged. "I mean, he was here Thursday, and last night, and he's gonna be here tomorrow too. It just seems." She shrugged again. "Seems nice to have him around."

Really?

Oh. Maybe because she missed her father, and Jon was filling that niche? Sure, Erin had enjoyed having Jon around the past couple of days, but things had become weird between them somehow, and Erin couldn't nail down why. Part of her enjoyed having him around, but another part wanted to run far away from him. He'd be here tomorrow. That was enough closeness for the weekend. "Today it's just us."

"Oh." Her shoulders sagged just a bit. "Then I'll do the kitchen," she said with far less enthusiasm than she'd initially shown. Erin couldn't compete with a dad figure—another reason Clara needed a different home. She deserved to have a mom and a dad raising her.

On the way to the living room, she checked the bathroom. Hadn't she just cleaned it four days ago? Ugh! Someday when she became independently wealthy—ha ha ha—she'd hire a maid to clean the kitchen and bathroom. But first she had to task Clara with putting away her toys.

She returned to the living room and shook her head. These toys had to be escapees from *Toy Story*. Somehow in the short time Erin had been talking with Mik, they'd scattered further across the living room as if on their own power. Clara sat in the middle of it adding voice to her stuffed crocodile that was scolding a toy tractor. Oh, that child had an imagination, just like her father.

She probably would do anything to avoid work, too, like her father.

The question now was, how to make cleaning up fun? Bribing the child by offering a penny per toy would be one solution but being paid to pick up after yourself wasn't a lesson she wanted to teach Clara.

There had to be another way. She glanced around the room, her gaze landing on the three shelf baskets for toys. All empty, of course. A race maybe? Her gaze drifted up the shelving to the ancient CD player/radio, and an idea sprouted. Maybe if they'd race along with a kids' song. She still had Mik's favorite CDs. The problem was, if they cleaned up the toys now, by the time Erin finished the bathroom, the living room would be back to its disaster state. Which meant Erin should clean the bathroom first, and then maybe she could enlist Mik to help with the game.

Yeah, that could work.

Before starting the cleanup, though, she began hard boiling a dozen eggs. Then, with her hair pulled back in a messy bun, she spent the next hour scrubbing the bathroom until it sparkled. This was one time she was grateful for having one bathroom in the house, and a tiny one at that.

Then she checked on Mik in the kitchen. Her earbuds were in, as they'd been when Erin had removed the eggs from the hot water and set them in a bowl of cold water. Even on her hands and knees on the floor, scrubbing a spot that was no longer dirty, she was dancing to whatever tune played.

The kitchen even sparkled as much as the bathroom. Her daughter may not like cleaning, but she did it well.

With all Erin's failures as a wife and mom, it was nice to see that she'd done one thing right. After setting the eggs on a towel to dry, she tapped Mik on the shoulder.

Her daughter startled and jerked to a sitting position. She yanked out her earbuds. "Scare me much?"

Erin raised her hands, hoping to convey that she was sorry. "Didn't mean to frighten you. Just wanted to let you know the kitchen looks marvelous."

Mik blinked as if trying to absorb the rare compliment—Erin needed to work on that—then a smile broke out on her pretty face. "Thanks."

"Want to join me in a game?" Erin nodded to the disaster area also known as the living room.

Mik looked into the messy room and wrinkled her nose. She excelled at that almost as well as she did rolling her eyes. "She's such a pig."

"Yeah, she's got a lot of her father in her for sure." Corey had made messes faster than a hummingbird flapped its wings. That was one thing she hadn't missed when he'd moved out. Erin walked to the living room and knelt in front of Clara. "Want to play a game?"

The girl's eyes grew as round as lollipops, and she nodded. "I wike games."

"I know. We're going to play race with music."

"I wike race with music." Clara clapped her hands together. Even Erin had to admit the child looked adorable.

"Good. It's one of my favorite games."

"Mine, too." Mik mimicked her little sister's clapping. Another proud mommy moment. For all Mik's bluster about her annoying sister, she really did love her. The two loved each other.

"I'll set up the game." Erin took the three empty toy baskets and set them a few feet apart by the wall separating the kitchen from the living area. Then, with her feet, she swept the toys into three lines pointing toward the baskets.

She gestured toward the middle lane for Clara. "When I turn on the music, we race to put toys in our baskets." She pointed to the lane closest to the door. "Mik will put her toys in that basket." She stepped over to her line. "And I get these toys. Whoever gets all their toys in first gets to color the first Easter egg."

"I wike Easter eggs!" Clara jumped up and down.

Oh, to have some of that energy.

Erin placed a CD in the boombox and hit Play. "Pick up time!"

Keeping her eye on Clara, Erin picked up a book from her lane and walked it slowly to the front where she dropped it into the basket. Mik copied her mom's speed, while Clara bustled around getting toys from all three lanes, dropping in whichever basket was closest. Whatever worked.

Well before the end of the three-minute song, Clara clapped her hands. "I did it!"

Well, not quite. A couple of puzzle pieces had escaped her notice, but it was good enough for Erin. "Yes, you did!" She picked up the child and gave her a kiss on the forehead. "You are the winner, and you get to color the first Easter egg!"

"Yippee!" She wiggled from Erin's arms and ran to the kitchen.

"Oh, hold on there, Lolli. We're going to color eggs in your art studio."

Did she just say, Clara's art studio? Oh, boy, this child was already affecting how Erin thought, and Clara was becoming far too comfortable. When the child would have to move to a new home, it could be traumatic for her, once again.

But Erin couldn't treat her any differently. The child deserved to be shown love in this interim, even if Erin could never feel it.

She waved the girls into the kitchen. She handed Clara a container of Cool Whip and had Mik find food coloring and plastic gloves while Erin dried the eggs and placed them in a bowl. She also grabbed a square cake pan, a cookie sheet, paper towels, and a handful of spoons. The three of them carried their items out to the garage and set them in the middle of the doggy bed circle. Since the temperatures were nearing sixty and bugs hadn't hatched yet, she kept the garage door open, allowing in fresh air and plenty of sunlight.

Erin opened the whipped cream container, gave Clara a spoon, and pointed to the cake pan. "Lolly, can you and Mik put the whipped cream into the pan?"

"I make cake."

"Yes, you do. Whipped cream cake."

When the pan was full, Erin dotted the whipped cream with drops of different shades of food coloring. Then with a spoon handle, she drew a grid in the cream, swirling and distributing the food coloring.

"Now, it's time to color." Erin set four eggs in front of each of them then demonstrated how to do it with her egg. "Put on your gloves." She helped Clara fit the oversized gloves on her pudgy little fingers. "Good job." Erin clapped. "Now take your egg and put it in the pretty whipped cream." Erin set her egg among a color swirl. "Then spin it around." With her gloved hand, she turned the egg in a bunch of different directions until it captured color on every white part. "Take it out." She set the whipped-cream coated egg on the cookie sheet. "And let it sit." Erin had never done this before, so she prayed it worked as well as online friends said it would.

The girls both followed Erin's directions.

"Good job!" A familiar voice and clapping sounded from behind Erin.

Jon.

She turned to him, knowing the proper greeting would be a smile, but his arrival set off a whirlwind in her stomach.

"Uncle Jon!" Clara leapt up and hopped over to him.

"Lolli, don't touch." Erin grimaced as Clara embraced Jon's jean-covered knees.

He just laughed and squatted to her eye-level. He took her wrists, held up her hands, and his gaze flitted back and forth. "Are you painting again?"

"Uh-huh? Auntie Erin paints eggs!"

"Well that sounds like fun. Can I join in?" He looked to Erin.

Erin rubbed her forehead then realized she still had on messy gloves. Yay. Now she'd be going to church tomorrow with a rainbow forehead. "You're here." She nodded to the empty dog pillow. "Have a seat."

"Don't mind if I do."

He sat across from Erin and a scent wafted toward her? Cologne? Jon was here wearing jeans, an old polo, and cologne?

He picked up an egg. "How do I do it, Lolli?"

"I show you." She demonstrated, followed by licking the whipped cream off her gloves.

He followed her directions to a T, including the licking. "Yum."

May as well join in the fun instead of being a party pooper. Erin licked her gloves. "Yum." It really was good.

Mik joined in. "Yummy!"

A laughter-filled hour later, the eggs were colored, the whipped cream was eaten up, and Clara was out cold. Jon laid her in her bed then helped Erin clean up.

Once clean, Erin spread out on the couch and Jon plopped down in the recliner. Erin closed her eyes and relished the quiet. It had been a good day. A memory maker.

"I like seeing your smile."

Erin jerked open her eyes.

Jon was sitting up on the edge of the chair, leaning toward her. "You look content."

Well she was until he had to go and . . . and what? Compliment her on her smile? What was wrong with that? She'd advise Mik to say, 'Thank you.' Perhaps she should follow her own advice.

"Thanks." She looked toward her feet, avoiding his gaze. "We had a good time and painted very pretty eggs."

"Corey would have been proud."

That quickly stole her smile.

He raised his hands in the air. "I'm sorry."

"And I'm too sensitive when it comes to him."

"You have reason to be."

"Maybe, but you'd think I'd move on by now. Isn't forgiveness what this weekend is about?"

"You're working on it."

"And failing miserably."

"Are you?" He nodded toward the hallway. "I see someone who's doing an amazing job of providing a loving home for an orphan."

"Not like I had much of a choice."

"Don't you? Did you have to turn your office into a nursery? Your living room into a playroom? Your garage into an art studio?"

She shrugged. "It keeps her happy."

"Sounds like love to me."

"Sounds like someone being a decent human being."

"If that's what you want to call it. Fine."

He stood and came over to the couch. "May I?"

She gulped. "Isn't it time for you to go home?"

"Do you want me to?" He squatted beside the couch, his cologne drifting her way, and his line of sight even with hers.

She sat up, breaking that line. "You have food coloring around your mouth."

Jon quickly took the open space on the couch. "Why are you avoiding me?"

"I'm not." She grabbed a pillow and held it to her chest. "We spent Thursday together, and Friday, now today, and you're coming over tomorrow. That's not what I call avoiding. That's what I call you overstaying your welcome."

Something in his eyes shifted. If only she could read what that meant. He backed away, resting his chin on hands, and his elbows on his knees. "Is that what I'm doing?"

Now that she could read. She'd hurt him. Touch would help. It always did with Corey anyway, so she set a hand on his shoulder, and he looked her way. "I don't know. I just know that something's changed between us, and I don't know what I feel about it, and that scares me."

"That's okay." He sat up and created a bit more distance between them.

She almost breathed a relieved sigh, but held it in.

"Just do me one favor."

"Okay?" She hugged the pillow tighter.

"Please don't shut me out."

Blank space filled her mind, leaving her with no clue how to respond. In this little bit of time, she'd already gotten used to having him around, like when they were teenagers.

But not like as teenagers. And that was what frightened her.

He sighed as he slapped his knees then stood. "Guess that's my cue." He aimed for the door.

Get on your feet. Go to him. Her legs reluctantly obeyed, stopping within a foot of him. Close, but not too close. "I want to see you tomorrow." And that was the truth.

A smile edged up his lips, and he nodded. "Only because I'm bringing the dessert."

"Well." She grinned. "As long as you know the truth."

"I do, Pearl." He touched her cheek.

She flinched, then chided herself. She forced her hand forward and touched his arm. That was safe. "I want to see you, even if you forget the dessert."

Chapter Eighteen

Erin
Easter, 2019

Jesus, I love Easter, really I do. I love that we're celebrating your resurrection and are reminded that you buried all our sins when you died. For someone who's lived as messed-up a life as I have, I cling to that.

So, I was really looking forward to today. The early church service, time spent with family, watching Mik, and even Clara, hunt for their Easter baskets. I should have realized today wasn't going to turn out as planned from the very beginning. Mik woke up complaining. Clara spent half the night crying for her mommy and daddy. I probably looked like a zombie in church.

Which leads me to the next disaster. Jon wanted to accompany me and the girls to church, and I agreed, even though I wasn't comfortable with the shift in our relationship, whatever that shift is. I figured I could introduce him to Wendy, a friend who's never been married. She's an attorney, too, so they'd have that in common. And I hoped that Russ, that good-looking single guy I've had my eye on, who just moved into town from Colorado, would take me up on an Easter lunch invitation. Maybe that would help solve my Jon problem.

Well, as always happens whenever I make plans, they went completely awry. I was able to introduce Wendy to Jon, then I slipped away to the bathroom so they could talk. When I came out, they were still talking. Russ was there, too. Holding Wendy's hand. Even worse (or better, depending upon your perspective) is that Russ and Wendy make a completely adorable couple. Yay for them. Boo for me.

BUT the church service was amazing. You know I usually like the contemporary service, but on Easter and Christmas, I need the traditional. I love the brass and the choir and hearing the congregation sing out to familiar Easter hymns. It's one of the rare times I feel something. When singing those hymns, the Holy Spirit digs my feelings out from wherever they're hiding, and I sense his presence. Overwhelmed is a better word, to the point of tears, which you know, I don't let fall. I'm unable to sing or speak. But I am able to shut out Clara's squirming, Mik's slumping, Jon's too-closeness, my self-pity. Sensing feelings happens so rarely, I cherish the moments.

Too soon we had to leave for home and ham and family. The first time in four Easters I haven't spent the day alone. Sure, the Beldens had invited me along with Mik, but with Corey and his new family there too? No. Way. Yeah, I know, spending the day at home, alone and sulking wasn't really wise either.

But today, I actually enjoyed the first part of the afternoon with this untraditional family: me, Mik, and Clara. Henry and Joyce, Belinda and Charles. And Jon. Thank you for them. And thank you for the really good food! The ham turned out eye-roll-back-in-your-head delicious, if I do say so myself. Thank you for the laughter and even the tears the others shed.

Then there was that discussion about Corey and Lilith's will. With the prices Corey's paintings are demanding, Mik and Clara should have no worries about their future. That gives me relief. But what I want to know is, if he had all this money coming in, why didn't he adjust his support?

Guess wondering about the past won't get me anywhere, will it?

So, moving forward, this probate process could take a while. Problem is, by the time it's complete, Clara will have bonded with me, and it'll be even tougher on her moving to a new home. Can you speed up the process at all? Maybe help me find a better home for her?

I am sorry, mostly, for how the evening ended. Though it really wasn't my fault . . .

"Your pies were good, for being restaurant-bought." Erin accepted the wet plate from Jon and dried it with a towel.

"Much better than if I'd tried to bake them myself." Jon scrubbed what was left of a peanut butter pie from the dessert plate.

"Very true." Erin tucked plates into the cupboard. "Better to pretend it's home baked than to have your actual homemade."

"Yeah." He said too quietly as he handed the clean plate to Erin.

A change in tone meant a change in thought, right? "Something wrong?"

He shrugged. In other words, yep, something was wrong. "I don't really want to get into this tonight. It's been a good day." He let the soapy water out of the sink and dried his hands.

"It *was* a good day." Why did he have to go and ruin it? She leaned her backside against the kitchen counter and crossed her arms. "What's up?"

He copied her stance, by her side so she couldn't see his face. Not that she'd be able to read it anyway. "Do you trust the Caldwells?"

Ah, that was the issue. "I do. They've been nothing but kind. They're babysitting Clara for free and have nothing but praise for how I'm dealing with her. They came up with the art studio idea which has saved my house. So, yeah, I trust them."

"Okay." He pushed away from the counter. "Guess that's what matters. See you sometime this week?" He aimed for the front door, his walk rigid.

Fine. If he wanted to leave like that, so be it. The guy had become a drama king. She followed him to lock the door behind him.

He reached the door, gripped the handle, and then spun back around, almost bumping into her.

"Whoa." She stepped back.

He splayed his hands. "I don't want to hurt you, Erin."

Oh, boy, she'd heard those words before. "You can't hurt me any more than I've already been." She crossed her arms and glared at Jon. She had no intention of begging him to stay like she had with Corey. If Jon wanted to walk out of her life again, that was his choice. This time she'd be smart enough not to let him back in.

"I'm begging you, don't trust them, Pearl."

"Coming from someone who intimately knows what it's like to be untrustworthy."

He cursed under his breath. "I've apologized for that. A million times."

"Maybe you need to do more than apologize." She stepped closer to him, and he stumbled backward a step. "Why did you abandon me when Corey left? I needed you." She poked him in the chest. "I needed my best friend."

"I'm here now."

"Uh-uh. Until you tell me the truth, I have no reason to trust that you won't do it again. And I certainly won't listen to you smear people who've shown me nothing but grace."

"I have my reasons to doubt them."

"Just like I have my reasons to not trust you."

"Pearl . . ."

"My name is Erin.'

He brushed his fingers through his hair and down his neck. Frustration. That was a body language she recognized. She'd done it enough herself.

She gestured to the couch. "Let's sit. Have it all out right now. Easter's about forgiveness, right? And I think that starts with truth."

His jaw shifted. Did that mean he was thinking about her proposition?

"It's complicated," he finally mumbled.

"Well, I'll tell you what's not complicated." She opened the front door. "You walk out to your car. Drive away. And don't bother me again." She swiped her hands up and down, hoping to give the signal that she was washing her hands of him. She wasn't desperate enough for friends that she'd accept wishy-washy relationships.

"I'm sorry, Erin." His hand lifted as if he was about to touch her face, but she stepped out of reach and nodded toward the door.

She wouldn't waste one more word on him.

"I'm not letting you shut me out." He stepped out onto the concrete steps. "I'll be back."

She slammed the door in his face.

He might come back, but he wouldn't be welcome.

Jon drove straight from Erin's house to the cemetery, breaking all the speed limits, thankful he wasn't stopped. Buried secrets and lies always seemed to claw their way back to the surface and demand to be dealt with. It was way past time.

He knelt in front of the grave marker he'd purchased for his mother two years ago, where he'd finally buried the urn his father had brought from their former home, and brushed off the dirt and debris. This was his biggest lie of all. He sat beside the marker and stretched out his legs in front of himself, while staring at the moon playing hide and seek in the clouds. "I've kept your secret—our secret—too long, Mom. It's hurting me. I've hurt Erin. I don't know if I can undo this one, but I have to try, and that only comes with telling the truth. Whatever happens, happens."

He laid his hand on the cold marker, and a shiver coursed up his arm and spread through his body. "Love you, Mom. I'll be back soon. Let you know what's going on. Hopefully have some good news for once."

Now, how was he going to convince Erin to listen to him? Even more importantly though, was coming up with evidence that would either acquit or accuse the Caldwells. All their questions today about the will and Corey's art had raised his suspicion antenna skyscraper high. Maybe the couple was as innocent as Erin believed, but if they weren't, he needed to be prepared.

He looked up beyond the stars, beyond the moon. "You'll give me a hand, right?"

All Jon heard back was, "Listen and wait."

Definitely not the answer he wanted. He'd wait, all right, to talk with Erin, but in the meantime, he intended to sniff out what the Caldwells were up to.

———————

Erin

Easter, 2019

I don't understand why he doesn't want me to trust the Caldwells. They've given me no reason to doubt their sincerity. What's wrong with the men I choose to have in my life? What's wrong with me that I select them?

Good thing Wendy and Russ got together. I'm done with men and the idea of romance. Thank you, God, for making that clear to me.

Chapter Nineteen

Erin set aside her book and her gaze landed on Corey's journal. She hadn't picked it up for a while, knowing it only fed the one emotion she easily identified. She was already angry, though, so what would it hurt to read more from him now?

She pulled out his journal, arranged the pillows behind her back, and turned to where she'd left off, right after their romantic weekend.

And her miscarriage.

July 17, 2014

I was a little bit dramatic last Sunday. Okay, a lot. Something happened with Erin, and I don't know what I did. We'd had such an awesome weekend, and then she disappeared inside herself and hasn't been the same all week. Even Mik asked what was wrong with Mommy. If this keeps up, I won't be the only one who needs to see a counselor. It's been a while since Erin went. Maybe she should start again.

Speaking of which, I haven't gone for several weeks. The journal and art therapy have worked just fine. Why pad a doctor's wallet when I discovered a much cheaper cure?

So yeah. I'm still going to the gallery. Really needed it after this past week with Erin. I saw Lilith there, too, but avoided her. I didn't want to talk about my failed attempt to begin painting again.

Everything I do seems to disappoint or fail, but when I study the paintings and sculptures in this museum, take in the raw emotions the artists put into their work, I feel understood.

————————

September 11, 2014

Mik is back in school now—third grade already! And Erin's going back to school too to finish her business management major. She'd be a great manager. Maybe that'll get her out of the funk she was in all summer. Honestly, the two of us should trade places. She thrives on working with numbers.

I talked with Lilith again and mentioned that Erin has classes on Tuesday and Thursday evenings. She made an intriguing suggestion. The museum holds art classes for elementary aged kids on Tuesdays. I could enroll Mik and have use of another classroom for myself. Erin wouldn't have a problem with that—I mean, she's all about learning.

And I can finally paint again!

————————

September 12, 2014

Erin said yes to enrolling Mik and didn't balk when I said I'd have access to a classroom to paint. I haven't felt this excited about something in years! Starting next Tuesday, I get to paint again!

Even better, it feels like Erin and I are getting back on track. Going to school has helped her, and maybe she's seeing how my art can help me.

———————

September 16, 2014

Mik hated, HATED! the art class. Said she was bored the entire time then complained about wanting to play softball with friends instead.

I'd pictured the two of us working in a studio together, sharing that special bond, but she wants to be an athlete.

And I hate sports. Was lousy at everything, while Zax could do no wrong. Growing up with a super athlete for an older brother is the pits. He even gets away with being a prodigal. Mom and Pop know he sleeps around. Yeah, Erin and I messed up, but we got married, didn't we? And my folks just complained that we were too young.

Would it be better if I catted around like Zax?

No. I'm not bitter. Not at all.

I won't treat Mik like that. I'll be a good parent and take her to softball. If she wants to be a softball player, then I'll be in the stands every game cheering her on. I want Mik to grow up strong and confident. She can be or do whatever she wants and not let anyone stop her or discourage her.

———————

September 18, 2014

Lilith made another intriguing offer, but I don't know. It

doesn't feel right. Her house is a block away from the softball fields where Mik will be playing a couple days a week. She offered use of her personal art studio.

But I should be in the stands, even though this isn't an official league. It's just something some parents threw together to keep their kids occupied. It's a perfect way for Mik to dip her toes into sports, and I need to be there for her.

And the other thing . . .

Going to a woman's home, even if it is just to use her studio, doesn't seem right to me. I know nothing would ever happen, but the offer's tempting. I've started replenishing my supplies, and my fingers are itching to grip a paintbrush again.

Soon!

If only we didn't live in this tiny home and actually had a basement I could mess up. If only Erin would let me use the garage. Supporting the family isn't cheap. Neither are houses.

Enough grumbling, and time to take action. I'll ask Mom for a raise. Tell her I've earned it. She can convince Pop to do anything. Then I'll give Erin a bigger home. With a basement.

Yeah. That's what I'll do.

———————————

September 22, 2014

I got a raise. A lousy fifty cents an hour. Whoopee. Do they think I'm just some high schooler working at McDonalds? Maybe it's time to look elsewhere, somewhere I'm appreciated and get paid accordingly. A place where I actually enjoy my work.

I have no clue where that would be.

But Lilith might.

———————

September 25, 2014

I'm in love.

With an art studio. Lil understood that I didn't want to go to her house, so she explained that it wasn't really her house, but an art studio, a cottage, really, on her property that she uses for teaching. Mik and I checked it out after practice. It has this wall of windows that overlook a lake and a perennial garden. I could spend all day just looking out that window, or maybe I should bring an easel outside.

Mik—she's so intuitive—said I should use it. Said she gets to play softball, so I should get to paint. Then everyone will be happy.

Plus, it'll be Mik's and my little secret, and that makes her feel special.

———————

September 30, 2014

I practically cried when I touched my brush to the paint-covered palette and began to mix colors. It's been so long. I didn't even have a plan, I just let my brush take the lead on the canvas, and then I did cry. I didn't create a masterpiece. Far from it. And I'm far from done. Not much painting gets done in two hours' time. But it's a start. Before Thursday, though, I need to pick up a palette knife, try a new technique that I think will be just right for this piece.

I can't wait to come back on Thursday!

____

October 14, 2014

Mik had a family softball picnic last Thursday following her game, so I didn't paint then, but going to the picnic inspired me. I set aside the painting I'd begun a few weeks ago and began a new one of Mik standing in the batter's box. She looks so determined and focused, traits she obviously gets from Erin. It felt good sitting beside Erin, both of us cheering our daughter on. We're getting back on the same page, I think. I hope.

Anyway, while watching Mik, Erin and I shared a bag of popcorn and the bag tore, dumping everything below the bleachers, leaving me with a scrap. I pocketed that scrap, intending to throw it out, but I found it in my pocket today when I got to the studio.

And inspiration hit. The painting focuses on Mik, but in the corner of the painting you see two hands holding onto the same bag of popcorn. I took the scrap from last week, stuck it to the canvas, and then completed that bag with paint, doing my best to make that scrap blend in. Goofy, I know, but I did it, and it filled me with a sense of accomplishment. The rest of the painting will take much longer to complete. It's important I get Mik at bat just right.

Then hopefully she'll have a memory from me to cherish.

Chapter Twenty

Erin woke up the next morning having dreamt about popcorn that overtook the house, eventually knocking down the walls and the roof. She'd never dreamed in metaphor before, though that bag of popcorn had been the perfect metaphor for her family. She remembered sharing that bag, being disappointed that it had torn. She'd probably ragged on Corey because of it too because they didn't have money to waste. It wasn't long after then that the rift between them had grown. The popcorn bag had ripped apart just like her family, scattering all the kernels on the ground. Unsalvageable like their marriage.

She didn't know how to feel about a piece of that bag being a remnant in a painting she'd always loved and now hung in Mik's room. She had wondered how he'd found the time or place to create it. She'd probably ragged on Corey for that, too. How could she not have noticed the bag scrap before? Once Mik left for school, Erin would give that painting another look.

But Clara awoke crying about two seconds after Mik went out the door to catch the bus. Probably because Mik was in a mood and slammed the front door hard enough to wake everyone on the street.

What was Erin going to do with her?

Erin opened the door to Clara's room and immediately smelled urine. Wonderful. She lifted the crying child, felt her backside, and sighed. Well today was starting out fabulous. She gave Clara a bath, dressed her, fed her, played with her, read her books, took her to the park, fed her again, and finally Clara laid down for her afternoon nap. Erin prayed that her wet pants this morning had been an anomaly.

At last, Erin went to check out Mik's painting. She waded through her daughter's jungle of a bedroom to the painting Corey had given her that Christmas in 2014. If only Erin had known where that artwork had been created, maybe she could have salvaged their marriage. She leaned close to the painting and eyed the popcorn bag in the corner, touching it. There! She felt her eyes pop open. The edges were seamless. How did he do that?

She stepped back and took in the painting as a whole. It was clearly created with love. He'd captured Mik's determination perfectly, putting the focus on her, with the crowd and field blending in in the background, and a secondary focus on two hands united on a bag of popcorn. Ha! Their marriage had been just as fragile as that bag.

Should she read on in Corey's journal? Maybe if she read during the day, she wouldn't have nightmares. She hurried from Mik's room to her own and checked the time. She had about an hour before Mik got home. Clara would likely wake up around that same time. Not enough time to get any work done. So, she sat on her bed once again, pulled out Corey's journal, and read.

November 24, 2014

I've been coming to Lil's for almost two months now. Last week I finally finished Mik's portrait. It'll be a perfect Christmas gift to her. But how do I explain it to Erin? I can't very well say I've been spending a couple evenings a week at a women's art studio when I'd said I was taking classes.

After Mik's softball ended, that was the best I could come up with. And now, I don't have to worry about Mik tattling on me.

I especially can't tell Erin what I'm working on now. Lil, as payment for use of her studio, asked if I'd paint her portrait. How could I say 'no' after all she's done for me? To be honest, I can't wait to arrive at the studio each week.

And let's face it, Lil is hot. She's young. Sexy. Smart. Lil gets me. She doesn't nag. She applauds. She encourages. I need that positive energy in my life.

Erin just drags me down, always reminding me of my responsibilities to my job, to her, to Mik. I get it! I should be responsible, and I am. I support the family. But shouldn't marriage have a little fun now and then too? I mean, Erin and I rarely make love anymore.

I don't remember marriage being this difficult for Mom and Pop.

This Thursday is Thanksgiving, and we're spending it at the folks' place. I feel I should talk to them, ask them how they made it through tough times.

———————

November 27, 2014

I never did get Mom and Pop alone today. Zax is in town, so he got all the attention, of course. Jon joined the family, too, and he told me he noticed something was off between Erin and me. We're still friends, but I don't think he ever forgave me for being the first to ask Erin out. Not like he hadn't had the opportunity. He asked what was up with me and Erin. I told him we're going through a rough patch.

He said, "That better be it" as if he knew I wasn't taking an accounting class and was painting instead. Regardless, what happens between me and my wife is none of his business, and I told him so.

Sometimes I wonder how different life would have turned out if Jon had been the first to ask out Erin. Would I be stuck doing bookkeeping during the day? Would I be a dad? Maybe I'd be flying around the world like Zax, leaving a trail of broken hearts.

Nah. I'm a one-woman man. Sure, I'm attracted to Lil. I mean, what red-blooded man wouldn't be? I mean, she's hot. She's eight years younger than I am, has long, muscular legs she shows off with her short skirts. I don't mind that one bit. Her blonde curls make me want to wrap my fingers around them. And those lips. Man, they were made to be kissed. We haven't talked about it, but I'll bet she's got a horde of boyfriends. So, am I attracted? I'm alive, aren't I?

———————

December 16, 2014

I'm despicable.

I don't know how it happened. One second I was working on Lil's portrait, the next we were lip locked.

I was just painting, then Lil got up to see my progress. She loved it. Do you know how good it feels to have someone appreciate you? Appreciate your gifts?

So, she was there. Her hand was on my back, and I turned to her. I don't even know who started it, all I know was that I liked it. A lot. I mean, in that moment I was ready and willing to forget my marriage vows.

Thankfully, my phone rang preventing me from making the worst mistake of my life.

The kiss was bad enough.

So, I told Lil I couldn't do it anymore. I can't trust myself around her, and she apologized.

But she promised it wouldn't happen again. Besides, I have to finish her portrait so she can give it to her parents for Christmas. A couple more visits to her art studio should do it. We both got caught up in the moment. I'll make sure it doesn't happen again.

———————

December 18, 2014

Okay, that was a lie about not letting it happen again. Or not really a lie because I really had no intentions of kissing her again, but I couldn't help myself. It's like she has me under a spell, and all of a sudden, we're having a make-out session. We stopped before going all the way, I mean, I'm not that type of guy. I won't cheat on Erin.

But I finally get my brother. There's an adrenaline rush when you're doing something dangerous, something you shouldn't be doing.

As long as we don't have sex, I'm not hurting anyone. I even read an article yesterday that said a little fling is healthy for a marriage. I get certain needs met from Lil and that takes the pressure off Erin.

Pretty soon, Erin and I will be back to where we were.

———————

December 23, 2014

I've been found out.

Jon was standing outside, in the freezing cold, when I stepped out of Lil's cottage. Said someone called him with an anonymous tip. I've never seen him so angry. I thought he was going to punch me. Instead he pointed to my lips, said I better wipe them off if I didn't want Erin to find out. I begged him not to tell her. I said I messed up big time and promised it wouldn't happen again, that we just got carried away in the moment.

He said the only reason he wouldn't tell Erin was because he loved her too much to hurt her, and he'd seen too many marriages ripped apart by affairs. I insisted we weren't having an affair. It hadn't gone that far. I don't think he believed me.

Still, it's a good thing I finished Lil's portrait tonight. What I told Jon was true—we hadn't had sex, but I'd be lying if I said I didn't want to. Especially when Lil started reaching for my zipper. Oh, man I wanted to make love to her.

I couldn't do that to Erin. To Mik. I'm not an adulterer.

I know I can't ever go back, because I can't promise myself I won't cross the line. After all, I'm only human.

Only human? Erin slammed shut the journal and tried to calm the shakes overwhelming her body.

That despicable, good-for-nothing pig! Convincing himself in a matter of days that it was okay to kiss another woman? Good for their marriage, even? What she'd give to drag him from the grave and send him right back in.

She had appreciated him, but he was gone so much that fall, he wasn't around to notice how much she needed him. Now she finally knew where he'd disappeared to. How had she been so clueless?

And to think Jon had known about the affair—yes, even without sex, the jerk had been cheating on her—and hadn't said anything. The rat. When she saw Jon again, she'd give him a piece of her mind.

Maybe that was why he'd stayed away from her. He probably felt guilty for being complicit with Corey's affair, and he couldn't face her. Now that his co-conspirators, the only ones with evidence were gone, he was no longer afraid of being found out. Oh, now it all made sense. She didn't need him around anymore. The problem was, how would she let Mik know that she'd chased another man from their life?

Chapter Twenty-One

Erin stopped at the nursery door and blew Clara a kiss. "Goodnight, Lolli."

"Night-night, Auntie." Clara cuddled her pet crocodile, Chomper, and rolled over on her side. She'd acclimated to the toddler bed very quickly. Was this house becoming too familiar to her as well?

Erin shut the door, leaned against it, and slowly breathed out, helping to erase stress. Quiet permeated the house. Today was filled with another client rejection. More arguments from Mik, this time over a boy. Why couldn't she get it through her head that a thirteen-year-old was too young to date? All she needed to do was look at Erin and her father. And even her grandmother, who Mik had never met, thank goodness. Not a tear had been shed when Erin's mom passed away shortly after she and Corey got married. Instead they'd been relieved.

As for Clara, she didn't have an icy vein in her entire body. She effused joy, especially when painting out in the garage. Living here would only rob her of that joy. Especially without Jon around.

Nope. Not thinking about him tonight. She strode to the kitchen and pulled out a pint of German chocolate ice cream. That, along with a non-romance movie would be the perfect way to spend the evening.

She sorted through her DVDs and finally found one that

always made her laugh: *Galaxy Quest*. Yeah, she used to watch it with Jon and Corey when they were teens, but that was a long time ago. One thing she'd learned to do—mostly—was separate good movies from the people she'd enjoyed them with.

The phone rang as she sat down with her pint and spoon.

Jon again. He'd called a lot, and she hadn't answered, though she wanted to tell him what she thought of their so-called friendship and him keeping Corey's affair a secret. Her finger hovered over the green phone symbol, but then she swiped the red phone to the left, rejecting his call. Someday he'd get the hint and leave her alone.

Apparently, he caught the hint as she watched the rest of the movie in peace.

When it was over, she turned off the television and sat in darkness in the living room. She'd barely laughed tonight. In the olden days, she and Corey and Jon knew the movie so well, they'd laugh well before the punch line.

Now the movie made her feel . . . she processed what was going on with her body. Her shoulders felt heavy, her back slouched. Sadness. That was it. And nostalgic for the good times. She, Corey, and Jon had had a lot of good times. And she and Jon had found a real family with the Beldens. They weren't perfect, but they'd been close knit and faith filled. They'd shown Christ to Jon and Erin through their actions, through their love, which made Corey's behavior all the more perplexing and hurtful.

He'd not only cheated on her and Mik, he'd hurt his family, and turned his back on God.

How?

She had to know what happened with Corey, why he turned his back on God and family. There was one way.

Like a bee to a flower, she returned to her bedroom and dug out Corey's journal.

December 25, 2014

I've never had such a stressful Christmas Eve. I spent the evening afraid Jon had told Erin about Lilith, or that she'd find out some other way.

This morning as we sat in church, singing traditional Christmas songs that usually connect me with God, I felt as if he'd cut our connection. I guess I haven't experienced that connection in a long time, though. He's abandoned me.

I look at Mom and Pop and see what a great marriage they have, and I want the same thing. I just don't know how to get it.

On the plus side, I gave Mik the painting as her gift this morning. She LOVED it. Erin, as expected, was skeptical. She didn't say anything, she didn't have to. I could read it in her body language, and the way she turned away from me tonight when I needed a little Christmas lovemaking . . . I couldn't stay in our bedroom after the rejection. It hurt too much. It's like she knows I've been unfaithful.

I needed to know she still cares for me.

I need to know if I still love her.

Erin slapped the journal shut. Her rejection hurt *him* too much? Please!

She remembered that Christmas, how he'd given Mik that beautiful painting, and his gift to her was a bottle of expensive perfume that she'd never use. Now she understood that he was trying to buy her affection. But perfume? When had she ever asked for or wanted perfume? And then he'd wanted to fool around? Ha!

Maybe that was her first hint that their marriage was irreparably broken. Her gut had probably known it, but hadn't conveyed the message to her brain.

The perfume was possibly Lilith's favorite. Or maybe he'd even purchased it for her, then thought better of it and gave it to Erin. Jerk!

She raised her arm, planning to hurl the book across the room, but that would wake Clara, and probably draw Mik. What she should do is burn it. This stupid book was making her crazy, yet she was drawn to it like a stressed-out woman to chocolate, somehow hoping for a happy ending which no one would get.

Rather than put the book away, she opened it up planning to read just one more entry.

January 1, 2015

A new year. A fresh start. That's what I'd planned.

I woke up this morning frustrated from a New Year's Eve of Erin and I avoiding each other, and that's hard to do in our little house, especially with Mik staying at a friend's place overnight. I decided saving our marriage was up to me, no matter what it takes. And that means breaking off all contact with Lil, and no more trips to the art gallery. Both will be hard, but if Jon keeps dogging me like he has this past week, it'll be easy to stay away. The guy's threatened to introduce his fist to my nose if I don't straighten up. As buff as he's gotten, I don't dare mess with him.

Funny how roles are reversed. Twenty-some years ago when I met Jon, he was the scrawny troublemaker whose mother had abandoned the family and whose Dad loved the bottle more than anything. He needed a friend, a normal family, and we gave that to him. Jon always said I saved him. Guess it's his turn to save me.

Starting with giving Erin something she wants—definitely not perfume. So, I got up early this morning, let Erin sleep in, threw a roast in the Crock-Pot, and worked on cleaning the house. I know I'm not the neatest guy in the world. Okay, I'm probably one of the messiest. No wonder Erin would get frustrated with me.

Well, Jon was right about cleaning. I think Erin almost cried when she saw there were no dishes in the sink, no mess on the kitchen table, and my junk from the living room put away.

Then came the really hard part, telling Erin what I'd been doing. No, I didn't mention Lil, I'm not stupid! But I did tell her about going to the art gallery and painting at a friend's place. She just sat there, stoic, as I spilled my guts, crying, begging for her forgiveness.

And I realized I was no longer in love with my wife.

How could that happen? I've known Erin since we were in grade school. She and Jon were always my best friends, and then it grew into more. I'd loved how I could make her laugh and cry and love.

Now, it's too much work. She doesn't respond like she used to, and I miss that. I need someone I can share emotions with, and that's no longer Erin.

That broke my heart, and I started to cry. I kept thinking this couldn't be the end. It just couldn't.

But I heard Jon in my head reminding me that Erin processes before reacting, and that I needed to wait her out. How is it that he knows her better than I do? Probably still has a crush on her.

Well, he was right. I waited quietly, tearfully. Even talked to

God while I was waiting—I've really let my prayer time lapse over the past months.

Suddenly her arms were around me and she was saying how she forgave me and was asking if I could forgive her for not seeing I needed to paint. She even said I could have the spare room as an art studio. That was a huge concession for her as she'd been saving the room for a nursery. After two—or was it three?—miscarriages, she was ready to move on. She also volunteered to go back to work and finish her schooling later. Mom and Pop have always said there's room at the firm for her. Then we could move into the larger home we've always wanted.

I lie to her for months, and she forgives me. How do I wrap my head around that? I didn't know what to say, so I showed her the only way I knew how. Right there on the couch we made sweet love to each other, better than it's been for years. Who knows, maybe this will be what makes me a father again. Maybe that will help heal our marriage. Maybe that will make me fall in love with her again.

Because I'm in deep, deep trouble. When I closed my eyes during our lovemaking, I didn't see Erin. I saw Lilith.

———————

Erin's stomach turned topsy-turvy. She remembered that New Year's Day, all right. His confession and his lovemaking had convinced her their marriage was back on track. It had convinced her to try again.

She hurled the book across the room, and it crashed against the wall. She didn't care if Mik came running or if Clara woke up. What she needed to do was wring Corey's neck.

How he could make love to her while picturing . . .

That was the night Erin got pregnant.

She clutched her spasming stomach, and bile vaulted up her throat. She ran to the bathroom, making it just in time.

"Mom, are you okay?" Mik stood in the doorway, dressed in footy pajamas, cuddling her pet dragon to her chest, her makeup wiped from her face. She looked like the young child she still was.

Erin wanted to hold that little girl, make sure she never grew up, because adults are too messed up. All they did was hurt one another.

"Just an upset stomach." Erin sat back, leaned against the bathroom wall, and wiped her face with toilet paper.

"Can I get you anything? 7-Up? Crackers? Banana?"

That made Erin smile. Mik had never exhibited mothering before. A sign of maturity in the midst of puberty?

"I would love 7-Up and a banana. Thank you."

"You'll be okay, right?" What looked like worry crossed her daughter's face.

She looked straight ahead at the toilet. "Yeah. I'll be okay." A big fat lie. Sometimes Erin doubted she'd ever be okay again.

With her stomach finally settled, Erin lit newspapers she'd inserted between wood in her fire pit and retrieved the journal from her bedroom floor. Carrying the book out to the fire made her feel like Frodo Baggins bearing the burden of the ring across miles of dangerous, unfamiliar territory. The only way to free himself was to scale Mount Doom and throw the ring into the fire. Okay, that was a bit dramatic, but that was how Corey made her feel.

Yes, walking out the side door, she recognized she felt like a drama queen. But if she kept this journal around, it would make her crazy. She'd be drawn to read it, but then she'd despise what she'd read. It had to go, for her sanity and her family's health.

Especially Clara's. To think that Corey got his wish to be a father again. How could she possibly love that precious child?

Erin walked around the side of the house, and heard a door slam behind her.

"Mom? Mom! Hurry, it's Clara!"

No!

Erin glanced at the fire burning about twenty-five feet away. She could hurl the book and run back to the house, but with her severe lack of athletic ability, she'd likely miss by twenty feet.

"Mom?" Mik was suddenly behind her. "Clara's throwing up. Probably got your bug."

No, dear Mik, Clara definitely did not catch my bug. Still, Erin thanked her daughter and ran back to the house. A trail of vomit ran from Clara's bed to the bathroom, making Erin want to gag all over again.

Clara sat on the bathroom floor, her round face red and blotchy and messy. Vomit clung to her pajamas all the way to her footy-covered toes. A tiny blotch landed in the toddler toilet bowl she held in her hands.

"I sick, Auntie Erin."

"I'm sorry, Lolli." She found a clean place on the floor and knelt beside the child. She kissed Clara's forehead. A slight fever. She'd check again once she got the child cleaned up.

She took a clean cloth from under the sink, ran it beneath warm water, and wiped Clara's face and neck first.

Then the gagging began again.

Erin took the pot from Clara's hands and held it beneath her mouth just in time to catch the majority, thank goodness.

"I want Mommy, Daddy." Clara's lower lip stuck out and her chin shivered.

"Oh, baby." Ignoring the vomit-coated pajamas, Erin wrapped Clara in a hug. "I know. I know."

"Is she okay?" Mik stood in the doorway, holding a roll of paper towels.

"Just the flu." She slowly rocked Clara. "And she's missing her mommy and daddy."

Mik looked down, and wiped at her eyes. "I miss him, too."

"Oh, honey, I know." Erin stretched out her arm, and Mik tucked herself beside her mom, the three of them grieving on the bathroom floor. She kissed her daughter's cheek. "Your father loved you very much."

But did he? In all the journal readings, Mik's name had barely been mentioned. It was all about him and Lilith.

Chapter Twenty-Two

"You two okay?" a whispered voice broke through Erin's dream. She awoke on the living room floor to see Mik hovering over her. Erin shook her head and blinked her daughter in clearer. Mik was dressed and ready for school. All without Erin's nagging.

She sat up and stretched the kinks from her back. "I think we'll survive."

Mik grinned. "Good. I was worried about you two. Almost gave Uncle Jon a call."

Why would she do that?

Whatever.

"Well, I gotta go." Mik slung her backpack over her shoulder. "Bus'll be here any second. Remember to eat bananas, rice, apples, and toast. No butter. And get lots of sleep."

"Yes, Mom." Erin saluted her daughter. "Thank you for taking care of us."

Mik shrugged. "Just doing what you taught me." And then she was out the door.

Imagine that. Her daughter was learning. Erin knelt on the blanket-covered floor where she'd slept all night alongside Clara. How a small child could throw up that much was beyond her. Two hours of vomiting followed by another three of dry heaves before Clara finally rested.

She pressed the back of her hand to Clara's forehead. Didn't feel feverish. She kissed it as well for a second test. The low-grade fever was gone.

Still, Erin could not bring the child over to the Caldwells for the day. She called Belinda and gave her the sad news, and Belinda wholeheartedly agreed that Clara needed to stay home. She offered to babysit the following day instead. Hopefully, Clara would rest this morning so Erin could get some work done. That attorney Vanessa Martin was right when she'd said that a child would pull her attention away from work.

Letting the child sleep on the floor, her stuffed crocodile at her side, Erin got up to tackle the massive cleaning job Clara had left behind. She threw all the bedding into the wash, then, armed with white vinegar and rags, she got on her hands and knees to scrub vomit remnants from the carpet. She'd wiped it up last night, sprinkled baking soda over the trail and covered it with towels, but now it needed a deep cleaning. The one bright spot was that Clara's room was right across from the bathroom, so the trail wasn't long. Still, it was long enough.

An hour and a half later, Erin plopped down on the couch, her arms and knees sore from the work, and her eyelids pleading to close. Clearly, no bookkeeping work would get done today. Trying to work with numbers while fatigued never turned out well.

She carried Clara to her bed with its freshly washed bedding and tucked her in with Chomper.

Now what?

She yawned, informing her of her next move. Napping in her bed never felt right, so she brought a blanket and pillow from her bedroom and settled in on the couch.

And couldn't sleep. Really? Grrr. Surrendering, she got up, did some bookwork, checked on Clara, made a few phone calls, booked a new appointment (Yay!), and checked in again on Clara who was just beginning to stir. If Clara was anything like Mik, the day after being sick, she'd have a ton of energy and want to play the rest of the day, so Erin selected a book on her e-reader, got cozy on the couch, and mentally prepared herself for Clara's burst of energy.

"Auntie Erin?" The child climbing up on her lap pulled Erin from her story. Thumb firmly ensconced in her mouth, she snuggled into the crook of Erin's shoulder.

Erin kissed her forehead. Still no fever, thank goodness. "How are you feeling, Lolli?"

"I got sick."

"Yes, you did, sweetie." She slowly combed fingers through Clara's rat's nest hair, careful not to tug out the tangles. "But we got you all better."

"Uh-huh. I wuv you, Auntie Erin."

Erin froze, her fingers halfway through untangling a knot of hair. Was it okay to lie to a child? Well, Erin certainly wasn't going to tell her the truth, so she kissed her cheek and forced out the words. "And I love you."

Unlike Mik, Clara didn't want to play, she just wanted to be held. All afternoon. She ate small bits of bananas and apples and crackers then wanted to be held again. Anytime Erin put her down to get work done, Clara would whimper, so she finally gave up. Studies showed you couldn't hold a child too much, right? Even when Mik got home from school, Clara clung to Erin. And then thankfully, at eight that night, Clara fell asleep.

Erin's brain was too fatigued to concentrate on bookwork, so she picked up her e-reader, her pillow, and blanket from the couch and brought it to her bedroom. If she fell asleep while reading, so be it. She stopped in the middle of the doorway and stared at her bed. Corey's journal lay in the middle of the bed and seemed to be taunting her in a singsong voice, "Na, na, na, na, na, na."

She thought of the firepit, but she'd burned every scrap of wood she had last night. Throwing it in the garbage wasn't permanent enough. It was as if the book was staring her down saying, "I won!"

No. No it didn't.

She picked it up and started ripping out the pages, tearing each into miniscule pieces that looked like volcanic ash layering the carpet.

The words "Valentine's Day, 2015" leaped from the pages and stopped her. Memories of that day flooded through her mind. She'd never been sentimental, but being remembered on the holiday still had mattered to her, especially when they were supposedly trying to work on their marriage. But that year it was just another disappointment in a string of letdowns.

Valentine's Day, 2015

I am scum.

I tried to get my marriage back on track. Really, I did. Erin working at Belden Accounting drives me nuts. She's with me. All. The. Time. Even at home, when I can lock myself in my studio, I know she's there just beyond the door, and my muse is nowhere to be found. My canvases become a mess of hostility rather than works of beauty.

I couldn't breathe.

And she wears this smiling mask all the time, too. She doesn't know I see her unhappiness right through it.

I knew if I didn't do something different, I'd go crazy.

So, when our receptionist brought me my mail that afternoon, including a flyer from the art gallery with a note tucked inside that said, "I miss you," I couldn't resist. I had to see Lil again. I had to feel alive again.

At the end of the workday, I stopped by Erin's cubicle and told her I had a meeting that night. She may not show a lot of emotion, but her disappointment was obvious. I couldn't help it, though. I needed to get away.

I went to Lil's art studio. I needed to release my emotions. I needed to paint in the place that inspired me.

And, yes, she was waiting for me with all new paint supplies.

All new because in the first part of January, Jon had accompanied me to Lil's to gather my supplies. He even stood in the room, chaperoning, until he got a phone call he had to take and excused himself. The look he gave me when heading out the door was clearly a warning not to try anything.

But how does a piece of metal resist the pull of a magnet?

Lil and I shared a heart-thumping kiss before Jon charged back in, angrier than I've ever seen him. I thought for sure he was going to lay me out.

That cold night in January, I believed the kiss was worth the risk because I needed to tell Lil goodbye.

And ever since, I've felt dead.

Until today. When I stood in the studio, life flowed through me. Lil asked if I'd do another portrait of her. After all she'd done for me, how could I say no? She stepped into the bathroom to pretty up, while I prepped my canvas and paints.

I called when I was ready, and she came out.

Wearing nothing.

Oh, man. My mouth went cottony dry as she reclined on a chaise lounge, and sweat must have oozed from every pore of my body. I concentrated hard on that portrait, trying to focus on my art and not the woman. I had to because my body was wanting something else. A kiss was one thing, but sex?

After what must have been a couple of hours, I said I needed to go. Erin would worry.

"Let her." Lil told me as she covered herself with a robe and sat down on the chaise. She patted the space beside her. I had to resist. Couldn't resist. Didn't want to resist.

She handed me a plate of fruit that had been sitting on a table by the chaise. Do you think I saw that while painting? Uh, no. She asked how it was going with Erin. I lied and said, "Good." As if she couldn't see through that. She replied with a nod and "That's good" which I knew meant something completely different.

I asked her what was up, and she said she sensed things weren't good with me and Erin. I denied it at first, but after prompting, everything spilled out of me, my frustrations with her, her nagging, her rigidness. Even her inability to get pregnant again.

Lil listened, really listened. Then helped me realize how Erin's been using me. Controlling me. Not trusting me. At work. At home. And I just bent to each one of her wishes. Our marriage was an unhealthy relationship that was doomed to fail. Why hadn't I seen it before?

Lil was right. How could I have been so blind? For the umpteenth time that year, I cried.

And then she kissed me.

Oh, man, I kissed back. And when she reached for my zipper, this time I didn't stop her, and she didn't stop me when I slipped off her robe. I completely understand my brother Zax now. There's nothing like the rush of doing something forbidden. Our lovemaking tonight was nothing like I've ever had with Erin.

When I finally put on my jacket to leave, she gave me one last kiss then whispered in my ear, "Happy Valentine's Day."

That's when it hit me, and I wanted to cry again.

I'd just cheated on Erin.

I'd just become an adulterer.

I am scum.

Holding in a scream, Erin tore the pages she'd just read from the journal and ripped them into shreds even a mouse would have difficulty detecting. Mik and Clara should never ever read his words. To think he'd put them down on paper! Their dad was pond scum. She slammed the journal shut. No, that was too nice. Bottom of the sewer scum, that was what he was.

He chose Valentine's Day to break their vows. The very same evening he'd forgotten she'd promised to make him his favorite meal. The evening his parents were watching Mik overnight.

The very evening she'd planned to tell him she was pregnant again, he was in bed with another woman.

Why hadn't she seen it then? Why hadn't it dawned on her when he said he'd signed up for additional accounting classes? She knew he hated accounting, yet believed he wanted to learn more?

She was a clueless idiot. Because she'd wanted to believe he still loved her, that she was worthy of being loved. Were all spouses who were cheated on as oblivious as her? She hugged her knees to her chest and rocked on the bed.

It was late or she'd call Debbie. She wouldn't mind the call, but her friend had a family of her own to care for.

This wasn't the kind of thing she could share with anyone at church. There was also Jon . . . She hadn't seen him, talked with him, since she'd kicked him out on Easter.

And she missed him. That was a feeling she did identify.

So, he'd gone with Corey to collect his art supplies from Lilith's. What else had he known about? And if Jon was so unhappy with Corey, why did he abandon her when Corey asked for—demanded the divorce?

Nothing made sense.

She pounded her pillow. Someday she'd get up the nerve to invite Jon over so she could ask him point-black why he left her, too. Tonight, though, she was too angry to have a decent conversation.

Chapter Twenty-Three

Erin flung her briefcase into her car, got in, and aimed for home an hour earlier than planned. The meeting with a prospective client had gone worse than anticipated, and she had ice cream at home to medicate her wounds, even though her waistline was beginning to reveal her stress eating. So far, the list of prospects she'd received from Jon had resulted in one lousy client. One. And she was nearly done with the list.

On top of that, she didn't want to think about what she was heading home to. The Caldwells had dropped off Clara shortly after Mik got home from school this afternoon, so Mik had been babysitting for three hours already. Not that she wasn't capable, but was she reliable? Two days ago, she'd been amazingly nurturing when Clara was sick, but that was two emotions ago. Last night she'd been sullen. This morning, backtalking.

Not what Erin needed after reading Corey's journal last night. It still rankled her, and that no doubt played a role in her failed attempt to sway another client. Mik's attitude tasted of arsenic on top of Corey's secret confession.

Erin didn't like not trusting her daughter, but since Corey died, and especially since Easter, Mik's emotions had been all over the place. One day happy. The next, weepy. Then angry. Nurturing. Defiant. Childlike. And sad again. Like she was experiencing every stage of grief in one week. Erin couldn't remember telling her daughter "no" to so many requests. Rather, *demands*. Erin prayed that today was another happy day.

She flipped on her blinker and watched the stream of cars heading toward the lakes for a restful and fun weekend. What would that be like? Restful and fun were no longer on Erin's calendar.

Stop with the pity party, would you? This was why she hated emotions. They took over her life and stole all rational thinking.

A half hour later, she turned onto her street and the low-gas warning went off. Shoot! In her hurry to get home, she'd forgotten all about needing gas and zoomed right past every station. She looked ahead toward her little house calling her home. Tomorrow, she'd fill.

Chalk drawings covered her crumbling, patchwork driveway that had needed to be replaced when she and Corey purchased the house ten years ago. She hit the remote control, and her garage door cranked upward. Art supplies were strewn throughout the garage. That she'd deal with by closing the door. Tomorrow was her day off, so she and Clara would make a game of cleaning again. Hopefully, she'd soon learn to clean without being reminded.

Like Mik had? Yeah, right.

She got out of her car and locked it, then walked across the sidewalk that was pieced together as well as the driveway. Someday she'd have a little extra to fix everything. Maybe even add another story onto the house. Dreaming was healthy, so she'd been told.

She unlocked the side door leading into the walkway between the kitchen and living room, and a noise like giant mice scattering, followed by a thump, put her on alert. She glanced to the left. Nothing was amiss in the living room. To her right, the galley kitchen was messy, but empty of people.

She set down her briefcase on a dinette chair, then walked through the living room to the hallway leading to the three small bedrooms and one bath. She pressed her ear to the nursery door. All was silent. The bathroom door was open, as was the master bedroom door. Both rooms were empty.

Mik's door was closed, so she pressed her ear to that. Too quiet. At seven in the evening, Clara might be asleep, but Mik was just waking up.

Erin knocked on the door. "I'm home. Got a moment?"

"Uh, yeah, one second." Shuffling could be heard, followed by Mik opening the door an inch, if that. "What do you need?"

Erin pushed the door open further.

"Mom!" Mik, dressed in those cheek-revealing shorts Erin hated and a midriff-baring top, tried to close it, but not before Erin saw the evidence. Whoever was hiding beneath the disheveled bed forgot to tuck their stockinged foot under all the way.

Erin easily recognized the emotion building inside: anger. This time, it was justified.

"Come on out," she said in her best scary-mom voice. This type of situation was exactly where Mik needed a father influence, someone who would frighten adolescent boys into obedience.

That never would have been Corey.

The foot slid out, pulling with it jeaned legs, a ratty, skull-covered T-shirt, and finally a pimple-faced head coated with shoulder-length, dust-bunny covered hair.

Erin jabbed her hand toward the front door while glaring at the unfamiliar teen. "Get out. Now."

"Mom!" Mik stomped her foot.

Erin would deal with her next.

The young man. No. Not a man, by any definition. The boy,

his eyes wide as the doorknob she gripped in her hand, pushed past her, mumbling something about "mom not supposed to be home."

The kid hustled out the front door, then closed it hard enough to make pictures shake on the wall.

This was it. She'd had it. Life needed to get back to normal, now. She didn't say a word to Mik, afraid of the venom that might spew from her. Instead, she pieced herself together temporarily and dialed Belinda Caldwell's cell.

She answered after one ring. "Hello, Erin."

"I have an emergency, Belinda. Can I drop off Clara for the evening?"

"Oh, I hope everything's all right."

Erin glared at her daughter, who returned the look. "Oh, it will be. I'll come by in about twenty. No, make that thirty." She had to stop for gas first. "See you soon. And thank you." She punched the End Call button then opened her daughter's door. "Change into something decent. You're coming with me."

"I don't want to."

"This isn't about what you want. Go." No way was she leaving her daughter at home alone tonight. It might be a long time before she trusted Mik again.

Filthy words spurted from Mik's mouth as she entered her room and slammed the door.

Every muscle in Erin's body tensed as she held back a similar retort. She glared upward. "Can't life be easy, just for once?" *Call Debbie* flitted through her mind. Erin let it keep on flitting. Right now, she didn't want to be counseled. If she were on speaking terms with Jon, she'd give him a call, maybe he could talk some sense into Mik.

Stuff your pride, Erin. Didn't matter if she was talking to Jon or not. Her daughter needed a male influence, so Erin would wave the white flag. She dialed his number, and naturally his voice mail picked up. She left a message, hoping he'd listen soon. "Jon, I need your help. Please."

Now to wake Clara. She went into the child's room, put together an overnight bag, then knelt beside the bed. "Lolli, honey." She touched her warm cheek. "We have to go to Gramama Belinda's house."

Clara rolled over and tucked herself in a ball. Well, then, Erin would just carry her. She picked up the child and the overnight bag and walked to Mik's room. She knocked, waited, then tried the door.

Locked. Of course.

She knocked again.

"Time to go."

"I'm staying home."

Oh, no you're not. Keeping the sleeping Clara at her shoulder, she hurried to her office and found an old keycard. She knocked on Mik's door one more time.

"Go away."

Not happening, sweetheart. Erin set down the diaper bag then, with one hand, jiggled the keycard in between the door latch and the door frame, pushing in the lock. She hip-shoved the door open as Mik leaped into bed and covered herself with her blankets.

"I'll behave. I promise."

One. Two. Three. Four. "Doesn't matter, right now. You're riding with me. It's not up for a vote." Clara stirred in Erin's arms and started whimpering.

"You're a witch!"

"Yeah, I know." At this point, insults washed over her. "Get ready for a ride on my broom."

Mik growled, but got out of bed. "You do realize that Clara is an innocent victim in all this mess."

"Say what?" Erin held the child tighter, wanting to cover her ears.

"You heard me. She's just an innocent kid caught up in everyone's drama. Yours, Jon's, the Caldwell's." She snickered. "Mine."

Erin tried to shake Mik's words that had too much truth to them. Her nerves were stretched so taut, she swore they were going to snap. Clenching her teeth together, she jutted her hand toward the door and said, "Get. Dressed."

A full five minutes later, with Clara now fully awake and as grouchy as her sister, Mik shuffled out of her room wearing yoga pants and a T-shirt that said, "I'm with stupid." At least it was better than that midriff-baring shirt and too-short shorts. Not by much, though.

Erin scooted both girls outside and to her car. Clara fought going into the car seat, begging for her art apron and art box. Erin checked the back and front seats and the trunk, but nothing. Maybe in the house? Belinda had brought Mik home yesterday, so hopefully she dropped off the apron and kit as well.

No such luck. With Clara outside with Mik, Erin scoured her little house, but they were nowhere to be found. How had Belinda brought home the child without either item? Didn't matter right now. Rather, she needed to find an alternative. Perhaps something of Corey's? She retrieved a box from the nursery closet, one that had Corey's old art supplies and found an adult-sized apron. This had better work.

She hurried back to the car, forced a smile, and showed the apron to Clara. "Look what I found! It was your daddy's. It protects even better!"

Clara's eyes widened as she reached for the apron. "I wuv Daddy."

Thank You, Jesus, for small favors. Erin helped Clara put it on, then buckled her into her seat. The entire time, Mik sat quiet as a stone. At least she wasn't talking back or using language Erin didn't allow.

Finally, Erin sat in the driver's seat and started the car. She'd told Belinda they'd be there in thirty minutes. Well, that had passed about five minutes ago, so she called her again and said it would be another thirty.

"Take your time, dear. I know what it's like dealing with strong-willed children."

Yeah, I suppose you would.

Erin stopped at a gas station and added just five gallons to her car. That would get her through the day. Tomorrow she'd fill the tank. Then she started the car and aimed for the highway.

"Lady, stop!" A muffled voice yelled as Erin turned on her blinker.

"Mom, someone's chasing you."

"What?" Erin checked her rearview mirror and saw a craggy-bearded man running toward her. She stopped and rolled down her window.

He huffed up to her and gestured sharply toward the tank. "You didn't pay for gas."

"Yes, I did. I paid at the pump." Her heartbeat suddenly raced faster than the gas had filled her tank.

"No, you didn't." He pulled a phone from his pocket. "Want to talk it out with the police?"

"No. I . . ." She looked back at the pump, and replayed her steps. She'd hit Pay Inside, as she usually did, but had been thinking *pay at the pump* to get on the road quicker. Oh, no, he was right. "I'm sorry, really. I had a brain toot and—"

Flinging words she forbade Mik from using, the man told her to get back to the store and pay before he called the cops.

"I'm coming. It was a mistake. Honest."

"That's what they all say." The man finally hustled back to the store.

And Erin backed up into a parking space.

"Good job, Mom. Now you're a thief. Way to set a good example."

"Just watch your sister." Clenching and unclenching her fists, and trying to ignore other gas station patrons staring at her, Erin got out of the car, locked it, and strode to the store. She paid with cash, then—keeping her head down—hurried back to the car, rubbing a sudden pain in her left shoulder. Her breath came out erratic.

Not now. She couldn't have a panic attack right now. She got in the car, locked the doors, then clasped her hands together and begged God to pull her together.

Call the Beldens . . .

Yeah, good idea. She took out her phone and, after a couple of fumbled attempts, dialed Joyce and asked her if they could watch Mik overnight. Mik even liked that idea, as opposed to living in a home occupied by a witch.

Now to drop off the kids and make it home before she went completely insane.

Like her mom had.

Fighting off the panic, she somehow managed to drop off both girls and then headed for home. She turned onto her street, barely remembering how she got there. She had to get into her home now, before she became a danger to other drivers.

Only ten houses down. Eight. Seven . . .

Was that someone on her front steps?

Jon.

She almost cried at the sight, both relieved and upset. Did he assume he could show up anytime? She pulled into her driveway, got out of the car, and marched toward him, still trying to suppress her body shakes. She started to wag a finger at him, but her hand trembled too much to be effective. Instead, she hugged herself.

"What are you doing here?" She said in the calmest voice she could summon, which wasn't calm in the least.

He splayed his hands. "You called, said you needed help."

Oh. She'd forgotten that, too.

"Hey." He leaped up and drew close to her, but didn't hug, though right now she really wanted one. "What's going on?"

She opened her mouth then slammed it shut. If she said anything, the dam she'd built up inside herself would burst and she might never stop crying. Instead, she brushed past him to the front door. She unlocked it, hurried inside, and contemplated closing it on him.

Yes, she'd wanted him earlier, but now she needed to be alone. She couldn't let him see her like this, so out of control.

And Mik's wise words, that Clara was an innocent victim in all their drama, filled her with shame that deepened the crack in her self-control.

She managed to stuff away the shakes, momentarily at least, and gestured to the door. "I'm good now." She stepped inside the house. "You can go."

But he pushed past her and closed the door behind him.

The shakes returned with a vengeance. "What part of 'you can go' don't you understand?"

"I'm not leaving you like this." Jon closed the space between them, took her arm, and led her to the sofa. She had no strength remaining to fight him. He kept a good two feet between them. "What happened, Pearl?"

She opened her mouth, and a sob hiccupped out. No. Not now. She couldn't break down in front of him.

"Hey." He inched closer to Erin. This time he touched her arm. "It's me. You can tell me anything."

She inched away and kept her arms tight against her chest. "I . . ." She clenched her teeth together, hoping to seal in her emotions, but the dam inside her burst open.

Words and tears flooded out of her. Reading Corey's journal. Clara's missing art kit. Mik's behavior. The gas station debacle.

Clara being an innocent.

He puffed out a breath with that confession and shook his head. "Mik is right. So right." He opened his arms. "Will you let me hold you? Please."

She hesitated, then fell into his open arms, and more tears flooded out. They were never going to stop, and someone would put her in a loony bin where she really belonged. She was more like her mom than she wanted to admit.

She closed her eyes, but tears still snuck out, soaking into Jon's shirt. Yet he held her. And it felt . . . it felt good. Relaxing. Caring. Loving. And sleep slowly overcame her.

A knock on her front door startled her. She blinked, adjusting to the sunlight streaming through her windows. Sunlight? When had she fallen asleep? And in Jon's arms?

Horrified, she pushed away, waking him as well, and hurried to the door. They couldn't be bringing home Clara now. She wasn't ready. Would never be ready.

She looked through the peephole and melted with relief as she opened the door. Seeing Debbie made her want to cry all over again. How was that even possible? Could women start menopause in their early thirties?

Debbie came inside and looked over Erin's shoulder. Some silent conversation happened between her and Jon that Erin couldn't comprehend.

Then Jon sidestepped them both, displaying his phone.

"Gotta take this call."

Right. Now she understood what Debbie had communicated with Jon. "Beat it."

"Come here." Debbie took Erin's arm and led her back to the sofa. "What's going on?"

The shakes from last night were gone, but Erin still barricaded herself with arms over her chest. "It started when I read Corey's journal."

Debbie's eyes grew wide. "His journal?"

Erin nodded. "Mik found it at his house, said her daddy didn't love her, then I had to read it for myself, see if that was true. And, honestly, I think the only person he loved was himself." Again, she recounted what she'd read in the journal and the mess from the night before, this time without out-of-control sobbing clouding her story. "I couldn't stop the tears last night. Now I'm as dry as a desert. There's nothing."

"You're feeling . . . normal."

"For me? Yes. I feel in control and like a fool for how I behaved last night. Jon must think I'm a nut case."

Debbie smiled. "I think he feels much differently about you."

"What does that mean?"

"You'll figure it out someday."

"I hate it when you talk in riddles."

Debbie laughed then turned serious. "About that journal. Where is it now?"

"What's left of it is probably in my room." She retrieved the book from her bedroom floor and returned, carrying it gingerly as if she were holding a poopy diaper. This was much worse. "Here. It's all yours."

"Do you want me to destroy it?"

"Absolutely. I mean, maybe." Erin shook her head, hating her indecision. "I mean, what if there's something good in it?

Something that his daughters should know? I don't want to take that from them, but I can't read it anymore either. All the anger I'd had toward him four years ago has returned with a vengeance, and I can't deal with that."

"I'll read it for you."

Erin jerked her gaze toward the door where Jon stood. All too often when she was super-focused on something, she became oblivious to what was going on around her. Thank God Mik hadn't inherited that trait.

"You will?" Erin held out the book, eager for someone to remove it and its evil from her house.

He crossed the room and took it from her.

She sighed as if a big weight had been lifted. "Thank you."

"If there's anything worth keeping, I'll let you know." He sat in the recliner across from the couch, set the journal on the lampstand, and leaned toward her. "I also have some important questions for you."

Uh-oh. She sat up and backed away. That hinted of lawyer-speak. This wasn't going to be good.

Chapter Twenty-Four

Erin ran her hands up and down her jeans, trying to calm her taut nerves. Every time she thought she was doing better, another problem cropped up like the weeds in her lawn. And when Jon transitioned into lawyer-mode, trouble always followed.

"Want me to leave?" Debbie sat on the edge of the couch.

"No." Jon held up a hand. "I'd prefer having you as a witness."

Yep. Lawyer-speak. She inhaled a breath while stuffing away worry and any other feeling that tried to sneak out. "What do you need to know?"

"I know that being a single mom is tough on you."

"No, it's a cake walk." She snorted. "I highly recommend it for everyone."

He smirked. "I'll always love your sarcastic wit, Pearl."

"Ha ha." She rolled her eyes. Maybe that was where Mik had learned to do it so well. "So, yeah, being a single mom stinks. And having to raise my ex-husband's love child on top of dealing with a hormonal teenager reeks like a manure pit."

"That's one way to put it." John leaned closer to her. "What if you had a man around more often? Someone who could take the pressure off you?"

"Well, sure, but I haven't seen any ads for guys volunteering to be a dad."

He shook his head. "Nothing's ever easy with you, is it?"

"You want me to be easy?"

Jon cursed and ran a hand over his mouth. "I'm sorry, Pearl, but you do tend to make me crazy."

"Well—"

Debbie's hand on her arm stopped her from saying something else foolish. "Jon, come out and say it." Debbie removed her hand. "The straightforward approach is always best."

"Okay then." His hands fidgeted in his lap, then his gaze bore into her eyes, giving her goosebumps. She couldn't figure out if they were the good kind or bad. "I'm talking about me, Pearl. Can I help you raise the girls?"

"What?" She shook her head. He was making no sense. Would he move in next door? Highly unlikely. And she couldn't afford to move near him. "How would you plan to do that?"

"Direct, Jon." Debbie again.

He sighed. "Okay. Pearl, if you marry me, I can be their full-time dad."

"Say what?" Had he just asked her to marry him? Now she was going deaf along with crazy.

He groaned, got up from his chair, and crossed the room. He knelt in front of her and held out his hand. "May I hold your hand?"

In a confused fog, she uncrossed her arms and laid her hand in his.

He gripped it loosely. "I know you probably haven't noticed, but I've had a crush on you since we were teens."

"What?" Jon had a crush on her?

"And I stepped aside when you chose Corey. I know you probably don't feel about me as I feel about you, but hopefully someday the feelings will follow." She started pulling away her hand, but he gripped it tighter. "I can be the father the girls need.

I can support you. Be your partner. And you'll always be able to trust me."

Now that made her angry. She tugged her hand from his. "Trust you? Really? Like when you disappeared for nearly four years when Corey left me? Oh, that's rich."

He settled on the floor in front of her and crossed one leg over the other. "Let me explain."

"Are you sure you want me here?" Debbie started to get up, and Erin gestured for her to stay.

"Please do explain." She recrossed her arms.

He ran both hands through his hair and looked toward the ceiling. "My mom left me when I was young, but not the way I've led you to believe."

Oh, sure, another dishonest man. Big surprise.

"When I was eight, she committed suicide. In the bathtub at home. I found her."

Erin gasped.

He sniffled and wiped an arm across his nose. "And she left a note just for me that said not to tell anyone. She preferred that she be known for running away with someone than having slit her wrists. What did I know other than to follow her instructions? It didn't occur to me that the medical personnel and the funeral home would know the truth. Dad moved us from Idaho to here, a place no one would know our story, so it was an easy lie to tell."

"I'm so sorry, Jon." This from Debbie, naturally.

Why couldn't Erin think to say something sympathetic? "I'm sorry, too." Mimicking her friend was better than remaining silent.

"So." His attention focused on Erin's wrist where the word Lulu was permanently inked. "When I found you in the bathroom after Corey gave you his news . . ."

Oh. Now it made sense.

His gaze flicked to Debbie and back to Erin. "Does she know?"

Erin covered her wrist with her other hand. "Everything." Back then, Debbie was the counselor Erin had been seeing following the incident.

He refocused on Erin. "When I broke into your bathroom and saw that razor in your hand, your wrist bleeding, all I saw was my mom. I couldn't do it anymore. I couldn't bear to lose someone I loved to suicide, so yeah, I disappeared, and I made it my goal to hound Corey until he repented and treated you like you deserve. I had no clue you wanted me around anymore. I was part of your broken past I thought you wanted to get rid of."

Erin closed her eyes, recalling the words she'd hurled at Jon when he interrupted her in the bathroom, saying something to the effect of completely erasing her past and memories of the 3 Sixlets. He hadn't run away, she'd chased him.

And he wasn't the only one who'd misled someone. Debbie knew the truth. Jon should know, too.

"The truth is, I never tried to commit suicide." She rubbed her tattooed wrist. "It's just what I led you to believe."

"You didn't?" How could it have been anything but? Jon had seen her on the floor in the bathroom, dark red blood oozing from her wrist, a razor in her hand. She'd hurled words at him he never knew were in her vocabulary as he pressed a towel to her wound while he called 911.

She crossed her arms, hiding her wrist beneath her armpit. "When he came to me that day in June, a month after I'd miscarried—"

"You were pregnant?" Something else he never knew. "He's

despicable." Made him want to wake Corey from the dead so he could blacken his left eye too. He'd punched the right one when Corey told him about Lilith and her pregnancy.

"Corey didn't know. Every time I planned to tell him, he was conveniently gone. It was as if he intentionally missed all our important dates, always having some lame excuse. Valentine's Day. Our anniversary. My birthday. Mother's Day. And after I miscarried, he missed Father's Day. Little did I know then, he was celebrating his fatherhood elsewhere. I even made a point of adding those dates to his phone so he wouldn't forget or make other plans. Lot of good that did me. It doesn't take a genius to know where he was. After a while, I gave up on trying to talk to him. He'd clearly given up, so why should I try? I figured if he ever touched me again, he'd figure it out. I was four months along when I miscarried. He should have noticed."

Oh, he had, but he'd blamed the weight gain on all the stress she was under, giving him one more reason for falling out of love with her and in love with the younger and svelte Lilith.

"And then he shows up here, says he wants a divorce. Said he'd fallen in love with someone else and that she was pregnant. So, yeah, I was upset."

Upset . . . So like Erin to understate things. Jon wanted to get up, hold her as she recounted her story, but held back knowing too well that wasn't what she wanted.

"Mik was at her grandparents', so I decided to gather up everything that was his in the house and throw it out. I started with the bathroom. I was tossing his razors when a thought passed through my head. Yeah, for a second, and only a second, I thought about ending it all, but I refused to do that to Mik. Then a different, more appealing idea took its place: cutting off his man parts."

John flinched and instinctively covered his crotch.

"No, I wouldn't have done it, but I felt an immense satisfaction thinking about it. And that's when you barged in, and I accidentally cut my wrist with the razor. When the EMTs came, I didn't discount your story because, in my screwed-up state of mind, I believed that attempted suicide was a lesser evil than castrating my soon-to-be ex-husband."

"And then she talked to me, professionally." Debbie rested her hand on Erin's arm, but Erin didn't flinch. "And told me the truth."

And here he'd gone and made things worse by abandoning her just as Corey had done, as the father she never met had done. No wonder she was skittish around men. Somehow, he had to change her perception.

But first he needed an answer to his earlier question, before he dropped the other bombshell.

He cleared his throat and got back up on both knees. "Can you forgive me? Please? Regardless of whether or not I knew the truth, regardless of what happened to my mom, I was wrong. I should have been here for you, and I promise that from this day forward, I will always be here."

Erin's face bore that stoic, far-off look he recognized as her processing look. It meant he shouldn't press. He should let her think. But man was it hard not to say a word. He sat back on his haunches, folded his hands together, and prayed silently like he'd done outside after taking the shocking phone call, and before he came inside and asked Erin the life-changing question. He'd felt so certain marriage was the direction God was leading him in, but now he had his doubts.

If she said "yes" to his proposal, he'd be shocked but ecstatic. If she said "no," he'd live with it and do as he promised, to never abandon her again.

"Okay." She finally broke her silence.

Okay? His head jerked up and he studied her emotion-free face. Okay what? That she forgave him? Agreed to marry him?

"I forgive you."

Whew. His tense muscles relaxed. "Thank you," he said, nearly crying at the weight she'd removed from his shoulders.

"But . . ."

Oh, he didn't like the sound of that. He knew what was coming, but made eye contact anyway.

"You're a dear friend, Jon, and I'm grateful for your presence and your help and I'll gladly let you be in Mik's life."

But not Clara's?

"I've already lived through a marriage where I wasn't loved. I can't do it again."

"But I—"

She held up a finger. "Tell me what this is really all about. I don't believe you came here last night planning to propose. Something happened with that phone call you took outside minutes ago that put your plan into motion. I may not be able to determine what your emotions are telling me, but I am capable of adding two plus two, and the math with you isn't adding up."

Of course, she'd seen through him. Jon got up and returned to the recliner. He took off his glasses and wiped his eyes, summoning the attorney side of him. "You're right." He dug his phone from his pocket and brought up a file that disgusted and angered him. "I heard from the Caldwells this morning. They've decided to fight you for custody."

Chapter Twenty-Five

"What?"

This was where Jon really hated his job. He had to deliver the facts, even if it hurt. "They're claiming you're mentally unstable and unfit to raise Clara."

A shadow crossed Erin's face, and her fists clenched. All her life, she'd struggled to distance herself from her mother's mental illness, and to have someone else accuse her had to be crushing. But she raised her chin, showing defiance to the charge. "I suppose my episode last night reinforced that."

He shook his head. "It didn't help."

"And my mom's history isn't a secret."

"Correct. Plus, they claim they have further evidence. What it is, I don't know yet."

"They wouldn't know about the suicide"—she made air quotes—"would they? Did Corey know?"

Jon looked down and nodded. He'd told Corey, hoping to get him to change his mind about leaving Erin, but it had further cemented his plan to leave. Corey had used similar words, mentally unbalanced, to insist that was why he'd fallen out of love. No doubt, words put into his brain by Lilith, the master manipulator.

Jon fidgeted with his phone as he waited for Erin to say more. She sat blankly while Debbie watched her friend out of the corner of her eye. More processing. More waiting. What was she thinking? He prayed she had more fight in her.

But then Erin lifted her chin, the defiant look again. Was she planning to fight for Clara?

"That's good then. Tell them I won't contest it. Clara will be in a home where she's loved—"

"No, she won't," Jon said more forcefully than intended and slapped the arm of the chair. "You don't understand." He stood and paced. "You don't know what I've found."

"Then enlighten me."

"I can't. Not yet." Because right now what he knew was intuition and not hard fact, but he had his assistant working on it. "Please, Erin, don't give in yet. Promise me you won't."

"So, I'm to keep Clara in my home, allowing her to become more attached to me and Mik so that a month, two months, a year down the road, whenever the legal system decides to get its act together, she's moved to a different home? When I said okay to being temporary guardian, I was told the system would do what's best for the child. Leaving her with me is not for the best."

"You don't . . ." He rubbed a hand over his mouth and looked at Erin. "Please, just think on it. Pray about it. Don't make a decision right now."

"Fine." She raised her hands. "I'll pray." She looked at Debbie. "We'll all pray, but I can't see a better solution."

"That's okay, because God sees from a different perspective." He grabbed Corey's journal off the side table. Maybe there was something in Corey's meanderings that would help Erin.

And if it would hurt her, no one else would ever have to see it.

"But for now, I'm going with you to pick up Clara. She's still in your custody, and I will make certain they surrender her to you."

"Fine. But I have one more question for you before we go."

"Shoot."

"What was up with the marriage proposal?"

Other than the fact that he loved her? Had loved her since their teen years. "I figured that you being married, having a two-parent household would look better to the court than you being single." That was true, but it felt dishonest in its incompleteness.

"Okay." She thought again, then nodded. "That makes perfectly good sense. Then what about this mystery woman everyone talks about?"

He couldn't believe she still didn't have a clue, so he crossed the floor and knelt in front of her again. "Pearl, that mystery woman is you. It's always been you. I love you Erin Belden, and *that*, more than anything, is why I asked you to marry me."

Feeling numb from the events earlier in the evening, and finally having time alone, Erin grabbed a spring jacket, her journal, a pen, and matches. She locked the doors to the house and brought the baby monitor to the backyard. She really needed to go for a walk, but wouldn't leave the girls alone in the house. Retreating to the backyard would have to suffice.

Seated on the three-person canopy swing facing her fireless firepit, she mentally reviewed the day's events:

Jon proposed. She still couldn't wrap her mind around that. Even more, she couldn't reconcile her immediate thoughts had been to tell him, "yes" and that her "no" didn't just disappoint him.

The Caldwells said they wanted custody of Clara. Fine. Then Clara would be loved as she should be. But . . .

Them using the "mentally unstable" claim was uncalled for. She was not her mother! If they would have just told her they wanted custody, she wouldn't have fought.

Jon had said he loved her, had always loved her, and that she was the mystery woman everyone pointed to for him. Or had she imagined those words? How could she not have realized that he loved her?

And what did she feel about him? He was a friend who'd messed up big time, but she'd forgiven him. She enjoyed having him around, missed him when he was gone. Even Mik seemed to enjoy their time together. Yeah, that was love, but not romantic love, right? Then why did she miss him now?

Pushing that . . . feeling aside, she continued mulling over the evening's events:

Picking up Clara at the Caldwells had gone better than she'd anticipated, especially since they'd employed the good cop, bad cop routine. Jon went in as the bad cop, and Erin told them she understood and explained her turmoil of last night was caused by learning something devastating. All true. They'd been kind in return. But Jon said they were being passive-aggressive. Had they been?

She honestly didn't know.

She rocked on the swing while gazing up at the stars and the sliver of a moon. Jon had said he loved her. Proposed to her. Those thoughts kept creeping in, even making her smile. She shook her head, trying to erase them from her thoughts, but they wouldn't stay gone.

Maybe the real question was, how did she feel about him? She'd be lying to herself if she denied feeling something different between them than before.

Before leaving this afternoon, Debbie had encouraged her to examine her feelings for Jon, beyond liking him as a friend. With his image at the front of her thoughts, she closed her eyes and searched deep. He was kind, intelligent, willing, no, eager to fight for her. And yes, he was good looking—he'd outgrown the geek stage and was very attractive.

But those were all facts. What did she feel?

She searched deep, an image of Jon at the forefront of her mind. She felt giddy. Scared. Excited. Confused. Was that normal? If only she could identify feelings like normal people did. Maybe she was mentally unstable. Maybe she was going to turn out just like her mom.

This was where Debbie would tell her to write, so Erin lit the tiki torches on either side of the swing and opened her journal. She poured out her heart in written prayer.

May 2, 2019

Dear Jesus, please help me!

The Caldwells claim I'm mentally unstable and unable to raise Clara properly. That hurts, Lord, big time. After all the years of fighting the stigma of growing up with a mom who suffered from mental illness and refused treatment, it's come full circle.

Debbie would tell me to examine that idea, and who better to unpack it with than you, so here goes:

- Like Mom, I'm a single parent who apparently chased off my child's father.
- I have difficulty feeling and identifying the feelings I do have.
- Mom was overly dramatic. We were exact opposites—neither are healthy.
- Mom believed literal demons chased her and the only safe place was the bathroom. Maybe that's where I go to hide

from my inner demons. Guess that's another thing we have in common.

BUT . . .

- Even as a single mom, I feel I've done a good job with Mik. I ~~never~~ rarely put down Corey and Lilith around her. Yeah, Mik is having an attitude right now, but she's thirteen, and her dad just died. I'd have an attitude, too. I guess I do.

- I seek help, where Mom refused it.

- And then Mom scared herself to death. After I moved away for college, I wasn't around her to try to keep her sane. Her heart just couldn't take the struggle anymore. Sure, there are times when I don't feel sane—like last night—but I have friends who I can turn to. More importantly, I can turn to you.

Big difference there.

So, yeah, I get it, God. I'm like Mom in some ways, but unlike her in others. And I don't have to be defined by who she was. In your eyes, I'm unique. If the Caldwells want to label me as mentally unstable, I'll fight that. Besides, just because someone is mentally ill, that does not mean they're a poor parent.

Do you want me to fight for Clara? Would she be better off with me than the Caldwells? They love her. I think. And I don't know how I can possibly love her. Clara deserves to be loved. As Mik said, Clara is an innocent victim in this mess, but I don't know how to remedy that. Do you?

On another topic, what do I do about Jon? Do you want me to take his proposal seriously? I don't need to be rescued, but the idea of having someone to come home to at night, of having a man around to help shoulder the joys and burdens of parenting is more than appealing. I care for him, he does make me happy, and he says he loves me. But would he get bored with me as Corey did? Is it possible for me to love him back as he deserves to be loved? Will I know it if I do? My feelings are all over the place, and I can't package them into a sane box.

I don't have answers to any of these questions, Lord, so I'm going to need your help once again.

Thanks for listening!

―――――――――

"You did what?" Jon's assistant stared across the office, disbelief widening her eyes.

He shrugged. "I asked her to marry me."

"And what made you think that was a good idea?" Gina stepped inside the office and closed the door.

Another shrug. "I thought that's what God wanted me to do."

"Oh, really?" She stood on the other side of his desk, glowering down at him. "Or is that just your excuse? And don't shrug those shoulders again."

"I also thought it would help with the custody battle, if there is one. Having a two-parent household would work on her behalf."

"How noble of you."

"Well, she said 'no,' so it doesn't matter anyway." Jon shuffled papers on his desk to make it appear as if he were attempting to work. "For now, our goal is to get some facts to support our theory that the Caldwells are after Corey and Lilith's assets. They both warned me not to trust her parents, but Belinda and Charles have charmed their way into Erin's life. When I saw them on Easter, they were too interested in the value of Corey's artwork.

Why?"

"Greed?"

"Could be, but my gut says it's more than that."

"Aren't you the trustee? Can't you control what they get?"

"Yes, and Corey and Lilith set aside funds for the guardians, but not in the amount the Caldwells are used to living on." He drummed his fingers on his desk. "Contact Chuck Blue, have him do some nosing around."

Gina perched her hands on her hips. "And just who is going to pay for the private investigator?"

"Guess that'll have to be me."

"Then you make sure you don't go broke handling this case. I like to get paid, you know. I might even like to make a trip overseas, meet up with Zax."

"What?" It was Jon's turn to glare his disbelief. "You do realize, the man's a player."

"I thought he was your friend."

"He is, but I'm also not blind to his faults. Just be careful, okay."

"Yeah, yeah, yeah." She waved her hand. "I'll give Chuck a call, have him check out the Caldwells, then I'm off for the weekend. You should take off soon, too."

"Don't worry." He had a date with a book back home. If the PI couldn't find what the Caldwells' motivation was, maybe Corey's journal would reveal something.

Jon finished up the brief he was working on and left the office just as the sun was touching the horizon. Far later than he intended to leave, but he'd had difficulty focusing.

Before Erin had been thrust back into his life, focusing had not been an issue in the past.

Twenty-five minutes later, he was navigating his gravel driveway twisting its way through a forest of white cedars and pines to his lakefront A-frame home. Compared to the other homes on the lake, it wasn't much, but it had four bedrooms and a two-car garage, plenty of room to share with a family and the right someone.

"What am I going to do about her?" He really had messed up with Erin, proposing as he had. Why did his brain take a vacation around her?

He parked in the garage, went through his house, and onto the back deck overlooking the lake. Stress rolled off his shoulders and peace enveloped him as it always did on the deck, one of the reasons he'd chosen this home. In his demanding job, he needed a place to come home to and recharge.

But today, he didn't have time to recharge, he needed to dig into Corey's journal, as ugly as he knew it would be. If he were a drinking man, he'd add beer to his evening. It would make digesting Corey's thoughts a lot easier, but thanks to his father, he'd seen firsthand—actually, it was usually his dad's left hand—what alcohol did to people, and he wanted no part of it.

Instead, he went into the house and made himself a peanut butter and apple sandwich, added a handful of chips to the plate, and poured himself a glass of milk. He brought it out to the deck where he opened Corey's journal to what had likely been the midway point, before Erin had yanked out pages. Now it was the beginning. Jon knew Corey's story, and a fresh start was imminent, but he still had to slog through a bunch of mud. That was the part Jon wasn't eager to read, but knew he had to.

June 25, 2015

I'm going to be a father again!

It's taken a bit to digest that. When Lil broke the news on

Father's Day—when I once again forgot about Erin's plans and felt like the worst creep on earth—I was shocked. Angry. Scared to death. In just a few words, Lil turned my life upside down and inside out. I wondered, "What do I do now?"

I've wanted another child for years—it just didn't happen with me and Erin, but now with Lil . . .

After processing the information, almost in an Erin-like way, I could only take it as I'm meant to have a new life. On Monday I made the decision Lil has been urging me to make for three months, and today I put it in action. I told my parents I was quitting at the accounting firm—Lil made enough to support us, so I could paint—and snuck out of the office without Erin seeing me. I went to the house I shared with Erin for six years to pack what I needed to move in with Lil.

All I got in my suitcase was my underwear before I heard the side door open. I swore I was going to have a heart attack as I tried to figure out what to tell Erin. I left the suitcase in the bedroom, and hurried to the living room. She just looked at me with that stupid blank stare. I used to love trying to crack it, but now it makes me angry. Why can't she react like a normal person?

All she said was, "You quit."

How else was I supposed to respond, but with the truth? "I did."

"Why?"

I told her I'd fallen in love with Lil, that we were pregnant. I was filing for divorce and moving in with Lil. Her reaction? You guessed it, no comment, just that blank stare. I thought she'd care, at least a little bit.

So, I went back to packing. That's when Erin came in, and I saw a side of her I'm glad I'm escaping. She's more like her crazy mom was every day. Makes me wonder if Mik is safe with her anymore. She came in with a set of plates we'd purchased together when we got married. Just two ceramic dinner plates. That's all we could afford at the time. But they were unique and colorful with a sunrise painted on one and a sunset on the other. We'd purchased them together and used them for every meal.

They were special.

She held one like a frisbee, and I thought for sure she was going to throw it at me, but she just said in a super creepy calm voice, "How dare you!" She threw the plate at the wall and it hit our wedding photo. Both plate and portrait crashed to the floor. Then she threw the second plate and told me—I've never seen her eyes so black!—she told me to get the bleep out. I never heard her swear before either.

I'm no dummy, so I left. I called Jon, said I was coming over to his office. I gave him the scoop, and he tried talking me into counseling. What was left to talk about? Lil was pregnant with my child, I had to be there for her. Besides I love her so much it hurts. I didn't choose to fall out of love with Erin. I didn't choose to fall for Lil. It just happened. And I need to be happy. I'll be a much better man then. A better father to both Mik and the new baby. In the end, we'll all be better off.

Even after I explained, Jon drove his fist into my eye. I thought he was my friend.

Chapter Twenty-Six

Friend? The *plates* were special? Jon balled his fists, remembering that afternoon, and resisted the urge to punch something again. He wasn't a violent man, in spite of what his dad had taught him. That punch to Corey's face had been the only one he'd ever landed on a human being. Usually, he took his aggressions out on the racquetball court. He should go there now.

But instead, he kept reading, for Clara and Erin's sake, and mentally created bullet points:

- Corey talked about how Lilith convinced him that shared custody of Mik involved seeing her one weekend a month. Jon couldn't talk sense into him. That was perfectly fine with Erin. The amount of support he gave Erin and Mik was dismal because he no longer had a job, yet Corey complained about having to provide any at all since Erin was working.

- Corey wrote about the divorce, how he finally felt free. Then the wedding, a small justice-of-the-peace ceremony where only a handful of Lilith's co-workers were present. Corey was upset that his parents and best friend didn't have the decency to show up and celebrate with him.

Celebrate? No way. He and the Beldens were in mourning.

Jon laughed at the part where the "happy" couple opened a gift from Erin: the shattered pieces of the plates she'd thrown when Corey broke his news. Oh, he loved that attitude!

Then there was way too much detail on the honeymoon that Jon just skipped over.

If he didn't know that these were the dark days of Corey's soul, and that God's light was soon going to break through that darkness, he might have stopped reading. Peeking into his friend's messed-up thoughts was too heartbreaking. Loving him during those years had been tough enough, but the Holy Spirit had prompted Jon to stay at Corey's side then, as He was today.

Jon slogged through a few more entries about how amazing Corey's new life was, how excited he was to become a father again, before the first sign of reality hit, on Christmas day. Corey missed Mik.

———

Christmas Day, 2015

I've always loved Christmas day. Especially since becoming a dad. Watching the sparkle in Mik's eyes when she opened her presents. Getting her hugs. How she looked up to me . . .

That didn't happen today because Mik was with Erin and my folks. I'm their son, and yet I wasn't welcome. Yeah, I get it. They're mad at me. I'm now their prodigal son. But didn't the father welcome that son home?

Worst of all was missing Mik open her presents today. No hugs. No Daddy-is-the-best. Instead she now looks at me like I'm the enemy. I'm not. I love her. Just because her mom and I didn't stay together doesn't mean I wanted a divorce from the entire family.

I'll bet Erin's poisoning our daughter against me.

Why did I allow her to get custody all but one weekend per month?

I'm such an idiot.

———————

Jon slapped shut the book.

Yeah, Corey, you were an idiot, all right. You didn't even remember that Lilith was the one who insisted on one weekend per month when Erin felt it should be more, and that Mik spent Christmas with Erin and Easter with him.

That was all he could take for the night. He wanted to get to the good part, where Corey came to Jon and said, "I messed up big time. Can you help me?" but that was pages away yet, and Jon needed some encouragement to end the evening with, so he found Psalm 121 on his Bible app and read it on repeat, praying it over Erin, Mik, and Clara. And himself.

Erin pulled back her bedroom curtains and moaned. It wasn't supposed to rain today. She checked her weather app and rain was forecast all day long. Just yesterday, the same forecaster had predicted sunny and warm. She'd promised Clara a trip to the nearby park, the one she and Mik used to spend hours at. Tomorrow would have to suffice, but what would they do today?

Ideas skittered through her mind as she made a simple breakfast of scrambled eggs and fruit. Go shopping? With a three-year-old? No way. Children's museum? Couldn't afford it.

She stirred the eggs while googling ideas. They either cost money or they were outdoors. Which meant, they'd be staying home, but doing what?

Beyond the kitchen window, the garage caught her eye. Painting was a definite option. Clara would love it, even if Erin didn't.

"I hungwy." Clara walked into the kitchen, a blanket over one arm, the other both holding her pet crocodile, while sucking her thumb. The child version of multi-tasking.

"Climb on up, Lolli." Erin pulled out the step stool ladder that also served as a highchair. Clara appreciated the independence the stool brought her. She also pulled the bib over her head all by herself. "Scrambled eggs?"

"My favowite!" Clara clapped her hands together, her reaction to most any food Erin made, so unlike Mik who'd been picky from the day she was born.

Erin spooned eggs onto a sectioned child plate with *The Little Mermaid* cartoon figures on it. As a toddler, Erin had used the plate, then Mik, and now Clara. She cut grapes into quarters and a banana into slices and added both to other sections. Personally, Erin wouldn't mind eating off a sectioned plate even now. She hated it when food touched.

Clara had seconds of each food, *mmming* her way through the simple meal. Dramatic even in this, just like her father. He'd always vocalized his appreciation for a good meal, even when things started going downhill. That hadn't been enough to convince him to stay, but she'd tried.

Why couldn't she look at Clara for once and not see Corey?

Which was exactly why this darling child needed to be cared for by someone else.

"We go to park now?" Clara showed her empty plate to Erin.

Erin pointed to the window that showed rivulets of water streaming down. "I'm sorry, Lolli, but the park is all wet today."

The child's lip poked out. "I wike the wain."

"I do too, sweetie, but being in the rain too much can make us both sneeze. Ahh-choo!"

Clara giggled and mimicked Erin's fake sneeze.

"Exactly." She mussed the child's already-unruly hair. "But, what would you say to doing some painting in your art studio?"

"Wike Daddy?"

Erin forced a smile. "Just like Daddy."

"You paint, too?" Clara tugged the bib over her head, threw it onto the table, then climbed down the stool. "Go now!" She toddled toward the side door.

"Hold on, little one. Aren't you forgetting something?"

Clara's eyes and mouth pinched together as she turned around, then they brightened. "Oopsie!" She hurried back to the table, grabbed her plate, and put it in the dishwasher Erin had opened for her. Good thing the plate was empty, or a mess would have covered the floor, too. Would have been worth it for the teaching moment.

"Good girl." Erin clapped her hands. "Now find your umbrella, and we'll go paint some pictures.

"Okay!" Everything Clara said ended with an exclamation point, it seemed. The child ran to the closet by the front door and took her little umbrella from a vase on the floor. She popped it open by herself. "I ready."

Erin chose an adult-sized umbrella. "Then let's go."

Moments later they were skipping across the crumbling, puddle-covered sidewalk toward the garage, though Clara's umbrella became more of a rain catcher than a tool that kept out the rain. Well, she did say she liked the rain.

After opening up the car entrance so they could hear and see the rain, Erin set up a child-sized easel for Clara, a gift from the Caldwells. She uncurled an old poster of Corey's on a table for herself. She flipped it over to paint the all-white side and set stones on the edges to keep it flat. She wasn't an artist by any means, but maybe Clara would focus longer if Erin also painted. After putting on an apron, she sat and dipped a brush into blue paint.

"I help you?"

Okay, that focus lasted a short minute.

"Sure, why not?" Erin pushed back her chair and Clara climbed onto her lap.

And knocked over the jar of blue paint that puddled over the poster.

"Uh-oh!" Clara pressed both hands to her cheeks, and then those hands were playing in the spill. Her fingers drew squiggles across the paper.

Erin laughed. She couldn't help herself. This child could find joy in anything.

"Red, too?" Clara pointed at the red tube of paint.

"Of course, we need red." Erin poured a red streak across the poster.

Clara blew on the streak, creating a rather fun effect, so Erin joined in the blowing.

"Lellow now."

Erin squeezed dots of yellow on random parts of the poster, eager to see what Clara would come up with.

But the child climbed off Erin's lap.

"Done already?" Couldn't be. They still had far too many hours in the day for Erin to keep her occupied.

Clara hurried back to her easel.

Oh, she wants to work on her own. No problem. Erin turned back to the poster and chose a wide brush to whoosh the yellow across the paper.

"Auntie Erin, up please."

A paint-covered hand grabbed Erin's arm. The other hand

held a sponge. Interesting.

Erin lifted Clara onto her lap again.

The child pressed the sponge into the yellow paint then transferred it across the paper. Even though there was no pattern or obvious picture created, Clara's artwork really was beautiful. It made Erin feel . . . She closed her eyes and examined that feeling.

Joy.

Yes, it made her feel joyful and made her want to sing. So, she did. No surprise, Clara sang along, and when she didn't know the words, she made up her own.

The two continued painting, both the poster and the sheet on the easel until Erin's stomach growled. What time was it, anyway? Sitting once again with Clara on her lap, she glanced over her shoulder at the old plastic clock on the wall. They'd been out there for three hours already? Clara would certainly take a good nap after they cleaned up.

"Hey Lolli." She kissed Clara's cheek. "I think our paintings are done. We should sign them, don't you think?"

"Wike Daddy?"

"Yep. Like your daddy."

Instead of reaching for a paintbrush, Clara splayed her chubby fingers over a glob of paint that had landed on the table, then pressed that hand to the painting.

Erin looked for an adult-sized glob to do the same. Finding none, she poured a puddle onto the table and then pressed the side of her hand into it and then onto the painting.

Nice.

"I wike it!" Clara clapped.

"I do too, Lolli. It's beautiful. They're both beautiful. I think we need to get some frames and hang them in my living room. What do you think?"

"Uh-huh. Then I be just like Daddy!"

Erin kissed the cherub's cheek. The repeated references to Corey weren't as shocking as they had been earlier in the day. Actually, they were even giving Erin a newfound appreciation for her ex. Yes, he'd screwed up badly with her and Mik, but it was obvious he'd loved his daughter. She certainly adored him. If they could keep his spirit alive through painting, then Erin was all for it.

"Time to clean up." She set Clara on the ground and together they gathered up the brushes and capped the paints. They'd leave the artwork out here for now until it dried. With the rain still coming down, drying might take a while.

Erin removed her apron and took Clara's to hang them up, and heard a squeal. She spun around and laughed. The child was doing circles on the driveway, in the rain, her mouth open to the skies, catching raindrops.

Erin opened her umbrella and started to raise it over her head, but stopped.

Loosen up, Erin. Go have fun.

She stared at the umbrella and at the torrents of rain and at Clara dancing as if she hadn't recently lost both parents. If she could dance in the rain, so could Erin. She tossed aside the umbrella and ran outside. She took both of Clara's hands and they danced in a circle.

Clara giggled, and Erin laughed so hard she was certain tears came from her eyes.

"What are you doing?" Mik's yell came from the house, sounding way too motherly. She stood beneath the entryway, the door wide open.

"Dancing." Clara did a jig in a puddle, splashing mud up to her waist.

"I've got to catch this." Mik whipped out her phone and aimed it toward Erin and Clara.

Erin just stuck out her tongue and laughed some more.

"You're crazy!"

Probably. "Join us." Erin yelled back and motioned with one arm as the other wiped away the hair that had plastered itself to her face.

"You're not serious."

"Completely." Erin stomped her foot into a puddle while observing her daughter.

Mik stood there, unmoving.

Erin knew that look. Her daughter was processing.

Then Mik shook her head and hopped onto the steps with bare feet. She ran across the small patch of yard to the driveway, her smile growing as she neared. And then the three of them clasped hands and made a circle in the rain.

Laughing. Dancing. Splashing.

This was joy.

A car stopped at the end of the driveaway, and the three halted their dance.

Jon.

Oh boy, now he was going to agree with the Caldwells that she was unbalanced. But if laughing and dancing in the rain meant she was unstable, then she'd gladly own the label.

His passenger window rolled down, and he yelled through it. "What are you doing?"

"Having fun." Mik called back.

He shook his head. "You're all nuts."

"Yes, we are." Erin bowed. "Join us?"

"No. Way." He rolled the window back up.

Party pooper. She stuck out her tongue at him, and her stomach growled again. Well, maybe it was time to end the party. They'd all have a bite to eat and then take a nap. She grabbed

Clara's hands and swung her around, eventually landing on Erin's sopping wet hip.

She hugged the child and a whispered, "I love you, Clara," flew from her lips.

Clara circled her arms around Erin's neck. "I wuv you, too, Auntie."

Erin blinked. Wait. What? She shook her head, recalling the words that had somehow escaped her mouth. *I love you, Clara.*

She examined her thoughts—her feelings—and realized it was true. Somehow, someway this cherub of a child had broken through Erin's heart blockade. Yes, she did love Clara.

But then she focused on Jon and his grim face as he sat in the car. Had he already begun the process of changing over custody?

That couldn't happen.

Keeping Clara in her arms, she ran around to the driver's side of Jon's car. He rolled down the window and winced as rain sliced toward him.

She held Clara tightly and leaned down. "I need you to stop the guardian proceedings. Clara needs to stay with us."

The grim look on Jon's face told her that wasn't going to be an easy task.

$$Chapter\ Twenty\text{-}Seven$$

Jon still couldn't believe the words he'd heard come from Erin's mouth. After all this time of trying to convince her Clara belonged with her, a painting party and a rainstorm had done the best persuading. He still marveled at the sight he'd driven up to, with Erin and the girls dancing in the rain like they didn't have a care.

He'd never seen anything more beautiful.

But now he had to deliver bad news. Even worse now that Erin had changed her mind. "Have you got a few minutes?" he asked through the downpour.

She must have sensed the gravity of his arrival, as the joy slid from her face and she nodded, making him feel like a heel for adding a storm cloud to her declaration.

"I'll put on some hot cocoa." Clinging to Clara, she strode up to the house.

He followed her to the house, removed his wet shoes and jacket, and joined her in the kitchen.

"More news from the Caldwells?" Emotion was absent from her voice as she took a couple of coffee cups out of the cupboard.

"Can we talk somewhere private?" He didn't want either Mik or Clara to hear this.

"Sure, how about we got outside? A little rain never hurt anyone."

He just shook his head. Responding to her sarcasm would only fuel her on.

"Or, we can go to my private office." She snapped her fingers. "Oh, that's right, it's now a nursery."

Okay, his request was impractical. "Your bedroom?"

She said nothing as he filled a cup with milk and placed it in the microwave. She turned and reclined against the cupboard, her arms crossed in front as she looked him in the eye. Direct eye contact didn't happen much with her, so he knew she had wisdom to impart, and not sarcasm.

"I don't bring men into my bedroom and close the door. No exceptions. I don't want Mik to see me do something I tell her she's not allowed to do. She's already witnessed enough ambiguity from her parents, I will not add to it."

Of course, she made perfect sense, and he wouldn't ask her to bend the rules. He squeezed the tightening muscles in his neck. "Yeah, I get that." He splayed his hands. "I'm open to suggestions."

She looked at the linoleum floor Corey had promised to replace for her long ago. "I'm sorry I'm being a brat. I appreciate you thinking about the girls." She peeked around the corner into the living room where Clara and Mik sat on the floor coloring on blank pages. "How about this: I treat everyone to pizza, give Clara a bath, put her to bed, and then we talk? Mik'll spend the evening in her room."

"Good plan, as long as I get the pizza."

"Deal." She actually stuck out her hand to shake on it, like they used to in their teens. It seemed to impersonal, too businesslike for what he wanted from their relationship, but he still took her hand. And held it a little longer than she probably wanted, but he didn't care. He needed her to realize that working with her was far more than a business deal.

Her hand pulled from his too quickly.

And not so quickly, they had their pizza. Clara took her bath and went to bed without fussing. She already seemed acclimated to her new home. Mik hid in her bedroom, likely with earbuds blocking any outside noise. That was as private as they were going to get.

Erin aimed for the recliner, her way of telling him she needed space.

But he gestured toward the couch. "Please?"

She breathed in and her shoulders heaved with her breath. "Fine." She sat against one end and held a pillow close to her chest.

Okay, he could take the hint, so he sat against the other end. For now.

"What's the bad news?"

No pussyfooting around, of course.

He dug his phone from his pocket and brought up an informal document. The Caldwells hadn't officially filed for custody yet, which suggested they were bluffing, but that wasn't a certainty. It also could be that they wanted to avoid a battle as much as Erin did. Custody battles never turned out well for anyone, especially for the child who is yanked between two or more parties.

"Here's what the Caldwells are basing their suit on: your meltdown the other night."

"No surprise."

True.

"Your panic attack when they turned the garage into an art studio."

She blew out a puff of breath. "I'd forgotten about that. It compounds things, doesn't it."

"It doesn't help. And then there's your mom's mental illness."

"Does not mean it's genetic. And besides, if I did have mental illness, that does not mean I couldn't raise a child."

"Yes, I know that. It's just one more thing they're using to pile on."

She nodded, her jaw tightening. "What else?"

"Your attempted suicide."

"Which Debbie, my counselor at the time, will verify that it wasn't an attempted suicide."

That was one point for them. Maybe. He added the one item he'd mentioned the other night. "Being a single parent doesn't help either."

"Marrying you isn't a solution. I won't do that to us."

He sighed, wanting to reach across the sofa and take her hand, but he sensed she'd flinch at the touch and would only create more distance between the two of them.

She tightened her grip on the pillow, communicating more to him that what she realized. "Besides marriage, what solutions do you have?"

"We're researching that."

"Hmm."

"Yeah. Hmm."

"Do they have a chance? Do you think they'll win?"

"I'm good, Erin. We'll give them a tough fight."

"That doesn't answer my question."

He knew that all too well. "I'm sorry. That's the best I can do."

After a few additional minutes of small talk, Jon excused himself. It was time to go home and do some more reading. Corey had to leave some clues as to what his in-laws would be up to. Without that, Jon feared the Caldwells' money would overpower him. He was good, but even in the legal system, money spoke volumes.

Erin slowly opened the door to Clara's nursery and peeked in. The child slept soundly, comfortably, and already seemed adjusted to her new life. Still, Erin knew to be watchful for those times when Clara's losses hit her. Erin hoped she was up for the challenge. Even if she wasn't, God was.

She closed the door, went to her room, and stared at the queen-sized bed in which she'd become accustomed to sleeping by herself, and loneliness swept over her. Just because she was an introvert who didn't intuitively understand social cues didn't mean that she wanted to spend life as a single parent. Jon had promised to fill in the gap she didn't know was there.

Should she let him?

Grrr. She plopped down on her bed, clenching her jaw, holding in a scream. One minute she was eager to relinquish rights to Clara, the next she was needing to fight to keep her. One minute she thought Jon was nuts for proposing, the next she wished she'd said yes.

She took out her prayer journal and wrote only a handful of lines:

———————

Thank you, Lord, for helping me see that I do love Clara. Please guide Jon to information that will allow me to keep her.

And please grant me wisdom for what I should do about Jon, and give me clarity regarding my feelings for him.

———————

Jon hung up the phone after speaking with the private investigator. So far Chuck Blue had learned nothing, but he'd just begun his research. He promised to keep at it. Jon had to face the reality that maybe the Caldwells didn't have an evil plan. Maybe they did have Clara's best interests in mind.

His gut told him that wasn't true, but his gut wasn't always right. A little research would hopefully make the truth clear, and right now his best hope was in Corey's journal. He settled on his deck again, journal in hand. Tonight, he wouldn't go to sleep without finishing it. Erin and Clara deserved answers. Now.

He skimmed through the passages, mentally highlighting key moments.

- Corey spent most of his time painting while Lilith remained at the art gallery. With her influence, the gallery even promised to showcase a few completed projects.
- The luster was fading, though, on his new relationship. Lilith had become naggy and constantly complained about being pregnant. Corey couldn't wait to become a dad again.
- Clara arrived in January and he immediately fell in love with the towheaded cherub. Lilith couldn't wait to return to work, which was fine with Corey. The air was too tense with her around.
- After Clara was born, Lilith couldn't wait to get back to work, but Corey was okay with that. He loved to paint with her in her carrier. Jon had watched them in action— it was adorable. Corey would do anything for her. In caring for Clara, he finally started to see how selfish he'd been, and focused on "I." With Clara, he was learning to put others first.
- Ironically, Erin volunteered to babysit Clara, said she wanted Mik to get to know her sister better. No surprise,

Erin put aside her own comfort for Mik and Clara's sake. Quite the contrast from her ex-husband.

- His first hidden object painting sold, and for a price that shocked him. The gallery asked for more, and suddenly Lilith reverted to the woman he fell in love with. But he was naturally cynical about her attitude change.

- Especially when the nagging returned, this time for focusing too much on their daughter. She was also jealous of his weekends with Mik. Corey argued that he gave up everything for her. Everything: Erin, Mik, his morality, and his faith. He was through with compromising.

Jon set down the book for a breather. His friend had been an emotional wreck, and reading his intimate, often selfish, thoughts was exhausting. But at least Corey was now realizing what he'd given up.

Jon got up, stretched, made himself a peanut butter and apple sandwich then returned to the book.

March 11, 2017

I'm a complete idiot.

For months I've been missing important dates with Mik, events I swore I recorded in my phone. How do you explain to your eleven-year-old daughter that your calendar app is broken? Erin would have said something wise like, "Then write it down on a wall calendar."

I should have.

Turns out the only thing that was broken was me, and I'm a

complete mess.

I took Lil out tonight for her birthday. A pretty ritzy place at that. Funny thing is, I can afford it now. Two more paintings sold today for prices I never could have imagined. I really need to up my support for Mik, but every time I mention it, I get in an argument with Lil.

Everything ends in an argument with her. Especially tonight. This time, I don't know if I can forgive her.

I went to the restroom and when I returned, I saw her with my phone, watched her from behind as she went through my calendar and deleted scheduled times with Mik. I don't think I've ever been so mad or felt so sick.

How long has she been doing this? Since I was still married to Erin? The thought made me sicker, and I knew I had to learn the truth.

I didn't confront her until after we'd arrived home and made certain Clara was asleep. She denied it at first, then offered some lame excuse, but I wouldn't—couldn't—let her get away with it and kept hounding her. Finally, she admitted it, said she loved me at first sight, and this was part of her plan to get me to leave Erin and Mik.

The art studio was all part of the plan, too. Seducing me. Getting pregnant. She'd manipulated my every step, and I was too self-absorbed to see it. It's one thing to ruin my life, but Erin's and Mik's too? How could I have not seen it?

Dear God, what have I done?

March 13, 2017

I thought Jon would help me.

I'd spent forty-eight hours in my art studio, painting, sleeping, sometimes hurtling paint at the canvas before dropping Clara off at the folks' office and barging in on Jon. Like the friend he's always been, he excused himself and got me settled in a small conference room where we could talk in private. I told him what Lilith had done, and then asked him to help me with the divorce. Asked him to help me win Erin back.

He almost laughed me out of the office, and said, "And mess up more lives?"

I said something stupid about him wanting Erin for himself, which he logically said he could have stepped in any time to do that.

Yeah. I'm an idiot.

Then he told me to stop running from my problems and go back home. To Lilith. Fix my marriage. See a counselor. Be a good father to both Clara and Mik. Apologize to Erin. Maybe start with an apology to Lilith.

But most importantly, have a long overdue talk with God. He spread his fingers over the Bible that always sat on the corner of his desk and said, "I have it on good authority that God welcomes the prodigal home with open arms."

I have my doubts. I don't think this mess I've created can be fixed.

———————

April 15, 2017

I did what Jon said.

I went home, apologized to Lilith for not being the kind of man she deserved, for using her. Didn't faze her. All she cares about is how much money I'm making. I'm trying, though, honestly, I am. Since our relationship started with selfishness, I have to turn it around, so every morning I ask her what I can do for her. Her response is usually something dull, like clean the bathroom. But I do it, just as much for her as for me. Cleaning up crap fits my life right now.

And I'm learning, really learning that God is the best cleaner.

Yeah, I knew that growing up. It's what I learned from Mom and Pop. From my church. But I never took it to heart. Guess we have to experience brokenness before God makes us whole.

Also, as Jon recommended, I've been reading my Bible every day. To Clara as I put her to sleep. I want her to hear God's words, too, and hold them in her heart. I go on walks and have long talks with God. I'm seeing him again, hearing him again. Feeling him again. What the Bible says about the father welcoming his prodigal son home is true. He's welcomed me back with open arms.

I'm even finding more joy in my art, which is hard to believe. Clara loves to paint on her little easel right beside me. I love her so much it hurts. Mik, too, but I created a chasm between us that she doesn't want me to bridge. I will, though. I won't ever stop trying. I haven't missed a single event since I learned what Lilith did. I haven't forgotten a weekend. I always, always tell her I love her.

My paintings were popular before, but now they're in demand. But there's one project I won't rush. It has to be done right. And I'll never sell it. I don't know if it will be my masterpiece, but I do know when I put brush to canvas, I feel my heart bleeding along with it.

Brenda S. Anderson

———————

September 14, 2017

For our second anniversary, I treated Lilith to a trip to Minneapolis and their art institute, hoping to rekindle the spark we both felt when looking at art.

It wasn't there. To say we'd fallen out of love wasn't true. Love had never been part of our relationship, and selfishness and lust don't hold people together. I feel like I'm caught in that old '70s song, "I Don't Know How to Love Him." But I'm not giving up. Jon won't let me. God certainly won't let me.

So, I pray every day for Lilith, for our relationship, for Clara and Mik, and even for Erin that God will soften her heart to accept my apology.

I haven't apologized. Yet. I'm working on it through my painting. I know that probably sounds weird, but that's what I'm feeling led to do. When it's complete, I'll know that Erin is ready to listen.

———————

Christmas Day, 2017

When I asked Lilith what I could do for her this morning, she responded with, "Today, I need to ask what I can do for you."

Yeah. I wanted to cry. I didn't though. I just asked if I could read about Jesus' birth from the Bible. She said she wanted to hear it.

I couldn't have asked for a better Christmas present.

———————

April 1, 2018
Easter Sunday!

I wonder if the first April Fool's Day was the day the guards found Jesus' tomb empty. I'm certain they were hoping it was a joke. Today, we know it's not. Today, I know with my entire being that Jesus arose from the tomb, leaving all our sins behind Him. My selfishness. My affair. My dishonesty. All of it. He's forgiven me. Hallelujah! I don't think I've ever sung that word before with such feeling. Now I know in my heart what that word means.

Because, guess what . . .

Lilith gave her life to God today. Hallelujah! No, not during church or an altar call or anything, but at Mom and Pop's place, right in the middle of our meal, she said she believed.

Yeah, there was a lot of rejoicing at that table!

When we arrived home for the day, I asked if I could work on my "Forgiveness" piece. That's what I'm calling Erin's apology painting now. Can you think of a better day to paint what forgiveness looks like to you?

I made a lot of progress, but it isn't right yet. Hopefully, soon.

———————

September 2018

Three years married to Lilith, and our marriage has come full circle, from one of selfishness to one of selflessness and love. I can honestly say I love her now. Amazing, the work God can do in hearts!

We renewed our vows, this time Mom and Pop, Jon, and Mik were in attendance. This time everyone was happy for us. This time, God was the One binding us together.

January 5, 2019

Lilith told me something concerning today . . .

Jon read the rest of the passage and slapped the book closed. Finally, here was the proof he'd been searching for. Though it was well past midnight, he couldn't sleep now. He hurried to his office and brought up Corey's and Lilith's accounts.

With adrenaline pumping through his veins, he settled back on the deck and read to the end of the journal, and realized the final entry was dated the day before Corey died.

He cried for his friend again, this time knowing Corey was joyfully painting alongside the Master Artist.

This was one entry Erin needed to read.

Chapter Twenty-Eight

After feeding Clara, Erin planted herself at her computer desk with Clara playing happily behind her. The child effused joy, and Erin was learning to accept her presence as a gift, not a penance.

Per Jon's recommendation, Erin had ended the daycare agreement between her and the Caldwells. She'd thought she'd miss having the time alone to work, but Clara's chirpy voice added a calming effect to her workday.

Clearly, God knew that would happen when He orchestrated Clara's presence in her life.

Erin opened Lurch's—er, Larry's account and began the process of setting up his files. If only she could add one more client, she'd be fine. Two more would get her in the I-can-breathe zone. Regardless, God would provide.

Her cellphone rang in the middle of her project. She hated how the ring stole her focus, but she'd promised clients she would offer quick, personal service. Now to prove that.

"Belden Bookkeeping Services, how may I help you?"

"Erin?"

"Jon. Hi." The corners of her mouth involuntarily lifted. Seemed like forever since she'd heard his voice, though it had only been since last night.

"Do you mind if I stop over? I have news."

Her spine stiffened at his dry tone. "Good or bad."

"I'd prefer to tell you in person."

Which meant bad news. "Fine. I'll be here." She hung up without saying goodbye. And to think she'd been having a good day up until now.

Rather than immerse herself in her work, she prepared light appetizers and a bowl of Sixlets to share when Jon arrived. Food always made bad news more palatable.

Thirty minutes later, the doorbell rang, and she invited Jon in. "Thanks for letting me stop by on short notice."

"Did I have a choice?"

"Pearl, you always have a choice."

"Why do you keep calling me that?" She shut the door behind him. "The Sixlets were over and done with a long time ago."

"Uncle Jon!" Clara interceded before Jon could answer.

He picked her up and threw her in the air, her blonde ringlets flying like floating bubbles.

"Hey Lolli." He blew a raspberry on her tummy, and she giggled.

Watching Jon interact with Clara was rather intriguing. It was a side of him Erin hadn't known existed until Clara arrived. She'd be lying if she said she didn't find it attractive.

But she wasn't going to allow Clara to get in the way of Jon answering her question. She gestured toward the couch while she sat in the recliner.

Jon frowned, but sat, keeping Clara on his lap. As protection maybe with what he had to tell her? She certainly wouldn't throw anything—like plates—while he was holding her.

She folded her hands in her lap, squeezing them together, pouring her frustrations into them. "I asked you a question."

"What am I doing here?" He bounced Clara on his lap, and she giggled more.

Yes, he was attractive, but also infuriating. She covered her tattoo with her hand. "No. Why do you still call me Pearl?"

His leg stilled, and he kissed Clara's forehead before looking Erin directly in the eye, making her stomach do flip flops. "Because you are a valuable treasure, one that should be cherished."

Erin broke her gaze from his and looked down at her hands fidgeting in her lap. She'd never accepted compliments well.

Suddenly he was in front of her, taking her hands, holding them palms up so her tattoo was on full display. "You are precious. You are beloved, and I'm sorry so few people have valued you for what you're worth."

Erin tried to conjure a sarcastic retort, but her mind had gone blank. All she could do was yank her hands from Jon and hide her tattoo beneath her arm pit because she had a sudden, irrational urge to kiss him. She summoned her stoic face and changed the subject. "Why did you need to see me today?"

His eyes downcast, he returned to the couch without answering her question.

She chastised herself for hurting him, for not being honest about her new, frightening, exhilarating feelings. Releasing them might break open another dam, and that scared her to death.

Finally, he looked up at her. "I discovered what the Caldwells were after."

"And that's bad news?" She didn't have to summon her stoic face for that question.

He cocked his head to the side. That meant confusion, right? "Who said anything about bad news?"

"Well . . ." She replayed their conversation in her head, and the only one who hinted at bad news was her. But hadn't his body language indicated his news was bad? Like she was some expert. But he didn't seem excited or happy. Even she knew a smile meant happy. Usually. Or maybe not. Grrr. She needed to stop analyzing before her brain hurt.

He folded his hands together and looked down at Clara. "Apparently Charles Caldwell has a bit of a gambling problem."

Ah, okay, now his melancholy made sense. He was happy for Erin and Clara but the reason behind her getting custody gave him no pleasure. What a beautiful heart Jon had.

He cleared his throat. "Corey referenced the gambling in his journal, and their accounts affirmed it with Lilith having forwarded money to her mom several times over the past year. Her parents have come to depend on those funds. That's why Corey and Lilith specifically stated to me that they didn't want them to be guardians. The Caldwells were using their relationship with you to make you comfortable with them, while they were seeking anything they could use against you. With Corey's death, his artwork has become more valuable, and they hoped to use guardianship of Clara to access that artwork. This morning, I made them see the error of their ways. Besides, they really didn't like the sound of his gambling addiction being made public."

Erin sat back in the recliner, closed her eyes, and examined what Jon had told her. She was a chump. Jon had warned her about warming up to the Caldwells, and she hadn't listened. For once, couldn't she read people as others did?

"Hey." Jon's whispered word drifted across the room to her. "You won, Pearl. This is a celebration, not a funeral."

She won . . . Blinking, she looked to Jon. "So, Clara gets to stay?"

"The legal work isn't all done, but yes, Clara gets to stay."

Erin stared at the ceiling, her eyes still blinking.

A tear?

"Does that mean you're happy?"

She nodded but didn't dare speak. Nearly two months ago,

she wouldn't have believed it possible, but yes, she was happy. She could even feel it, name it.

"One more thing." Jon reached into his briefcase and pulled out Corey's journal. "His last passage—I have it marked—you should read it." He held it out but didn't cross the floor to give it to her.

So, did that mean he wanted her to make the first move? Didn't matter, really. She got up, walked the four- to five-foot distance between them, sat down on the couch, and accepted the journal.

"Will you stay here while I read it?" The last entry she'd read had resulted in a meltdown. She didn't want a repeat of that.

"I'd be glad to."

"I'll be out when I'm done." She carried the book to her bedroom, surprised by its weight. If it weren't good, Jon wouldn't want her to read it, would he?

There was one way to find out.

April 3, 2019

I finished it, finally. My masterpiece. And then I cried. No surprise, right? It represents so many things: selfishness, brokenness, sacrifice, forgiveness. Real, true love.

In some ways I identify with King David. The man was royally messed up. (Yeah, very punny. Glad I'm the only one who'll read this.) Anyway, the dude was an artist like me! No, he didn't paint, but he was a musician and a poet. And, like me, he had his demons. I mean, the dude not only had an affair, but then he basically put out a contract on Bathsheba's husband. So, David, king of Israel, a man after God's own heart, was an adulterer and murderer and polygamist, just to name a few things. Yet, God loved him. Forgave him.

I think my favorite chapter in all the Bible has to be Psalm 51. I've prayed that Psalm so much over these past years, especially the words, "Create in me a clean heart, O God, and renew a right spirit within me. Cast me not away from your presence, and take not your Holy Spirit from me. Restore to me the joy of your salvation, and uphold me with a willing spirit."

And you know what? That prayer's been answered, abundantly. God has forgiven me. He has cleansed my heart and restored joy. And someday, I'll get to hug him and thank him in person. I can't wait for that day!

So yeah, I get it now, although I wonder why I had to hurt so many people before God's grace made sense to me. I've apologized to all but one. Well, I've said I'm sorry to Erin too, more than once, but it hasn't felt genuine before. I think she knew that, too.

My heart still aches over what I did to her and to Mik. It was all me. A hundred percent my fault, though at the beginning I blamed Erin. When you're doing something you know is wrong, you have to shift the blame somewhere else to justify your actions. My finger pointed at Erin. I didn't realize then that the rest of my fingers were aimed back at me.

I don't know if she'll forgive me, but I have to tell her I'm sorry. I have to let her know she was an amazing mom, a loving wife, and a caring friend, although she might argue that last point. Still, it's true. She might not recognize what she's feeling, but her actions speak for her. The problem is, when you're focused on your own problems, you stop seeing all the goodness surrounding you.

That goodness was Erin.

It still is Erin.

Now the trick will be getting her to listen to me. I'm going to talk to her tomorrow night before we bring Mik to the hockey game, match, whatever it's called. I know Mik loves hockey, so I'll be there for her.

Hopefully, Erin will agree to meet. I need to apologize. I need to give her this painting of my heart, and I'd be stoked if she chooses to add her own final touch as Lil did. And my parents. Mik. Jon too.

The choice is up to her.

Christ paid the price for my sins and has forgiven me.

That's what really matters.

———————

Erin laid down the book on her bed. A normal person would blubber or at least tear up. She had nothing. What was wrong with her? Corey apologized. Took all the blame. Didn't that mean anything to her?

Maybe seeing the painting would help.

She picked up the book again and brought it out to the living room where Jon was watching a baseball game with Mik. The two looked natural together, and that warmed her heart. Even made her smile. What would it be like to see them like that all the time?

She shook away the thought, though it wouldn't leave entirely. She cleared her throat. "Have you seen this painting?"

His head jerked her way, startled, then he nodded. "It's by far his best work."

"I need to see it."

"I thought you would. The Beldens are on their way over to babysit."

She sat on the other side of him from Mik, hands clasped in

her lap, and stared blankly at the television. "Thank you. You're a good friend." Though, she believed they'd become much more than friends, whatever that meant. She had to work on pushing other words past her lips, but not with Mik around.

"Mom, you are so clueless." Mik got up and stomped to her room.

True, she was clueless, but she was also frightened of being abandoned again.

Jon sat silent. She'd hurt him again, hadn't she? She gazed at him through her peripheral vision, hoping she'd sense those tingles she read about it romance novels.

No. No tingles.

But she could envision sitting here watching ball games together, or just reading books. She could see him taking Mik to her games and Clara to dance class. In a few years, he'd be the perfect person to teach Mik to drive and to stand in the doorway greeting Mik's first date.

Was that love? Maybe tingles weren't necessary. She unclasped her hands and started to reach over to grasp his.

And the doorbell rang.

Seriously?

She did feel disappointed. Certainly, that was a sign.

"I'll get it." Jon jumped up before her brain made up its mind. He flung open the door and greeted the Beldens with hugs. "Thanks for coming over."

"Anything for family." Joyce kissed him on the cheek. "And where are my granddaughters?"

Erin joined them at the door. "Thank you for coming over. Mik is hiding in her room and Lolli's taking a nap." She practically pushed Jon out the door, eager to see this masterpiece Corey had created.

And to see if there was any kind of spark between her and Jon, something beyond gratitude and friendship. Not like what she'd felt with Corey. That had been reckless and wild, and she'd been escaping the craziness that had been her mother. Maybe being alone with Jon would ignite something more.

But they drove to Corey's house in silence. Maybe she'd gone too far and now he'd shut down his heart.

He led the way to Corey's studio, also in silence. He unlocked the door and motioned for her to enter ahead of him. Then he walked to a sheet-covered easel and flung off the sheet.

She gasped and realized Jon's silence was out of respect so she could absorb this moment. Never had she seen a work of art so beautiful. It literally stopped her breaths. He'd painted a rugged cross just to the left of the middle of the canvas. Storm clouds threatened to the left, and bright sun smiled on the right. On the middle left, open hands poured out what looked like dirty ceramic pieces. The pieces tumbled like a dirty waterfall toward the cross. The pieces that crossed to the other side were transformed. Bright and colorful and reflecting the sun's light, intermixed with . . . She squinted at the iridescent gems. Pearls?

She stretched a hand toward the canvas, then stopped. "Can I touch it?"

"He'd want you to."

She reached out slowly to feel the mosaic waterfall. Some pieces were real, but others were paint. How did he do that?

"Do you recognize it?" Jon said from behind her.

She studied the pieces on both sides of the cross and her eyes widened with realization. "The ceramic plates I threw at Corey."

"And then you gave them to him as a wedding gift. That was brilliant, by the way. He was ticked off, all right. But for some reason he saved them." Jon's voice drew closer, and she felt his breath tickle her hair. "Corey was hearing God even then, though he didn't realize that's whose voice he was hearing."

Then Jon's hand was on her shoulder. She didn't even flinch. More than that, she liked it.

He stood right beside her and opened his hand. In it were two items: a piece of that broken plate and a pearl. "He wanted you to complete it." Jon said softly, preserving the solemnity of the moment. "However you choose. He wanted you to know that he was sorry. For everything. And I can vouch for his sincerity. Pearl, you were precious to him, as you are to me."

Jon didn't need to vouch for Corey's sincerity. Erin could see it in this masterful piece. He'd understood what forgiveness was about.

As she studied the painting, Jon grasped her hand and caressed her tattoo with his thumb, stealing her breath.

Oh my. So that was what tingles felt like.

Keeping her hand in his, she accepted the two pieces. "How do I add them?"

Jon poured a dab of paint on a nearby palette. "Just dip and attach."

"How do you know that?"

"I already added my piece."

Oh.

Okay, she knew what she had to do. She dipped the ceramic piece and the pearl and added both to the right of the cross. "Corey, I forgive you."

Epilogue

Today, Erin was ready to begin living again, and she felt . . . Excited.

"How do I look?" Nibbling on her lower lip, she studied her image in the mirror. She thought she looked good, but would Jon?

Mik stood behind her, wrinkling her nose.

Erin knew what that meant. "Then you pick out what I should wear." She gestured toward her closet that had far too few choices.

"Gotcha." Mik broke out in giggles. "You look amazing, Mom."

"Are you sure?" Erin half turned, looking at her backside in the mirror.

"It's just a date. With Uncle Jon. You guys know each other inside and out."

"But we've never dated before." Something tickled inside her stomach. Was that what others described as butterflies? "I'm nervous."

"No kidding."

The doorbell rang.

"I'll get it." And Mik took off before Erin could say "Don't." Yes, she was nervous, and identifying it felt good. She took one more glance in the mirror before stepping out into the hall.

He whistled.

And heat warmed her cheeks, so she looked down, hoping to hide the pink glow he likely could see. Another sign that she was finally ready to take this next step with him. Yes, it was a dating step, but she believed it was important for them to see if romance was in their future.

Putting one high-heeled shoe in front of the other, she crossed the room to Jon on wobbly legs. When she finally looked up, her mouth went dry. Oh, my, he cleaned up nice. Tonight, she was going to be the envy of every woman at the restaurant.

He handed her a bouquet of mixed flowers. "I didn't know what you like, so I bought them all."

She dipped her nose into the bouquet and breathed in. "I like them all."

"Shall we go?" He offered his arm.

She accepted it and handed the bouquet to Mik.

"Now you two lovebirds get going." Mik shoved Erin in the back. "Clara and I are going to have fun."

"You have my number?"

"Really, Mom?" Mik rolled her eyes. "Now remember, be home by eleven. You can hold hands, but no kissing. Got that?"

Erin giggled. Giggled! When was the last time that had happened? To be honest, she wouldn't mind if she and Jon shared a kiss. Actually, she hoped for it. To think she'd let bitterness stand in the way of her caring for someone again.

Forgiveness had unlocked her emotional gate to the possibility of romance.

Jon opened the front door, let her step out first, then closed the door behind them. She started to take a step down, but his hand on her arm stopped her. She didn't flinch, and even liked his hand there. She turned to face him, looking up into his blue eyes, then down at his lips.

Heaven help her, she wanted to kiss him.

With his finger, he lifted her chin. "I know Mik just read us the rules for tonight, but I'm feeling like the rule breaker I used to be."

She gulped and closed her eyes as Jon's lips whispered across hers, leaving her hungry for more.

The door flung open. "Hey, you two. I saw that." Mik wagged her finger and grinned. "It's about time!"

Dear Reader,

Thank you for reading **A Beautiful Mess**. I hope you enjoyed taking this journey with Erin as she grew from bitter to forgiving. Isaiah 11:6 tells us, "...a little child shall lead them." That's exactly what Clara did in this story. And, as usual, I learned right along with my characters.

To read more about Erin and Jon, be sure to check out my short story, **A Beautiful Christ-mess**, in **Hope is Born: A Mosaic Christmas Anthology**. This story focuses on the prodigal brother, Zax, who has a big surprise for his family. But he's surprised by something that will turn his life upside down. This anthology features nine authors in The Mosaic Collection.

If you enjoyed **A Beautiful Mess**, please consider sharing a book review telling others why you liked the story. Your review doesn't have to be long or eloquent, just honest.

You'll find additional inspiration and encouragement at www.MosaicCollectionBooks.com and by reading other books in this uplifting series.

To be notified of all my upcoming releases, join my email list http://brendaandersonbooks.com/subscribe/. As a Thank You for subscribing, you will receive a Free copy of **Coming Home**, a Coming Home Series short story.

Thank you for joining me on this writing journey.

God bless,

Brenda

Acknowledgements

Before a book is released to the public, it passes through many hands, and many sets of eyes peruse its pages. I'd be remiss not to acknowledge their help in bringing this story to light.

Heartfelt thanks go to...

My family—Marvin, Sarah, Bryan, and Brandon—for putting up with my long hours and for your constant encouragement.

Belva Williams, Social Worker, for offering guidance regarding what happens when a young child is orphaned.

Geoffrey Dobbin, Attorney, for sharing legal guidance regarding guardianship for an orphaned child.

Marika Kim, RN, for helping me understand potential injuries caused by vehicle crashes.

Beta readers Gayle Balster and Stacy Monson for braving your way through a messy early draft and helping me make it better.

Editor Lesley Ann McDaniel for helping to polish the story.

My fellow Mosaic authors, Stacy Monson, Eleanor Bertin, Deb Elkink, Lorna Seilstad, Johnnie Alexander, Regina Merrick, Angela Meyer, Sara Davison, Hannah Conway, Janice Dick, and our invaluable Virtual Assistant, Camry Crist!

And thank you, God, for piecing together this story, turning my mess into something beautiful.

About the Author

 **Brenda S. Anderson** writes gritty and authentic, life-affirming fiction. She is a member of the American Christian Fiction Writers, and is Past-President of the ACFW Minnesota chapter, MN-NICE, the 2016 ACFW Chapter of the Year. When not reading or writing, she enjoys music, theater, roller coasters, and baseball (Go Twins!), and she loves watching movies with her family. She resides in the Minneapolis, Minnesota area with her husband of 31 years, their three children, and one sassy cat.

Let's Connect

Visit Brenda online at www.BrendaAndersonBooks.com and on Facebook, Goodreads, Instagram, and BookBub.

For news and encouragement about upcoming books, contests, giveaways, and other activities, sign up for Brenda's bi-monthly newsletter.

If you enjoyed *A Beautiful Mess*, please consider leaving a review. Your words bring hope and encouragement to the author, as well as other readers.

Coming Home Series

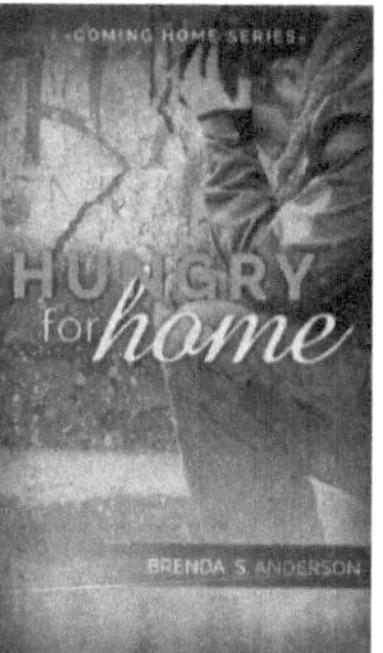

Praise for the Coming Home Series

"Anderson tackles family dynamics, tough issues, and gritty realism in her Coming Home series. From special needs babies to abortion and homelessness, you'll root for her authentic characters as they face real life struggles."

— Award-winning author, **Shannon Taylor Vannatter**

" . . . heartfelt, heart-wrenching fiction at its best, exploring relationships and family, love, faith and forgiveness in fresh, life-changing ways. I see myself in these endearing, enduring characters, their weaknesses and struggles and hard-won triumphs."

— **Laura Frantz**, author of *A Moonbow Night*

"Anderson thrusts her readers into the gritty underbelly of family life and she doesn't mince words or shy away from the difficulties that complicate relationships. The reoccurring themes of grace and restitution are delivered with heart-wrenching honesty. These compelling stories celebrate the joys and sorrows of ordinary living with an extraordinary God."

— **Kav Rees**, BestReads-kav.blogspot.com

Where the Heart Is Series

Praise for the Where the Heart Is Series

"*Risking Love* is a touching story of love and loss - and risking your heart! I can't wait to read the next in the series!"
—**Regina Rudd Merrick**, author of *Carolina Dream*

"Brenda does a great job bringing us into the story, capturing our attention and keeping it till the end. I read the first book in this series and look forward to the next. I highly recommend *Capturing Beauty* – it's an inspiring story of second chances and new perspectives!"
—**Angela D. Meyer**, author of *Where Hope Starts*

"*Planting Hope* is a lovely wrap-up to the Where the Heart Is series. The strength, or lack thereof, of a family unit has a profound impact on all of its members. Brenda Anderson expertly illustrates that in this story, and all of her books, as she deals honestly with the idiosyncrasies of families – the good, bad, and ugly. *Planting Hope* is about the hope God plants deep in our hearts, and the lengths we'll go to for those we love."
—Award-winning author, **Stacy Monson**,
author of *Open Circle*